W9-CIQ-451

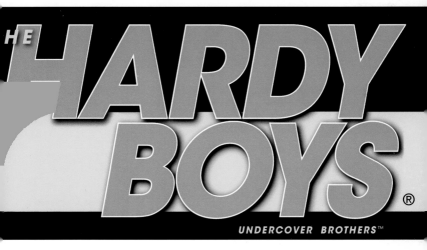

THE **HARDY BOYS**

UNDERCOVER BROTHERS™

PAPERCUT**Z**

THE HARDY BOYS®

Graphic Novels
Available from Papercutz

#1 The Ocean of Osyria
#2 Identity Theft
#3 Mad House
(coming November 2005)
#4 Malled
(coming February 2006)

$7.95 each in paperback
$12.95 each in hardcover

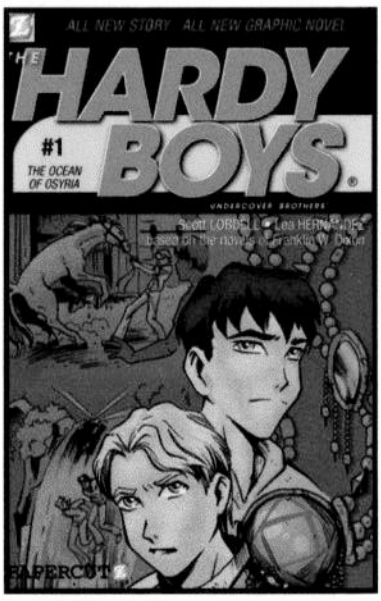
ALL NEW STORY ALL NEW GRAPHIC NOVEL
THE HARDY BOYS
#1
THE OCEAN OF OSYRIA
PAPERCUTZ

SPECIAL OFFER!

While supplies last, you may order the first three hard-to-find Hardy Boys collector's item comic books (which were collected in the first Graphic Novel) for $2.95 each!

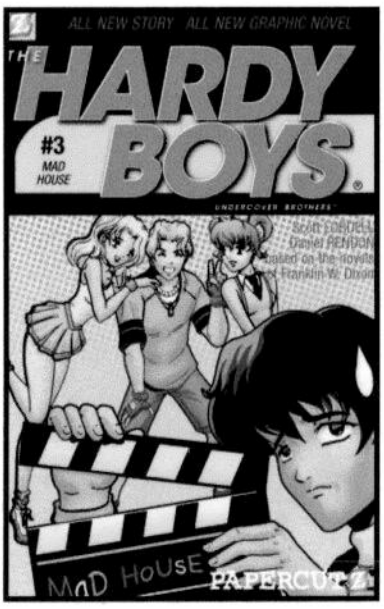
ALL NEW STORY ALL NEW GRAPHIC NOVEL
THE HARDY BOYS
#3
MAD HOUSE
MAD HOUSE
PAPERCUTZ

Please add $3.00 for postage and handling for the first book, add $1.00 for each additional book.

Send for our catalog:
Papercutz
555 Eighth Avenue, Suite 1202
New York, NY 10018
www.papercutz.com

THE HARDY BOYS®

UNDERCOVER BROTHERS™

#2

Identity Theft

SCOTT LOBDELL • Writer
DANIEL RENDON • Artist
Based on the series by
FRANKLIN W. DIXON

PAPERCUTZ™
New York

Identity Theft
SCOTT LOBDELL – Writer
DANIEL RENDON — Artist
BRYAN SENKA – Letterer
LOVERN KINDZIERSKI,
CHRIS CHUCKRY,
LAURIE E. SMITH — Colorists
JIM SALICRUP — Editor-in-Chief

ISBN 10: 1-59707-003-3 paperback edition
ISBN 13: 978-1-59707-003-4 paperback edition
ISBN 10: 1-59707-007-6 hardcover edition
ISBN 13: 978-1-59707-007-2 hardcover edition

10   9   8   7   6   5   4   3   2   1

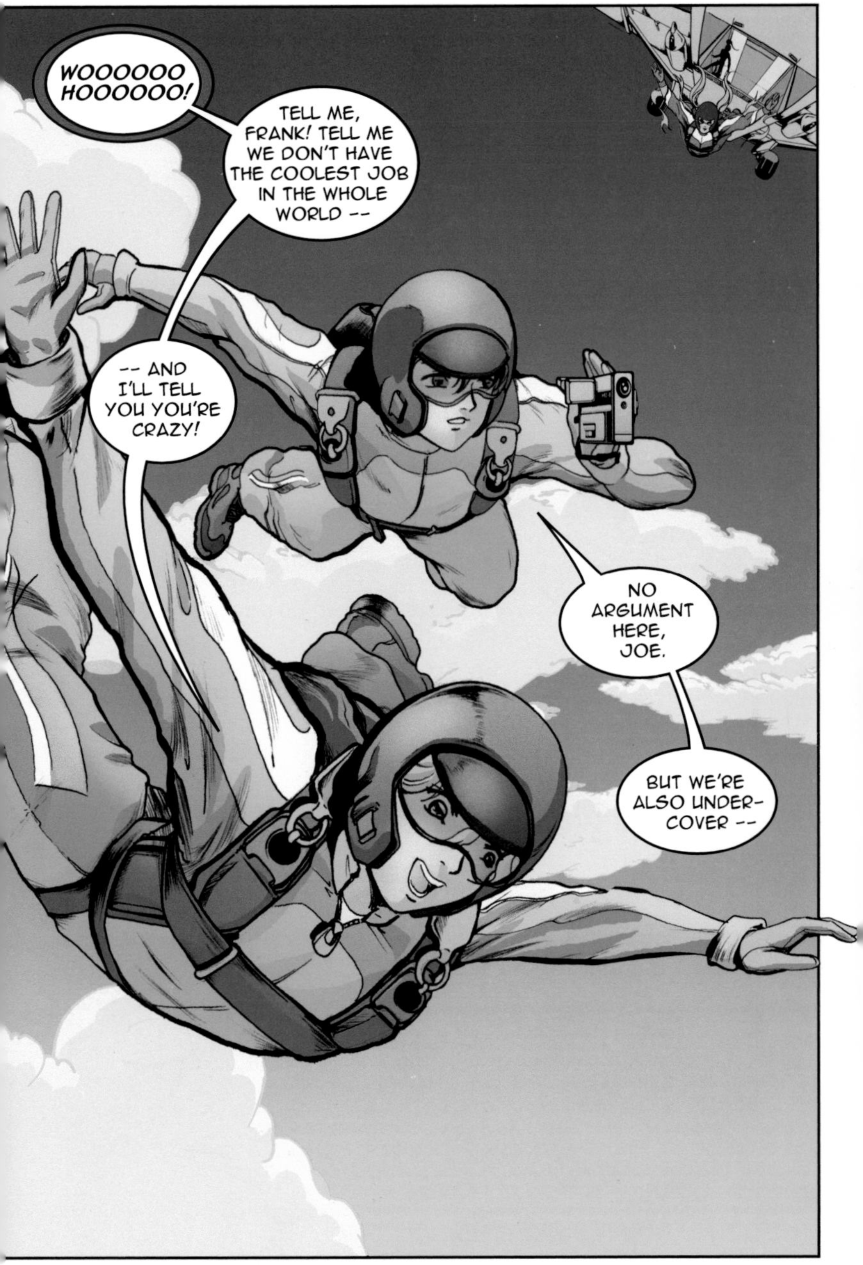
WOOOOOO HOOOOOO!
TELL ME, FRANK! TELL ME WE DON'T HAVE THE COOLEST JOB IN THE WHOLE WORLD --
-- AND I'LL TELL YOU YOU'RE CRAZY!
NO ARGUMENT HERE, JOE.
BUT WE'RE ALSO UNDER-COVER --

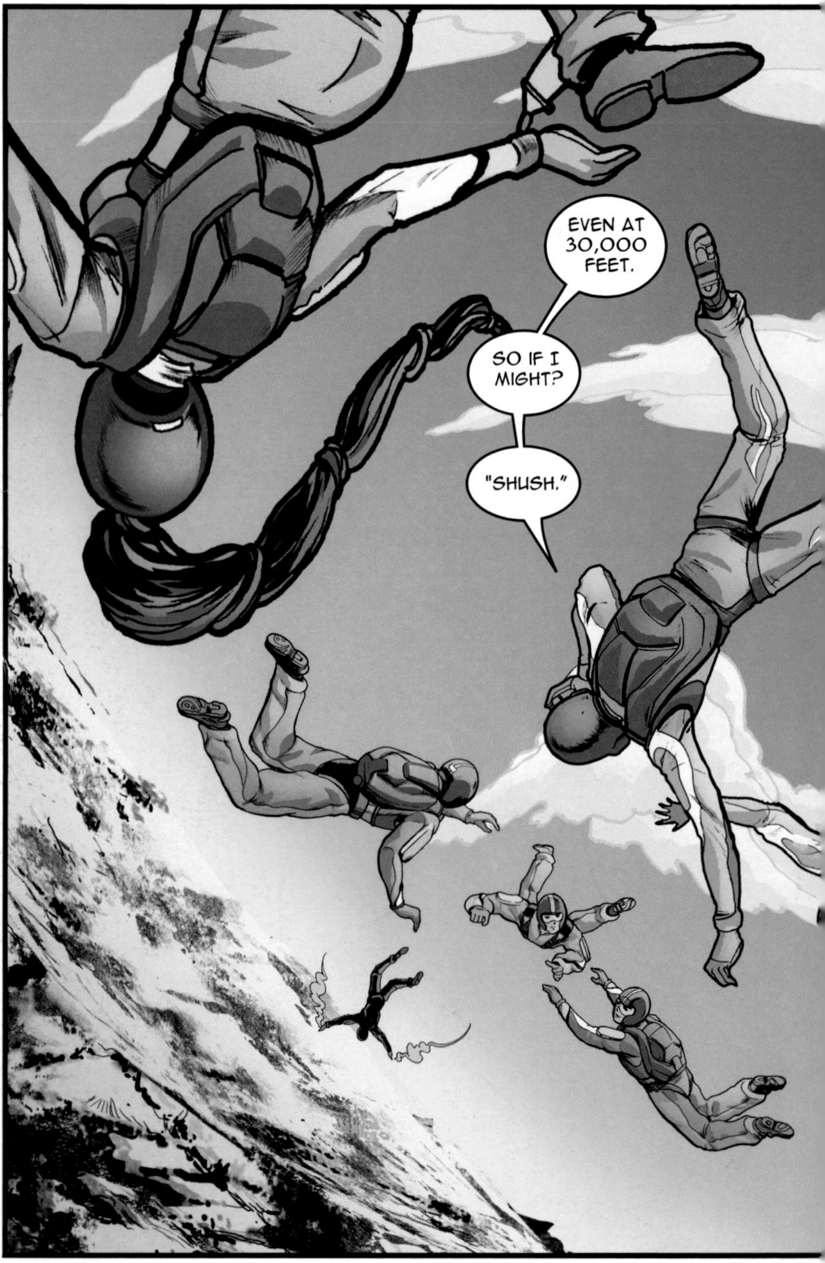
EVEN AT 30,000 FEET.
SO IF I MIGHT?
"SHUSH."

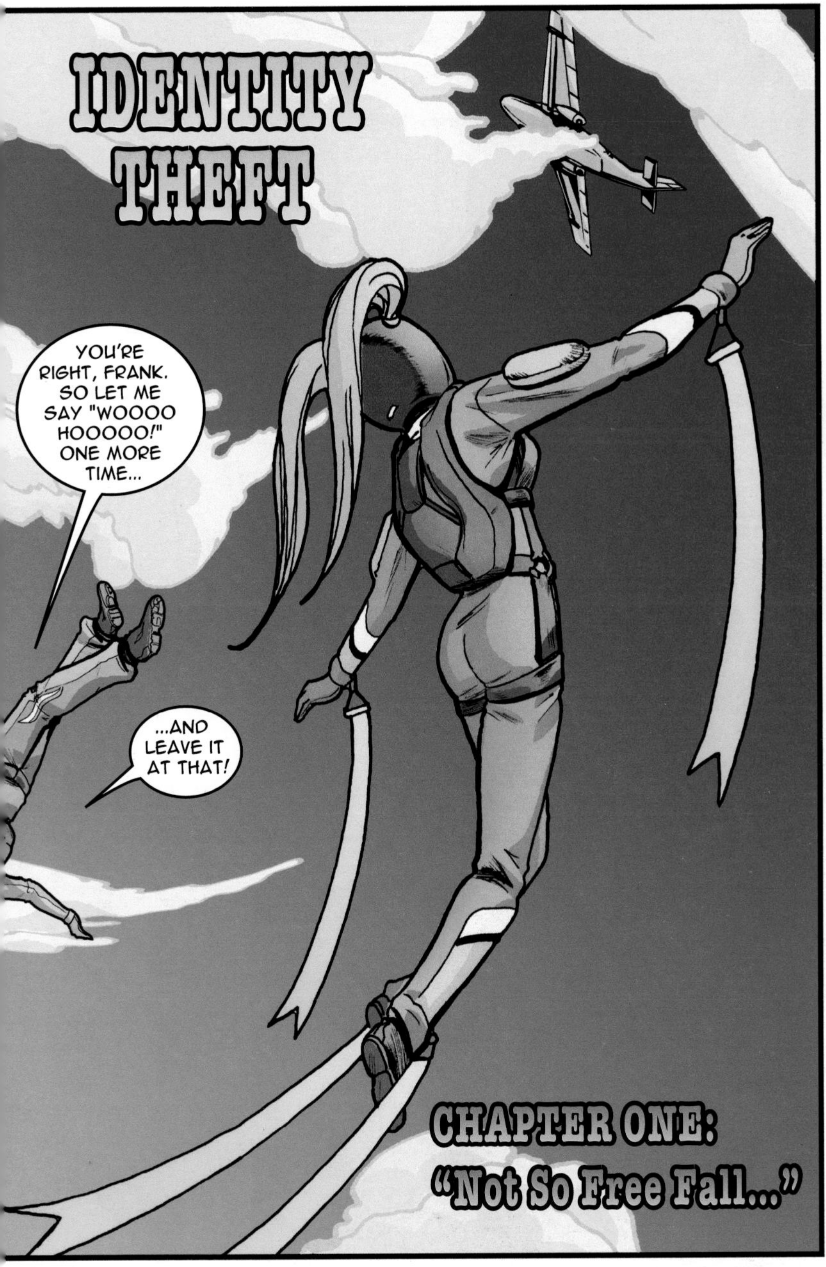
IDENTITY THEFT
YOU'RE RIGHT, FRANK. SO LET ME SAY "WOOOO HOOOOO!" ONE MORE TIME...
...AND LEAVE IT AT THAT!
CHAPTER ONE:
"Not So Free Fall..."

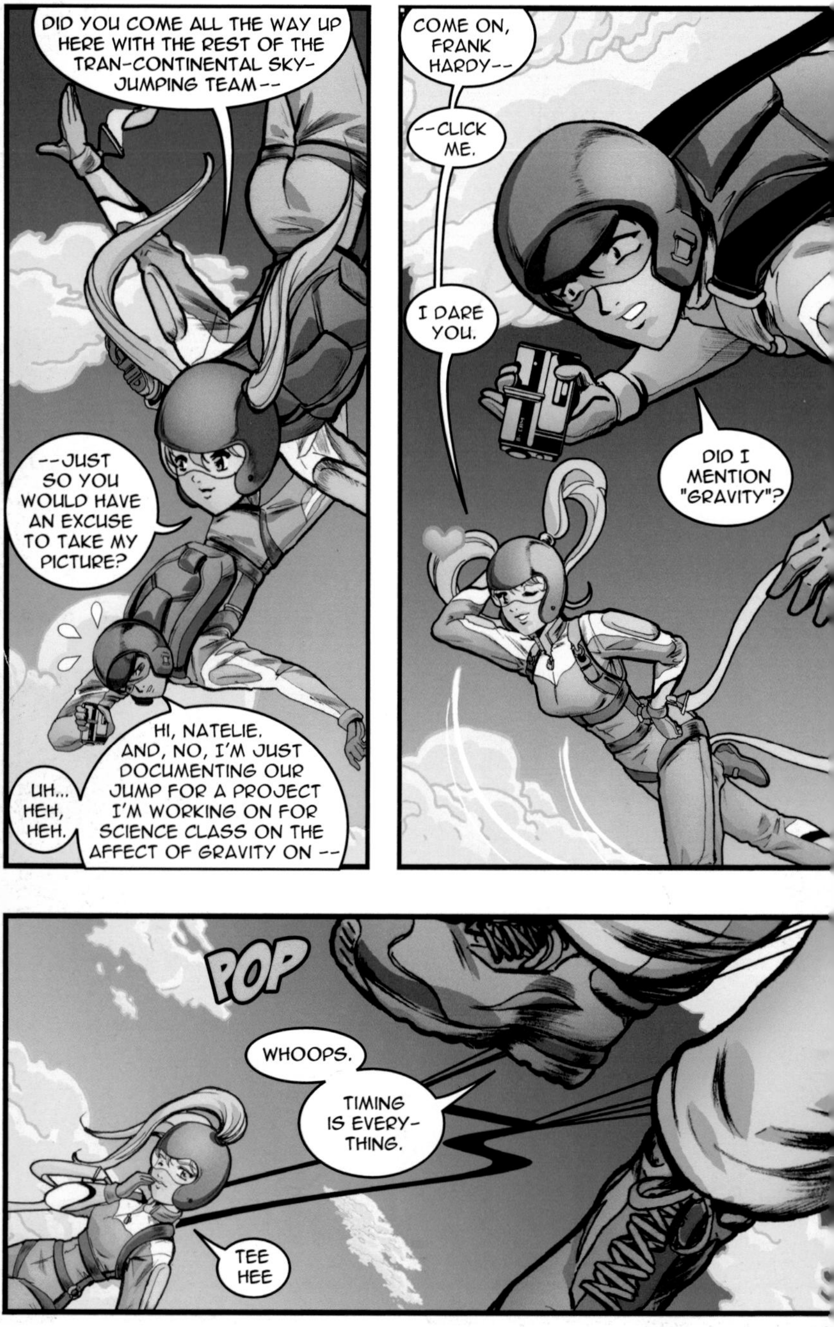
DID YOU COME ALL THE WAY UP HERE WITH THE REST OF THE TRAN-CONTINENTAL SKY-JUMPING TEAM--
--JUST SO YOU WOULD HAVE AN EXCUSE TO TAKE MY PICTURE?
UH... HEH, HEH.
HI, NATELIE. AND, NO, I'M JUST DOCUMENTING OUR JUMP FOR A PROJECT I'M WORKING ON FOR SCIENCE CLASS ON THE AFFECT OF GRAVITY ON --
COME ON, FRANK HARDY--
--CLICK ME.
I DARE YOU.
DID I MENTION "GRAVITY"?
POP
WHOOPS.
TIMING IS EVERY-THING.
TEE HEE

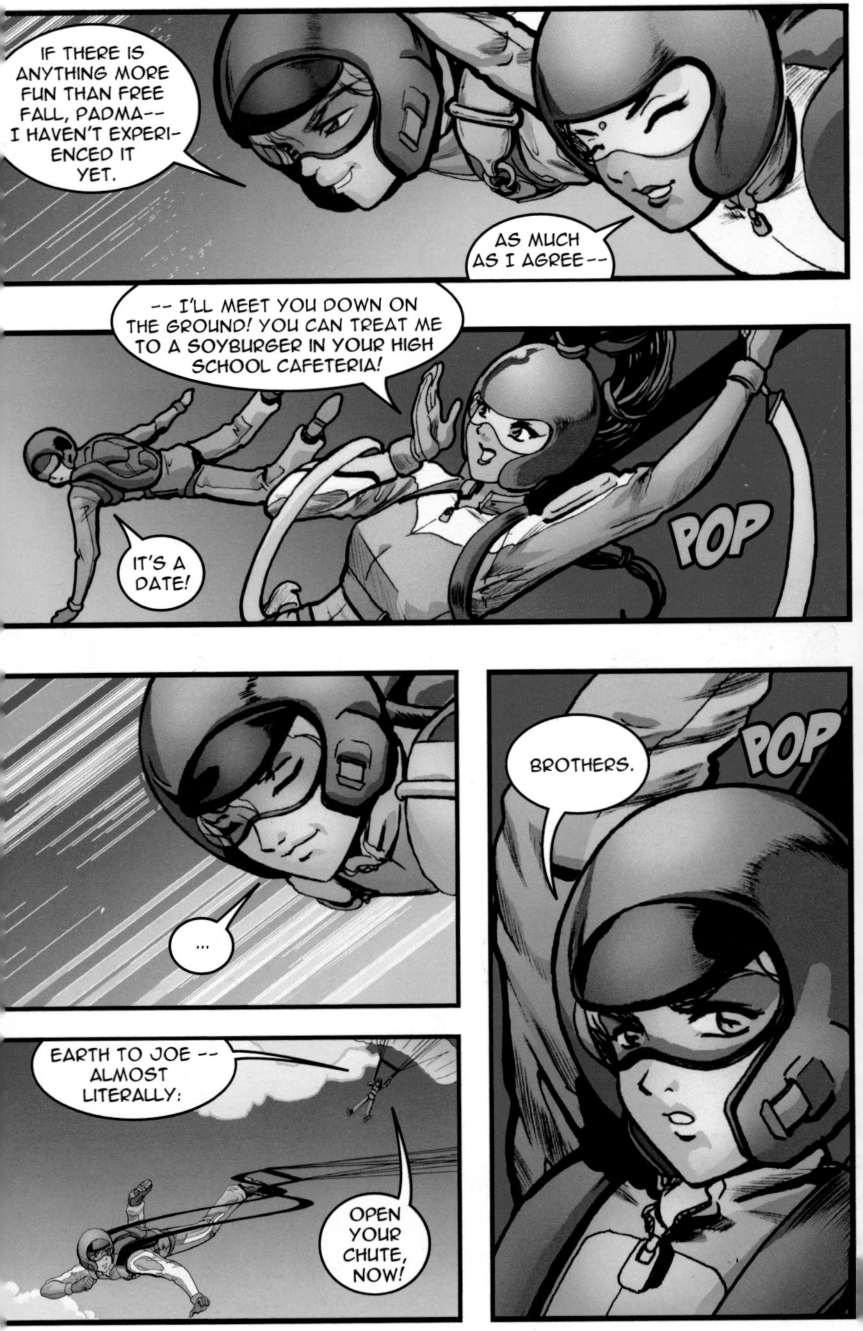
IF THERE IS ANYTHING MORE FUN THAN FREE FALL, PADMA-- I HAVEN'T EXPERIENCED IT YET.
AS MUCH AS I AGREE--
-- I'LL MEET YOU DOWN ON THE GROUND! YOU CAN TREAT ME TO A SOYBURGER IN YOUR HIGH SCHOOL CAFETERIA!
IT'S A DATE!
POP
...
BROTHERS.
POP
EARTH TO JOE -- ALMOST LITERALLY:
OPEN YOUR CHUTE, NOW!

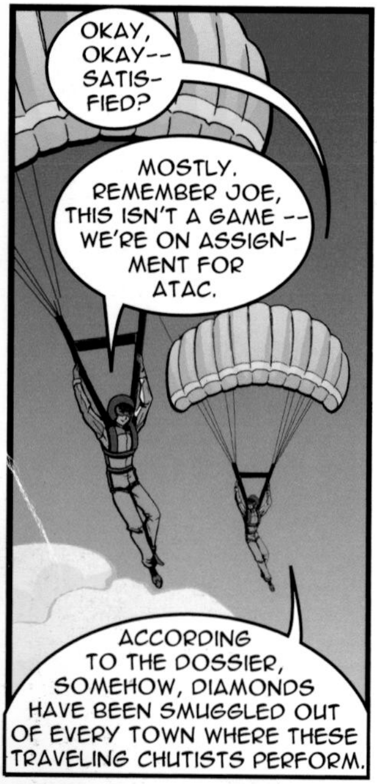

OKAY, OKAY-- SATISFIED?
MOSTLY. REMEMBER JOE, THIS ISN'T A GAME -- WE'RE ON ASSIGNMENT FOR ATAC.
ACCORDING TO THE DOSSIER, SOMEHOW, DIAMONDS HAVE BEEN SMUGGLED OUT OF EVERY TOWN WHERE THESE TRAVELING CHUTISTS PERFORM.

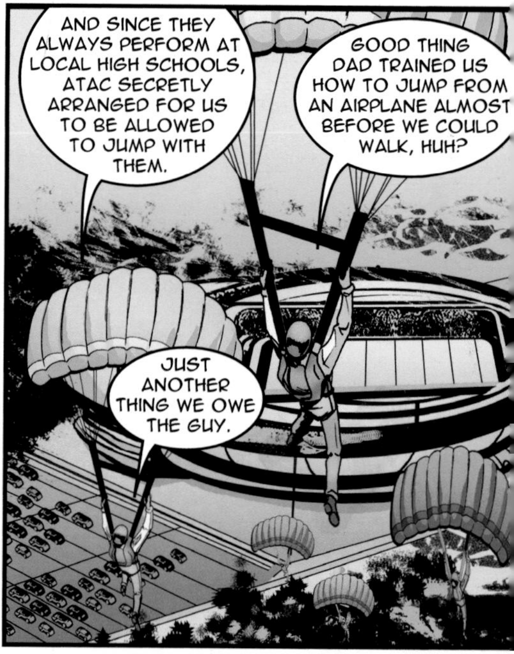

AND SINCE THEY ALWAYS PERFORM AT LOCAL HIGH SCHOOLS, ATAC SECRETLY ARRANGED FOR US TO BE ALLOWED TO JUMP WITH THEM.
GOOD THING DAD TRAINED US HOW TO JUMP FROM AN AIRPLANE ALMOST BEFORE WE COULD WALK, HUH?
JUST ANOTHER THING WE OWE THE GUY.

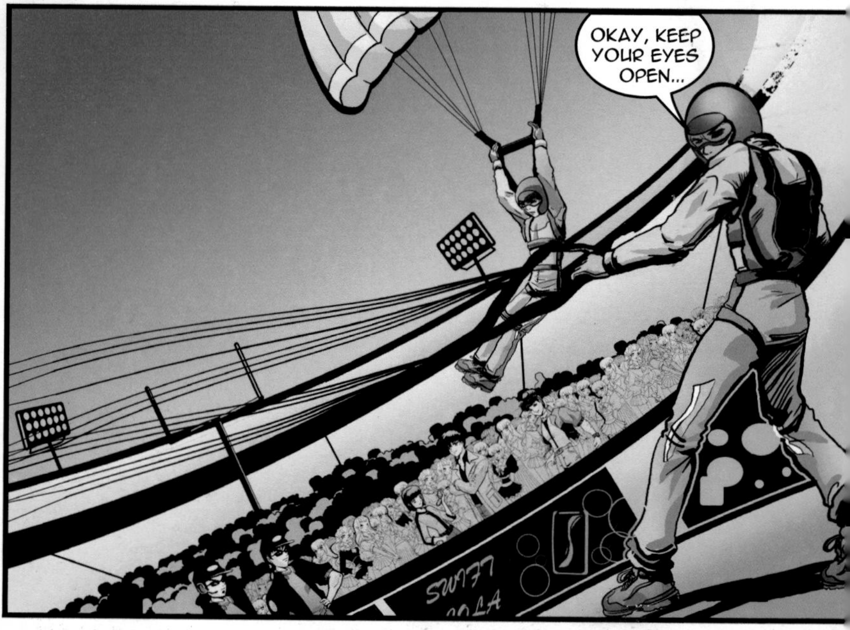

OKAY, KEEP YOUR EYES OPEN...

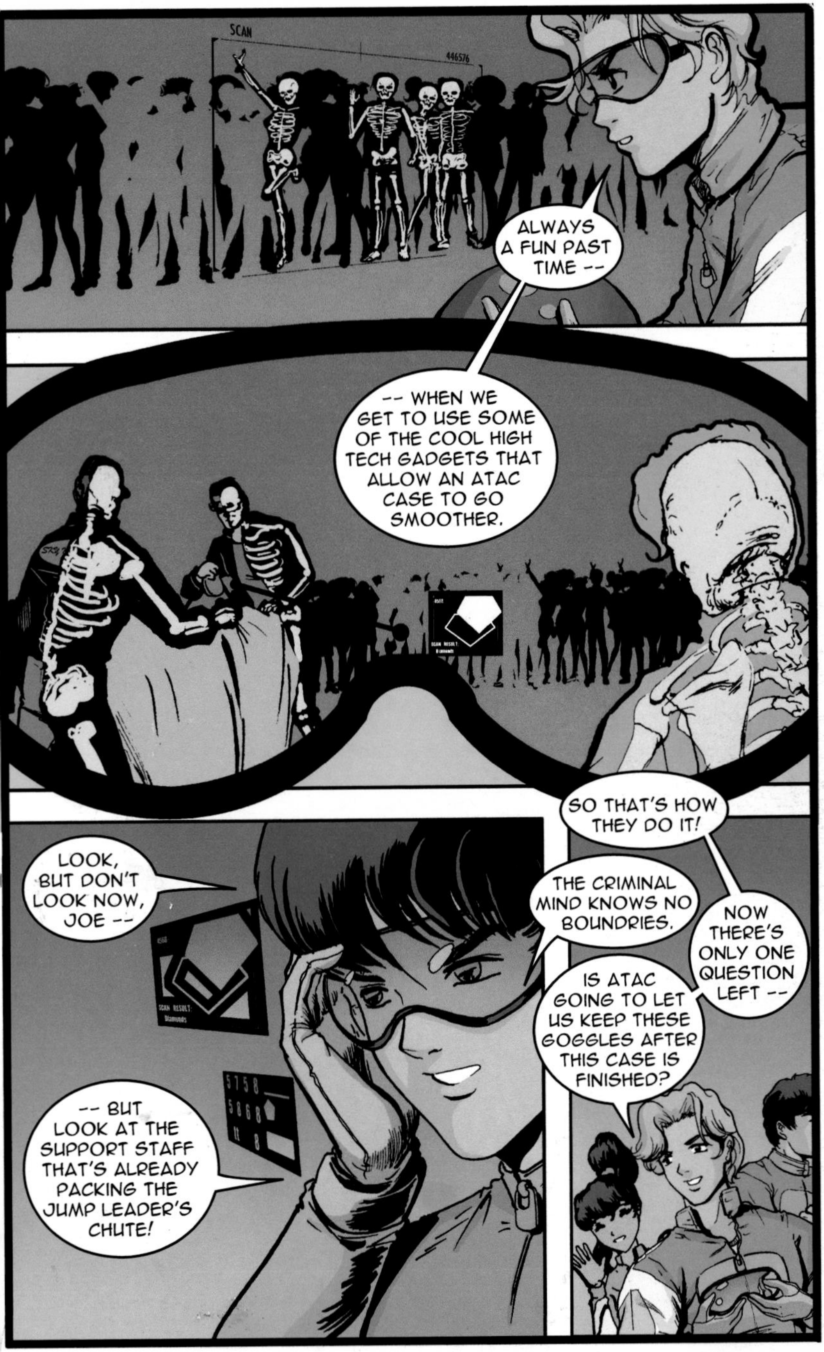
SCAN
446576
ALWAYS A FUN PAST TIME --
-- WHEN WE GET TO USE SOME OF THE COOL HIGH TECH GADGETS THAT ALLOW AN ATAC CASE TO GO SMOOTHER.
LOOK, BUT DON'T LOOK NOW, JOE --
SCAN RESULT: Diamonds
5758
5068
-- BUT LOOK AT THE SUPPORT STAFF THAT'S ALREADY PACKING THE JUMP LEADER'S CHUTE!
SO THAT'S HOW THEY DO IT!
THE CRIMINAL MIND KNOWS NO BOUNDRIES.
NOW THERE'S ONLY ONE QUESTION LEFT --
IS ATAC GOING TO LET US KEEP THESE GOGGLES AFTER THIS CASE IS FINISHED?

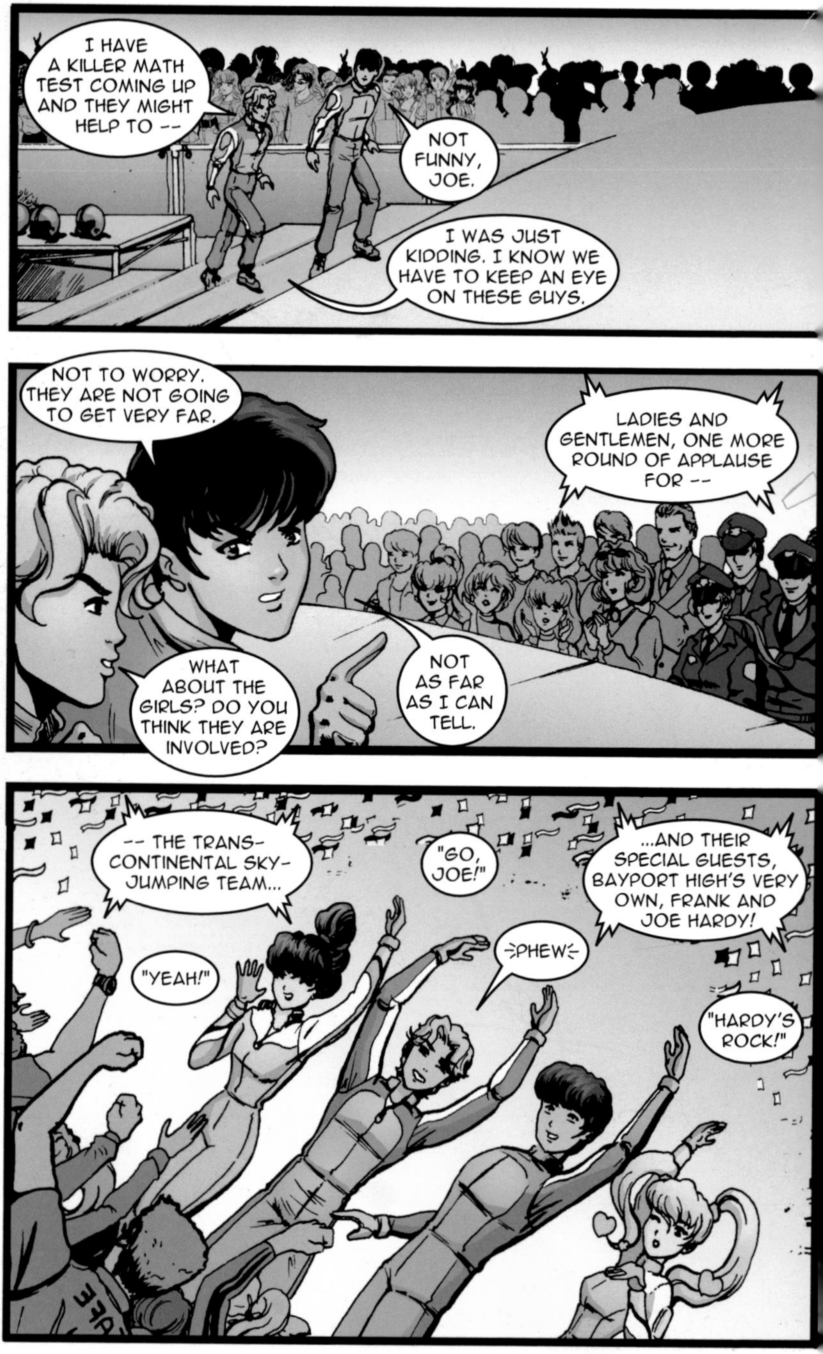
I HAVE A KILLER MATH TEST COMING UP AND THEY MIGHT HELP TO --
NOT FUNNY, JOE.
I WAS JUST KIDDING. I KNOW WE HAVE TO KEEP AN EYE ON THESE GUYS.
NOT TO WORRY. THEY ARE NOT GOING TO GET VERY FAR.
LADIES AND GENTLEMEN, ONE MORE ROUND OF APPLAUSE FOR --
WHAT ABOUT THE GIRLS? DO YOU THINK THEY ARE INVOLVED?
NOT AS FAR AS I CAN TELL.
-- THE TRANS-CONTINENTAL SKY-JUMPING TEAM...
"GO, JOE!"
...AND THEIR SPECIAL GUESTS, BAYPORT HIGH'S VERY OWN, FRANK AND JOE HARDY!
"YEAH!"
PHEW
"HARDY'S ROCK!"

CHAPTER TWO: "Home... For Now"

FOR ALL YOUR SKILLS, YOU HAVEN'T LEARNED HOW TO TALK TO A GIRL AND KEEP YOUR MOUTH FROM FALLING INTO YOUR LAP.

HA. I JUST DON'T WANT TO DRAW AWAY ANY OF THE HARDY CHARM WHEN YOU NEED IT MOST.

HA HA HARDER.

SOON, AFTER THE SPECIAL ASSEMBLY --

AND YOU BARELY TOUCHED YOUR LUNCH, FRANK.

-- AND THE AFOREMENTIONED SOYBURGER DATE.

SERIOUS THOUGH, IT IS HARD HAVING A CONVERSATION SOMETIMES WITH KIDS OUR AGE --

-- WHEN YOU KNOW YOU'RE A SECRET AGENT AND THEY'RE NOT.

UNTIL YOU REMEMBER THE WHOLE REASON WE AGREED TO BE SECRET AGENTS --

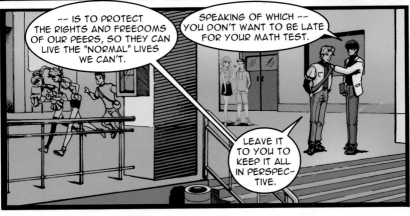

-- IS TO PROTECT THE RIGHTS AND FREEDOMS OF OUR PEERS, SO THEY CAN LIVE THE "NORMAL" LIVES WE CAN'T.

SPEAKING OF WHICH -- YOU DON'T WANT TO BE LATE FOR YOUR MATH TEST.

LEAVE IT TO YOU TO KEEP IT ALL IN PERSPEC-TIVE.

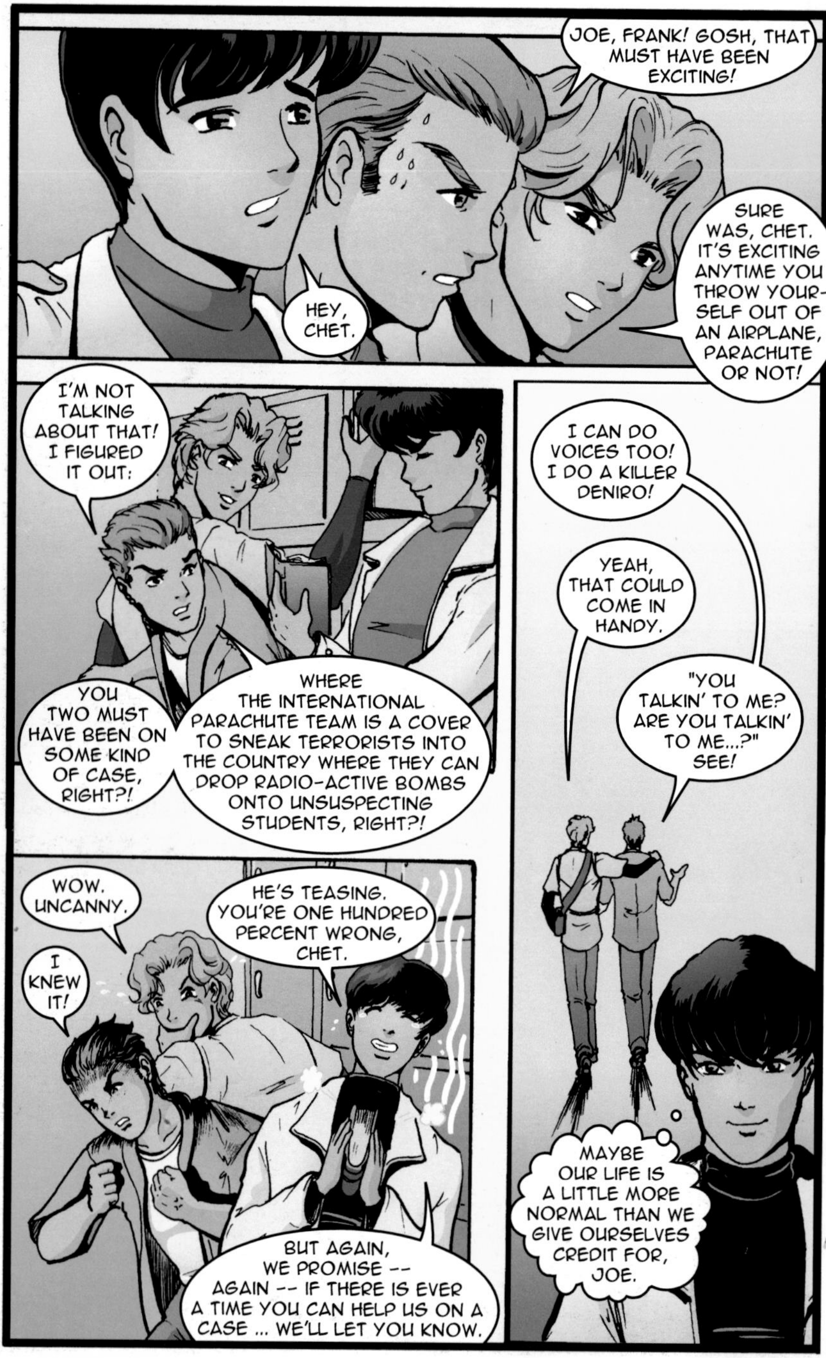
JOE, FRANK! GOSH, THAT MUST HAVE BEEN EXCITING!
HEY, CHET.
SURE WAS, CHET. IT'S EXCITING ANYTIME YOU THROW YOURSELF OUT OF AN AIRPLANE, PARACHUTE OR NOT!
I'M NOT TALKING ABOUT THAT! I FIGURED IT OUT:
YOU TWO MUST HAVE BEEN ON SOME KIND OF CASE, RIGHT?!
WHERE THE INTERNATIONAL PARACHUTE TEAM IS A COVER TO SNEAK TERRORISTS INTO THE COUNTRY WHERE THEY CAN DROP RADIO-ACTIVE BOMBS ONTO UNSUSPECTING STUDENTS, RIGHT?!
I CAN DO VOICES TOO! I DO A KILLER DENIRO!
YEAH, THAT COULD COME IN HANDY.
"YOU TALKIN' TO ME? ARE YOU TALKIN' TO ME...?" SEE!
WOW. UNCANNY.
I KNEW IT!
HE'S TEASING. YOU'RE ONE HUNDRED PERCENT WRONG, CHET.
BUT AGAIN, WE PROMISE -- AGAIN -- IF THERE IS EVER A TIME YOU CAN HELP US ON A CASE ... WE'LL LET YOU KNOW.
MAYBE OUR LIFE IS A LITTLE MORE NORMAL THAN WE GIVE OURSELVES CREDIT FOR, JOE.

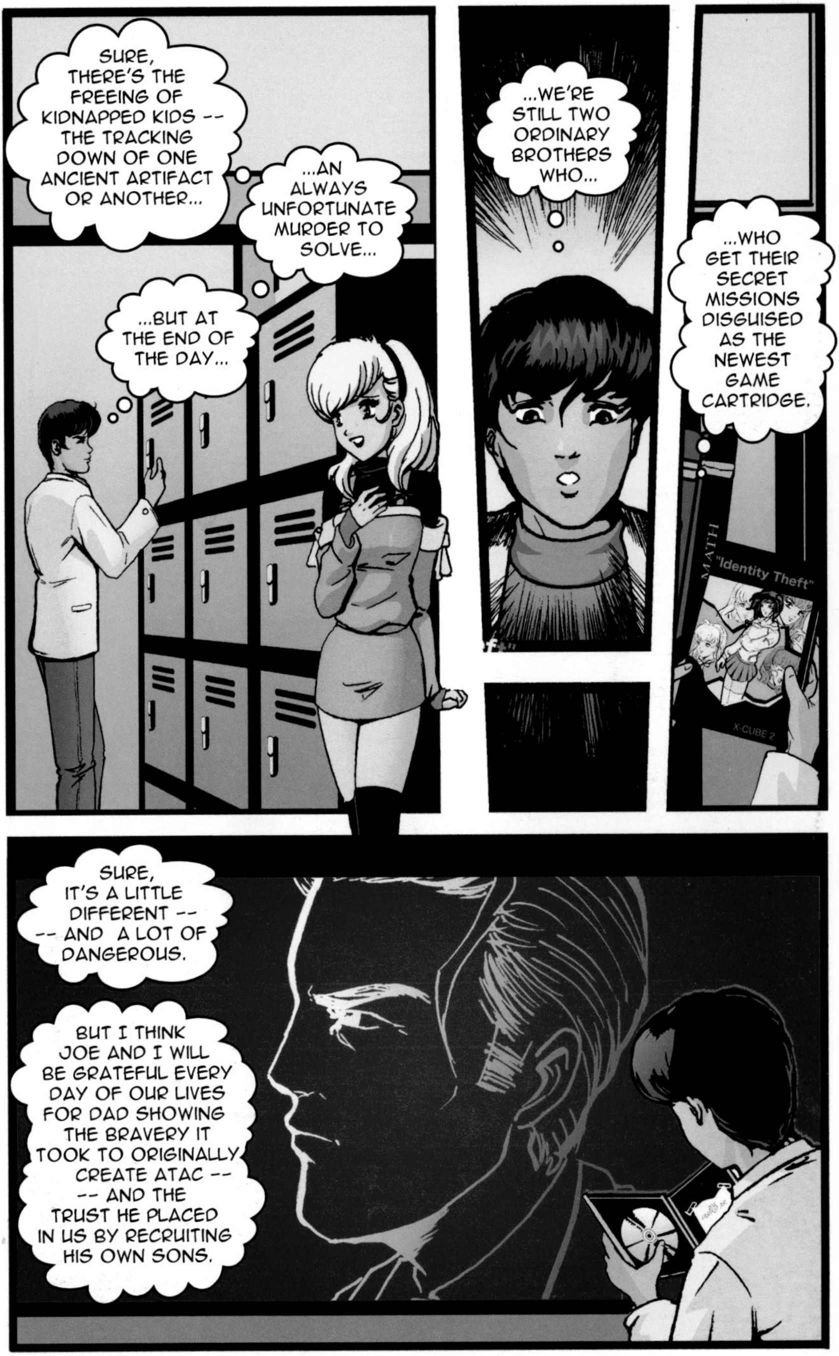
SURE, THERE'S THE FREEING OF KIDNAPPED KIDS -- THE TRACKING DOWN OF ONE ANCIENT ARTIFACT OR ANOTHER...
...AN ALWAYS UNFORTUNATE MURDER TO SOLVE...
...BUT AT THE END OF THE DAY...
...WE'RE STILL TWO ORDINARY BROTHERS WHO...
...WHO GET THEIR SECRET MISSIONS DISGUISED AS THE NEWEST GAME CARTRIDGE.
MATH
"Identity Theft"
X-CUBE 2
SURE, IT'S A LITTLE DIFFERENT -- -- AND A LOT OF DANGEROUS.
BUT I THINK JOE AND I WILL BE GRATEFUL EVERY DAY OF OUR LIVES FOR DAD SHOWING THE BRAVERY IT TOOK TO ORIGINALLY CREATE ATAC -- -- AND THE TRUST HE PLACED IN US BY RECRUITING HIS OWN SONS.

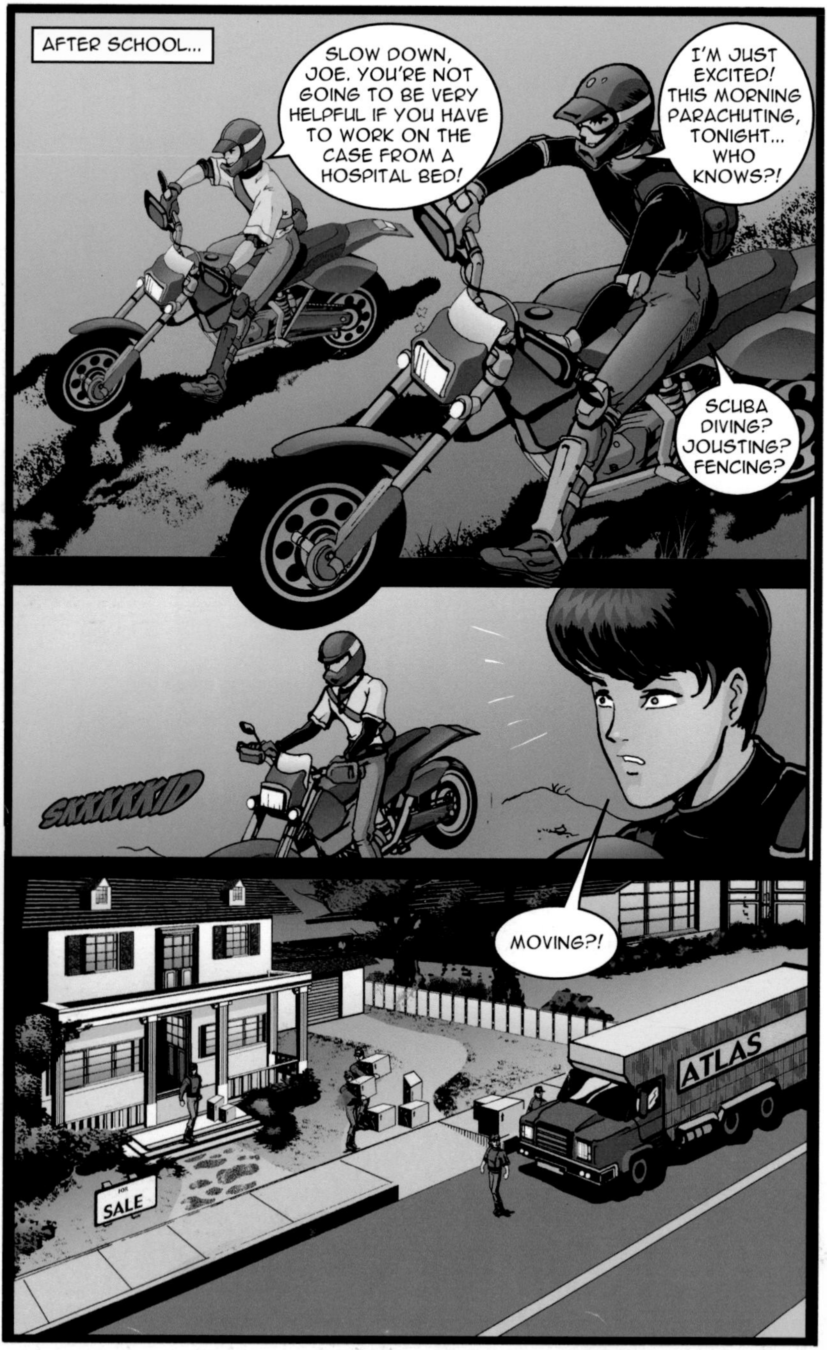
AFTER SCHOOL...
SLOW DOWN, JOE. YOU'RE NOT GOING TO BE VERY HELPFUL IF YOU HAVE TO WORK ON THE CASE FROM A HOSPITAL BED!
I'M JUST EXCITED! THIS MORNING PARACHUTING, TONIGHT... WHO KNOWS?!
SCUBA DIVING? JOUSTING? FENCING?
SKKKKKID
MOVING?!
ATLAS
FOR SALE

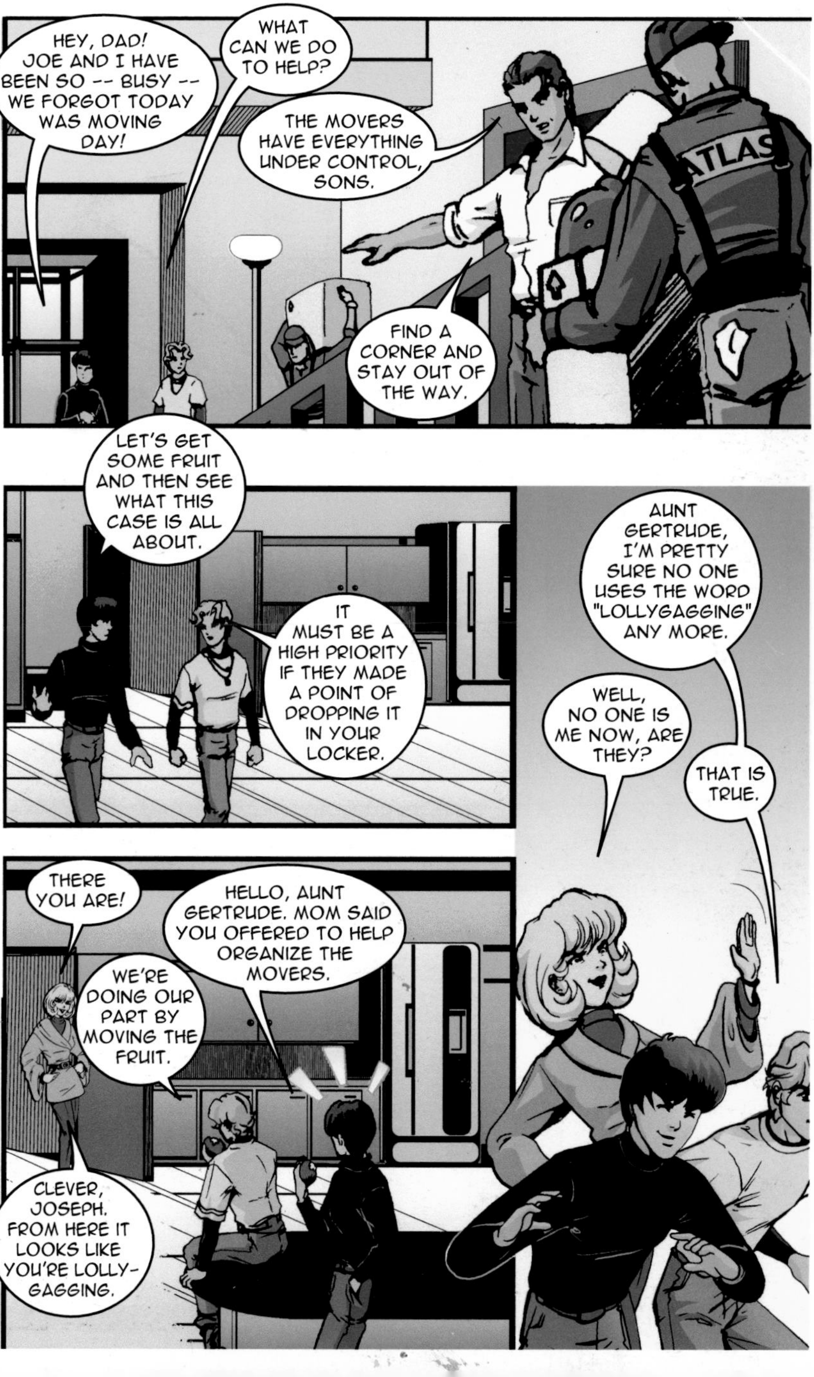
HEY, DAD! JOE AND I HAVE BEEN SO -- BUSY -- WE FORGOT TODAY WAS MOVING DAY!
WHAT CAN WE DO TO HELP?
THE MOVERS HAVE EVERYTHING UNDER CONTROL, SONS.
FIND A CORNER AND STAY OUT OF THE WAY.
ATLAS
LET'S GET SOME FRUIT AND THEN SEE WHAT THIS CASE IS ALL ABOUT.
IT MUST BE A HIGH PRIORITY IF THEY MADE A POINT OF DROPPING IT IN YOUR LOCKER.
THERE YOU ARE!
HELLO, AUNT GERTRUDE. MOM SAID YOU OFFERED TO HELP ORGANIZE THE MOVERS.
WE'RE DOING OUR PART BY MOVING THE FRUIT.
CLEVER, JOSEPH. FROM HERE IT LOOKS LIKE YOU'RE LOLLY-GAGGING.
AUNT GERTRUDE, I'M PRETTY SURE NO ONE USES THE WORD "LOLLYGAGGING" ANY MORE.
WELL, NO ONE IS ME NOW, ARE THEY?
THAT IS TRUE.

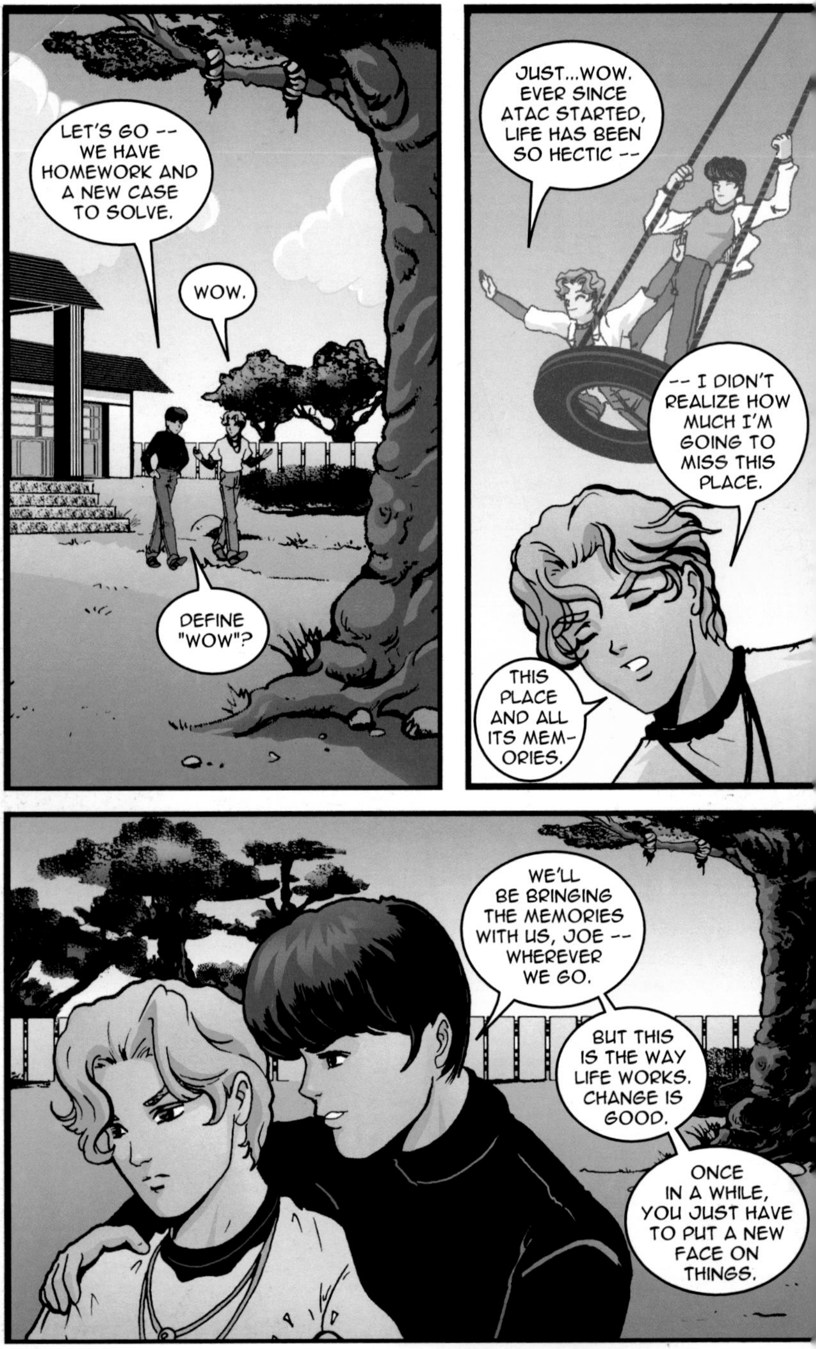
LET'S GO -- WE HAVE HOMEWORK AND A NEW CASE TO SOLVE.
WOW.
DEFINE "WOW"?
JUST...WOW. EVER SINCE ATAC STARTED, LIFE HAS BEEN SO HECTIC --
-- I DIDN'T REALIZE HOW MUCH I'M GOING TO MISS THIS PLACE.
THIS PLACE AND ALL ITS MEM-ORIES.
WE'LL BE BRINGING THE MEMORIES WITH US, JOE -- WHEREVER WE GO.
BUT THIS IS THE WAY LIFE WORKS. CHANGE IS GOOD.
ONCE IN A WHILE, YOU JUST HAVE TO PUT A NEW FACE ON THINGS.

INTO THE SPECIALLY CONSTRUCTED CONSOLE WITH YOU, MY FRIEND.

"IDENTITY THEFT."

WHAT? DID SOMEONE LOSE THEIR ID?

SWORD:
★★★

FOCUS, JOE. AS OF THIS MOMENT WE'RE OFFICIALLY ON A --

CA -- CA -- "CASE" IS THE WORD I'M LOOKING FOR.

HELLO, BOYS.

"HOT" IS THE WORD THAT COMES TO MIND.

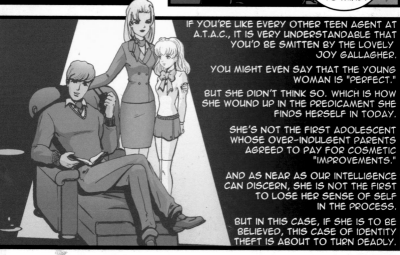

IF YOU'RE LIKE EVERY OTHER TEEN AGENT AT A.T.A.C., IT IS VERY UNDERSTANDABLE THAT YOU'D BE SMITTEN BY THE LOVELY JOY GALLAGHER.

YOU MIGHT EVEN SAY THAT THE YOUNG WOMAN IS "PERFECT."

BUT SHE DIDN'T THINK SO. WHICH IS HOW SHE WOUND UP IN THE PREDICAMENT SHE FINDS HERSELF IN TODAY.

SHE'S NOT THE FIRST ADOLESCENT WHOSE OVER-INDULGENT PARENTS AGREED TO PAY FOR COSMETIC "IMPROVEMENTS."

AND AS NEAR AS OUR INTELLIGENCE CAN DISCERN, SHE IS NOT THE FIRST TO LOSE HER SENSE OF SELF IN THE PROCESS.

BUT IN THIS CASE, IF SHE IS TO BE BELIEVED, THIS CASE OF IDENTITY THEFT IS ABOUT TO TURN DEADLY.

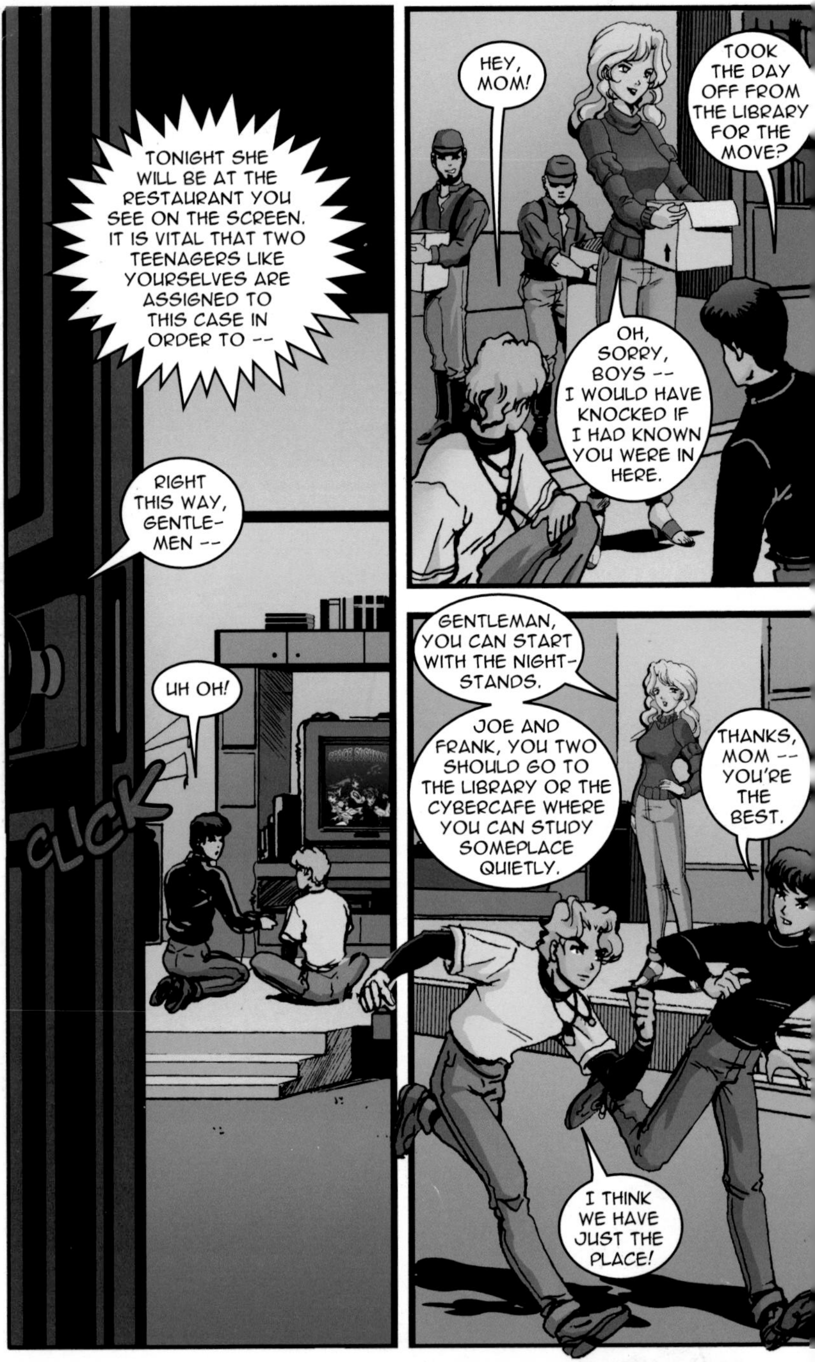
TONIGHT SHE WILL BE AT THE RESTAURANT YOU SEE ON THE SCREEN. IT IS VITAL THAT TWO TEENAGERS LIKE YOURSELVES ARE ASSIGNED TO THIS CASE IN ORDER TO --
RIGHT THIS WAY, GENTLE-MEN --
UH OH!
CLICK
HEY, MOM!
TOOK THE DAY OFF FROM THE LIBRARY FOR THE MOVE?
OH, SORRY, BOYS -- I WOULD HAVE KNOCKED IF I HAD KNOWN YOU WERE IN HERE.
GENTLEMAN, YOU CAN START WITH THE NIGHT-STANDS.
JOE AND FRANK, YOU TWO SHOULD GO TO THE LIBRARY OR THE CYBERCAFE WHERE YOU CAN STUDY SOMEPLACE QUIETLY.
THANKS, MOM -- YOU'RE THE BEST.
I THINK WE HAVE JUST THE PLACE!

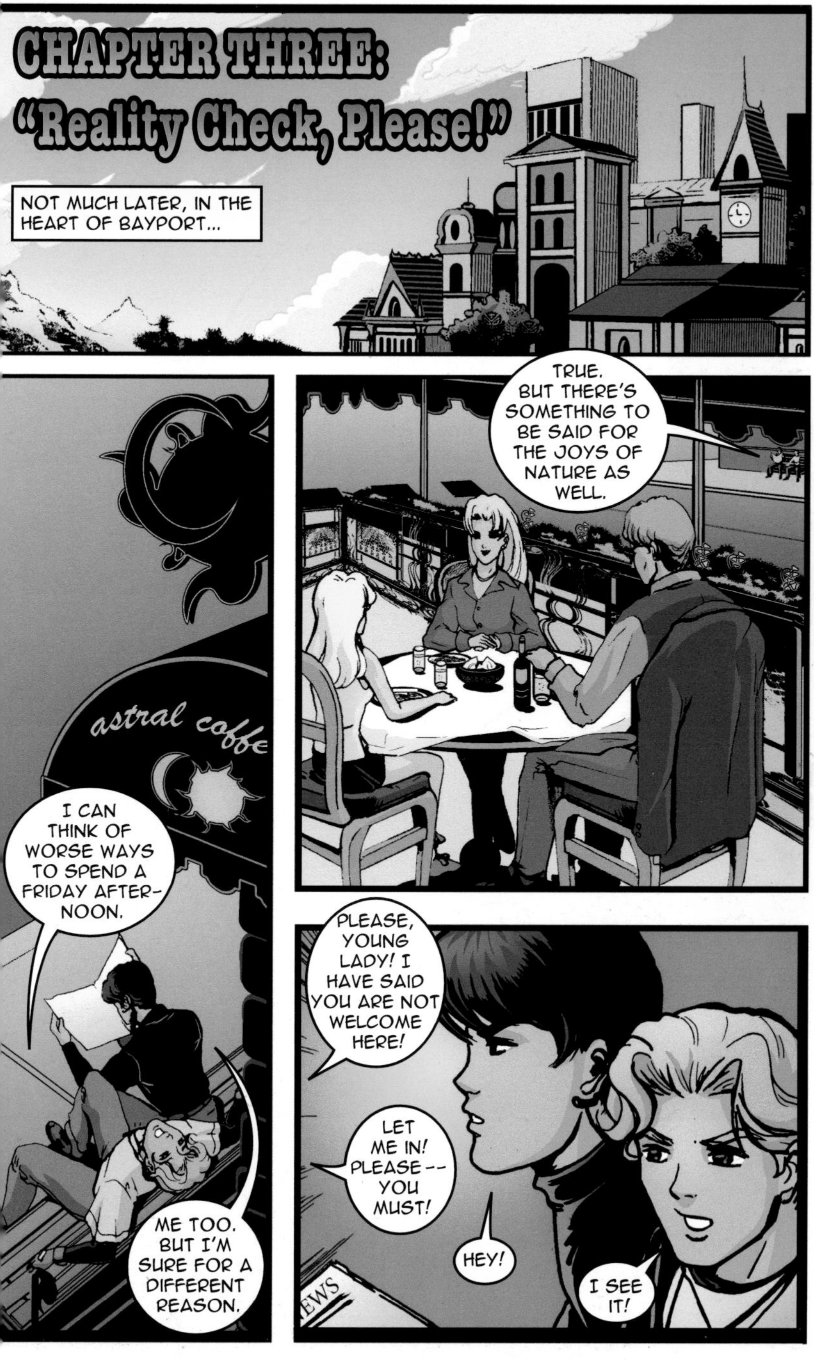

CHAPTER THREE:
"Reality Check, Please!"
NOT MUCH LATER, IN THE HEART OF BAYPORT...
TRUE. BUT THERE'S SOMETHING TO BE SAID FOR THE JOYS OF NATURE AS WELL.
astral coffe
I CAN THINK OF WORSE WAYS TO SPEND A FRIDAY AFTER-NOON.
ME TOO. BUT I'M SURE FOR A DIFFERENT REASON.
PLEASE, YOUNG LADY! I HAVE SAID YOU ARE NOT WELCOME HERE!
LET ME IN! PLEASE-- YOU MUST!
HEY!
I SEE IT!
EWS

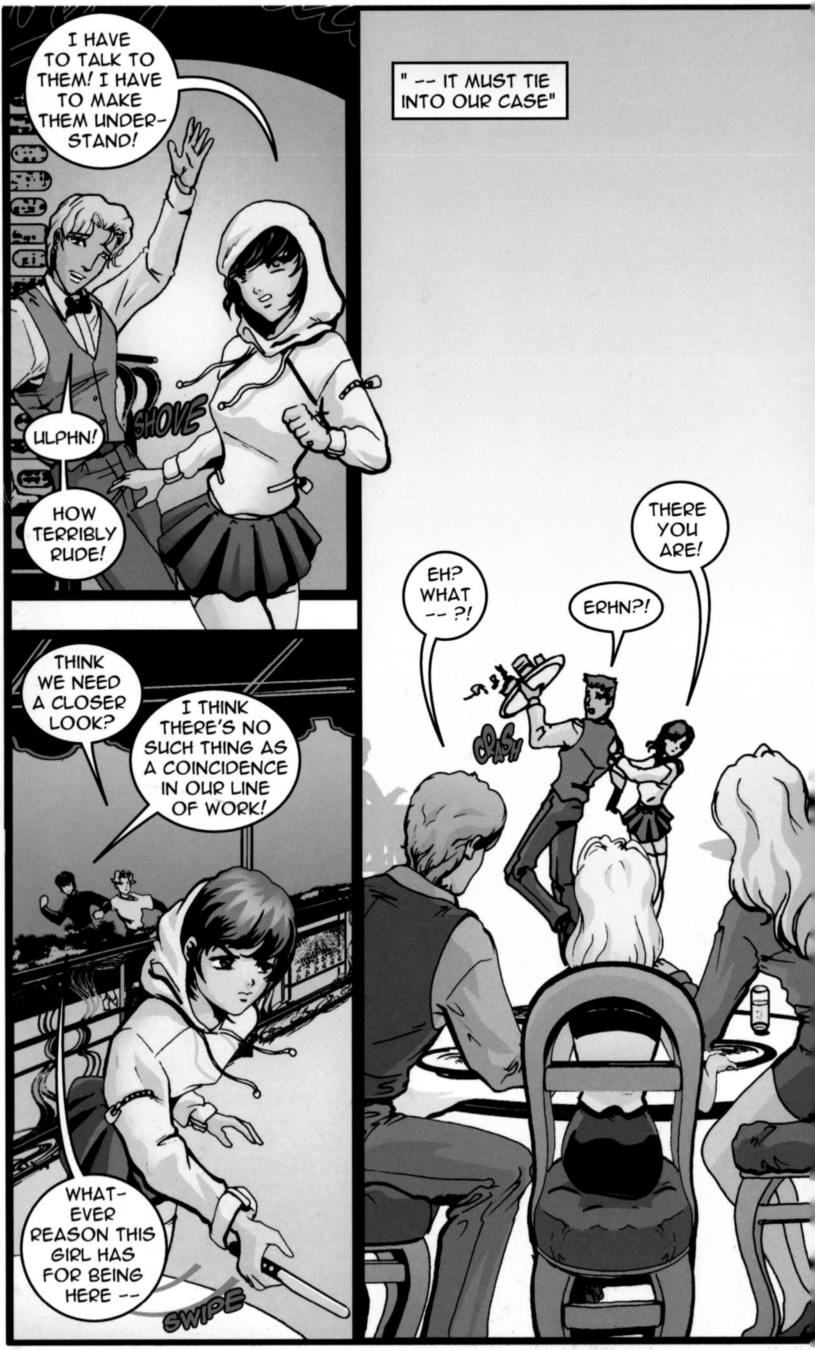
I HAVE TO TALK TO THEM! I HAVE TO MAKE THEM UNDER-STAND!
SHOVE
ULPHN!
HOW TERRIBLY RUDE!
THINK WE NEED A CLOSER LOOK?
I THINK THERE'S NO SUCH THING AS A COINCIDENCE IN OUR LINE OF WORK!
WHAT-EVER REASON THIS GIRL HAS FOR BEING HERE --
SWIPE
" -- IT MUST TIE INTO OUR CASE"
THERE YOU ARE!
EH? WHAT -- ?!
ERHN?!
CRASH

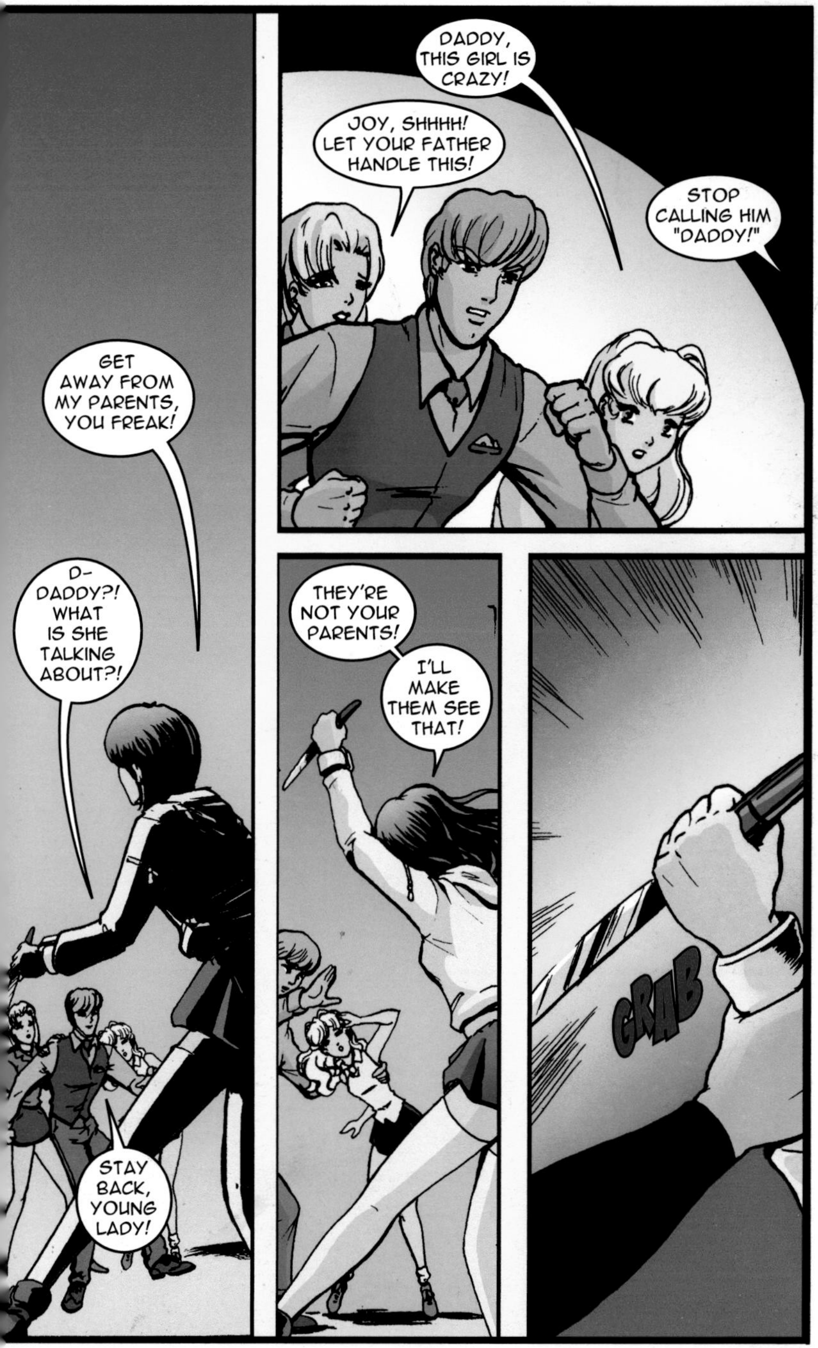
GET AWAY FROM MY PARENTS, YOU FREAK!
D-DADDY?! WHAT IS SHE TALKING ABOUT?!
STAY BACK, YOUNG LADY!
DADDY, THIS GIRL IS CRAZY!
JOY, SHHHH! LET YOUR FATHER HANDLE THIS!
STOP CALLING HIM "DADDY!"
THEY'RE NOT YOUR PARENTS!
I'LL MAKE THEM SEE THAT!
GRAB

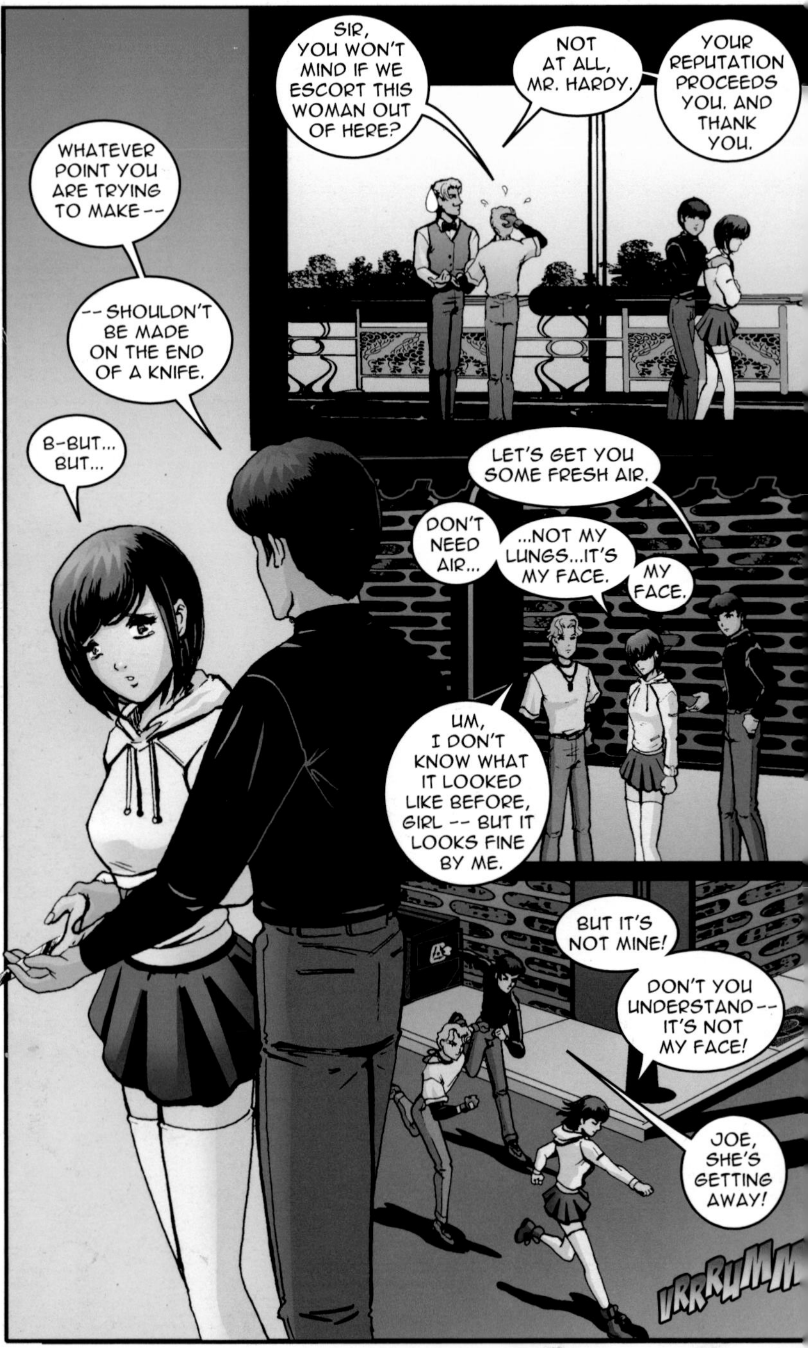
WHATEVER POINT YOU ARE TRYING TO MAKE--
--SHOULDN'T BE MADE ON THE END OF A KNIFE.
B-BUT... BUT...
SIR, YOU WON'T MIND IF WE ESCORT THIS WOMAN OUT OF HERE?
NOT AT ALL, MR. HARDY.
YOUR REPUTATION PROCEEDS YOU. AND THANK YOU.
LET'S GET YOU SOME FRESH AIR.
DON'T NEED AIR...
...NOT MY LUNGS...IT'S MY FACE.
MY FACE.
UM, I DON'T KNOW WHAT IT LOOKED LIKE BEFORE, GIRL -- BUT IT LOOKS FINE BY ME.
BUT IT'S NOT MINE!
DON'T YOU UNDERSTAND-- IT'S NOT MY FACE!
JOE, SHE'S GETTING AWAY!
VRRRUMMM

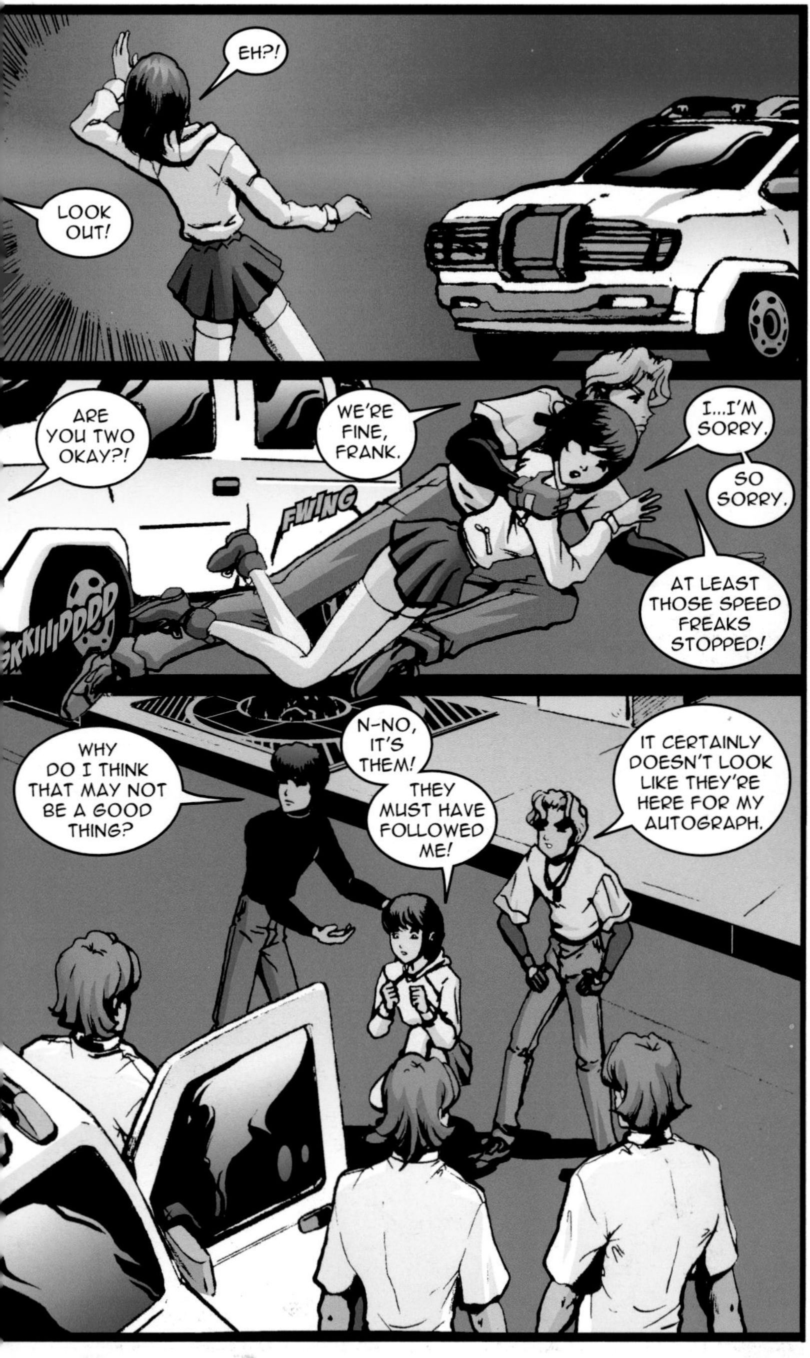

EH?!
LOOK OUT!
ARE YOU TWO OKAY?!
WE'RE FINE, FRANK.
I...I'M SORRY.
SO SORRY.
FWING
SKKIIIIDDDD
AT LEAST THOSE SPEED FREAKS STOPPED!
WHY DO I THINK THAT MAY NOT BE A GOOD THING?
N-NO, IT'S THEM!
THEY MUST HAVE FOLLOWED ME!
IT CERTAINLY DOESN'T LOOK LIKE THEY'RE HERE FOR MY AUTOGRAPH.

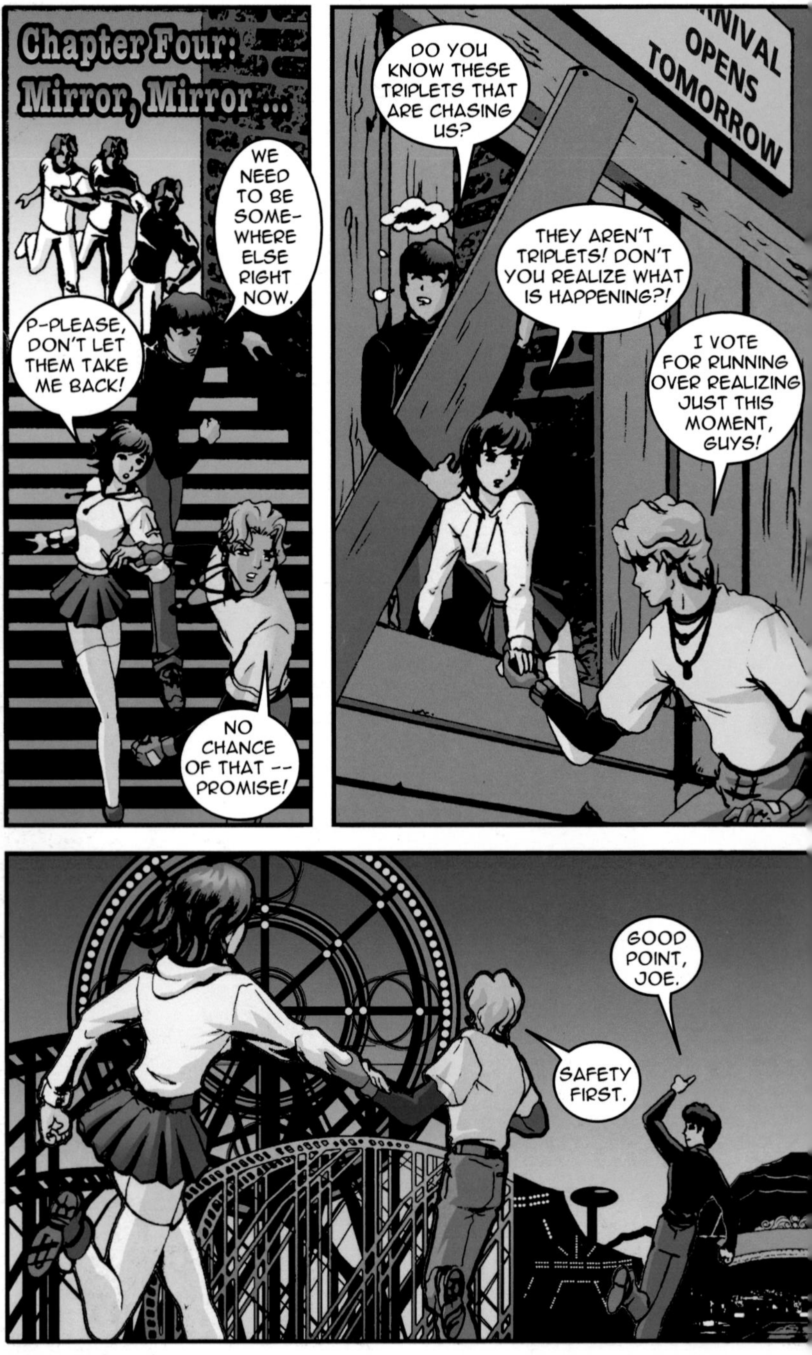
Chapter Four: Mirror, Mirror ...
WE NEED TO BE SOME-WHERE ELSE RIGHT NOW.
P-PLEASE, DON'T LET THEM TAKE ME BACK!
NO CHANCE OF THAT -- PROMISE!
DO YOU KNOW THESE TRIPLETS THAT ARE CHASING US?
NIVAL OPENS TOMORROW
THEY AREN'T TRIPLETS! DON'T YOU REALIZE WHAT IS HAPPENING?!
I VOTE FOR RUNNING OVER REALIZING JUST THIS MOMENT, GUYS!
GOOD POINT, JOE.
SAFETY FIRST.

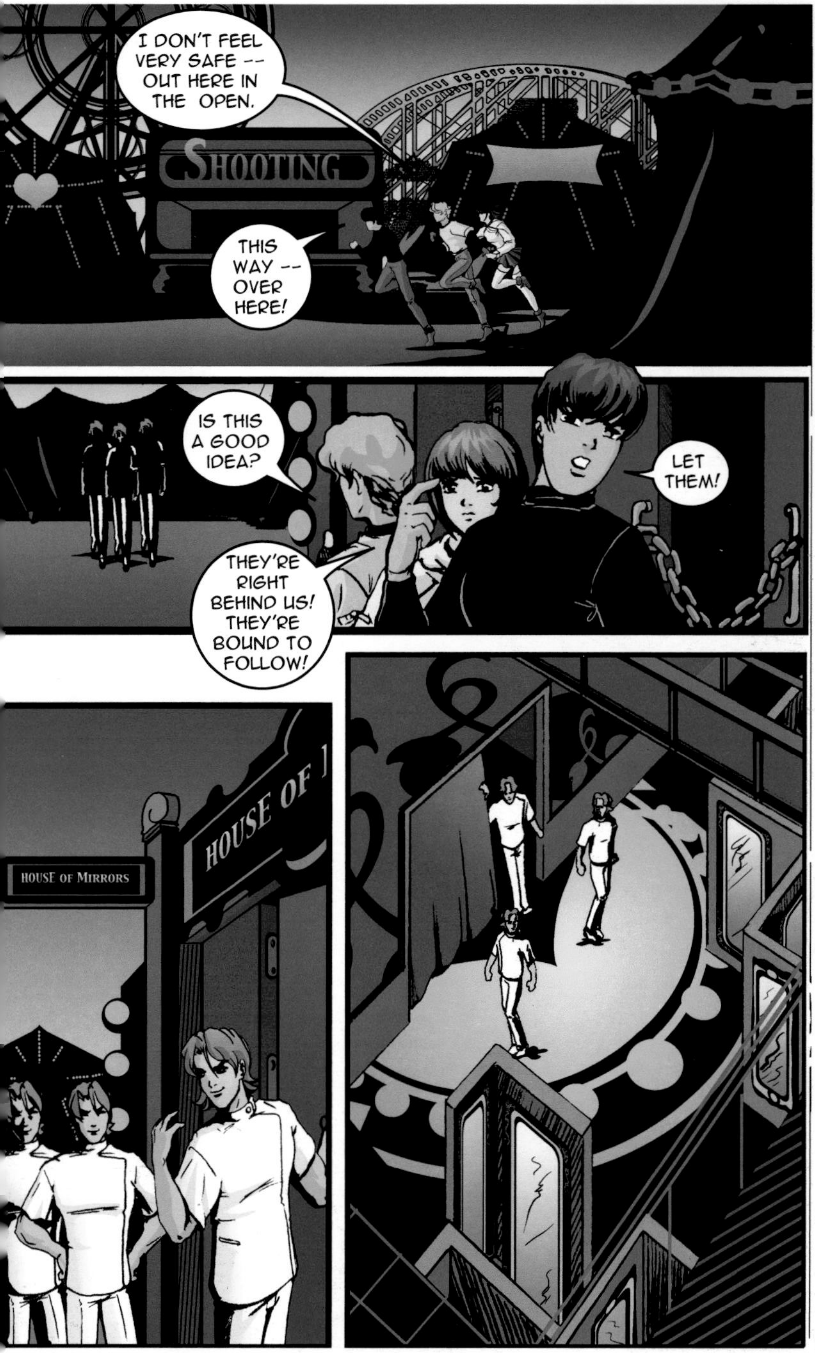
I DON'T FEEL VERY SAFE -- OUT HERE IN THE OPEN.
SHOOTING
THIS WAY -- OVER HERE!
IS THIS A GOOD IDEA?
LET THEM!
THEY'RE RIGHT BEHIND US! THEY'RE BOUND TO FOLLOW!
HOUSE OF MIRRORS
HOUSE OF

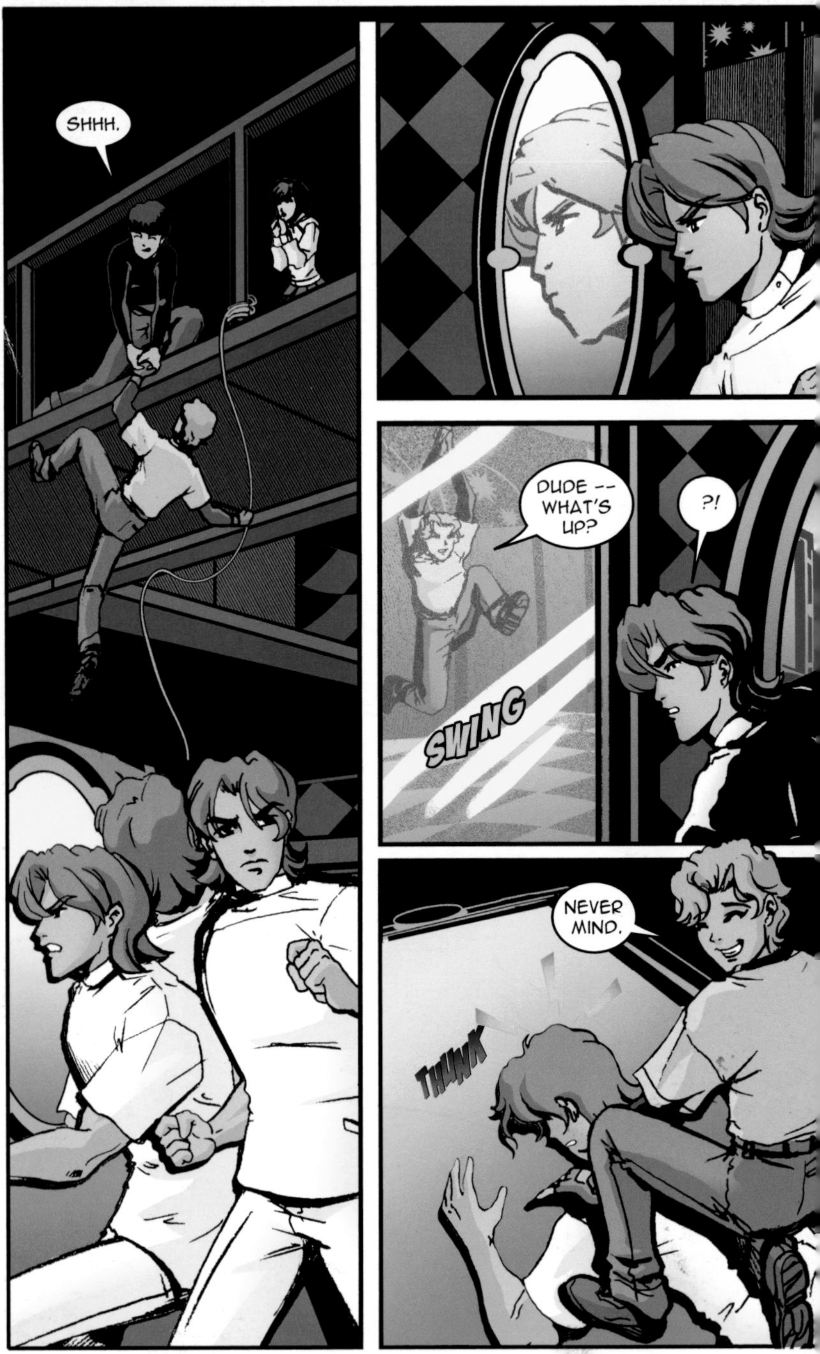
SHHH.
DUDE -- WHAT'S UP?
?!
SWING
NEVER MIND.
THUNK

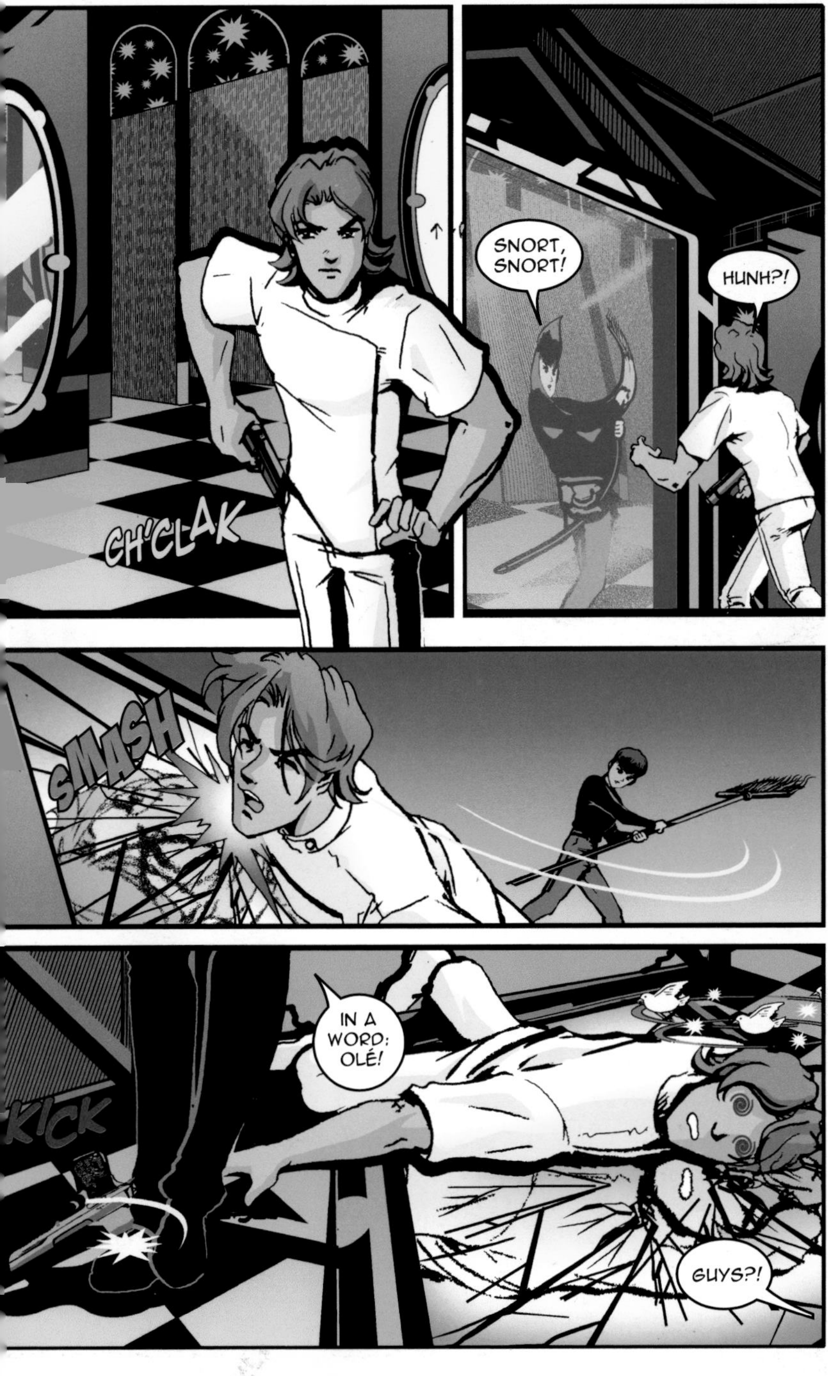
CH'CLAK
SNORT, SNORT!
HUNH?!
SMASH
IN A WORD: OLÉ!
KICK
GUYS?!

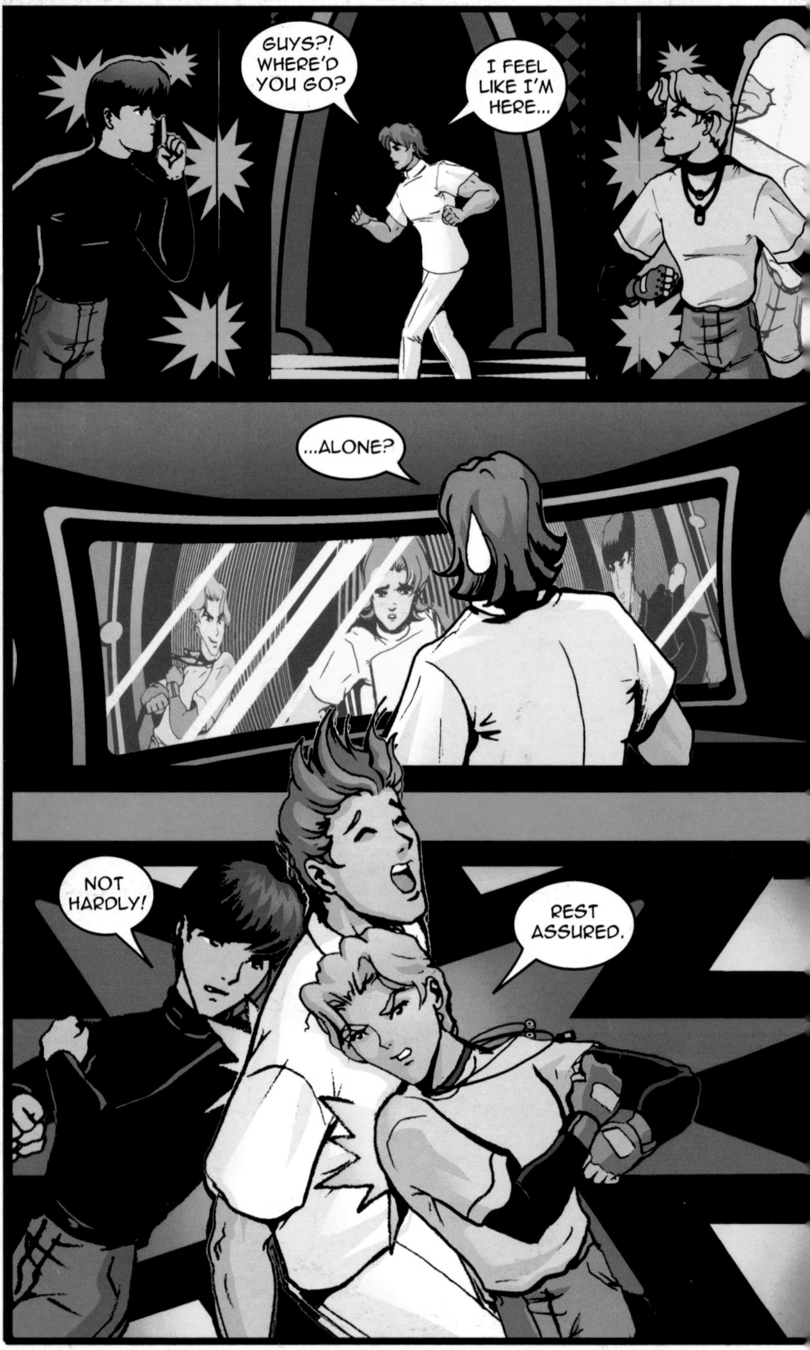
GUYS?!
WHERE'D
YOU GO?
I FEEL
LIKE I'M
HERE...
...ALONE?
NOT
HARDLY!
REST
ASSURED.

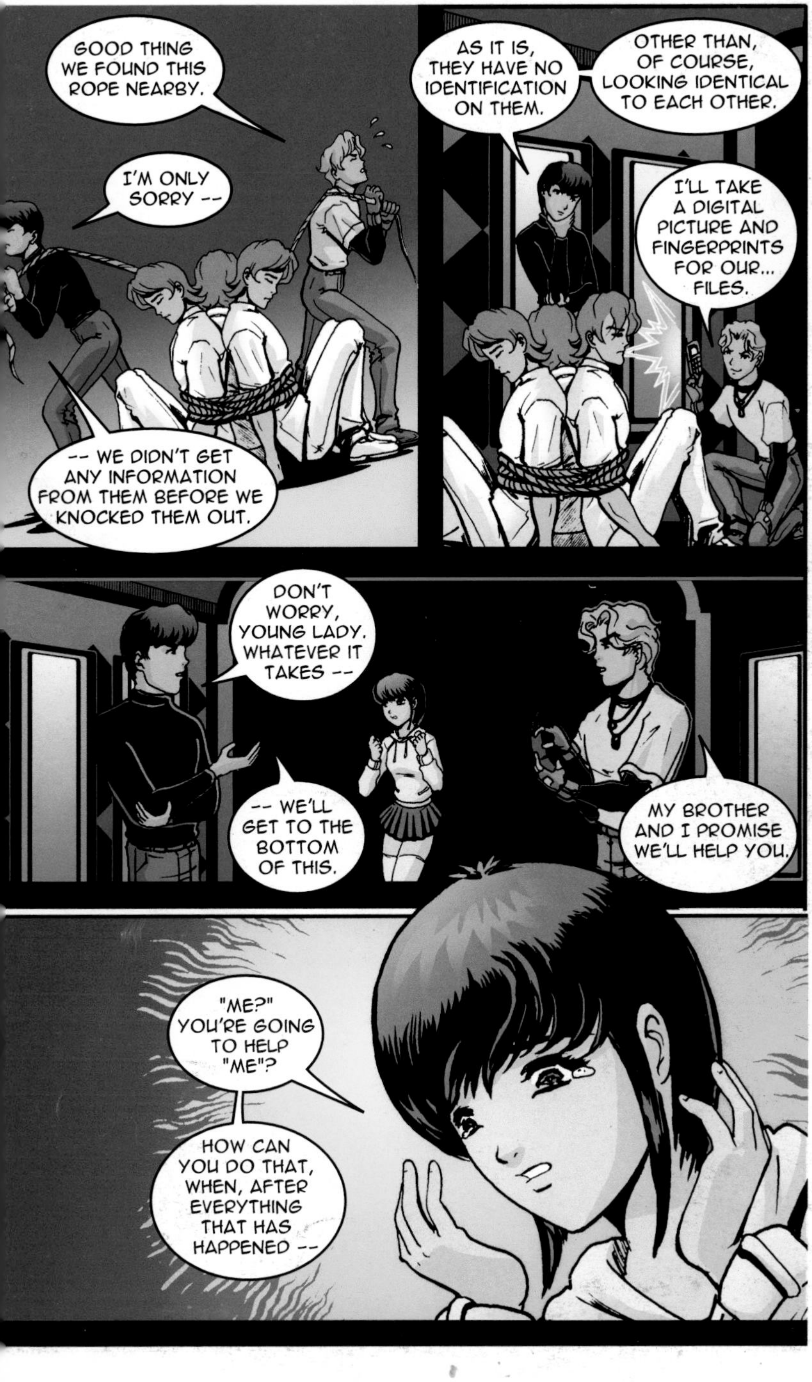
GOOD THING WE FOUND THIS ROPE NEARBY.
I'M ONLY SORRY --
-- WE DIDN'T GET ANY INFORMATION FROM THEM BEFORE WE KNOCKED THEM OUT.
AS IT IS, THEY HAVE NO IDENTIFICATION ON THEM.
OTHER THAN, OF COURSE, LOOKING IDENTICAL TO EACH OTHER.
I'LL TAKE A DIGITAL PICTURE AND FINGERPRINTS FOR OUR... FILES.
DON'T WORRY, YOUNG LADY. WHATEVER IT TAKES --
-- WE'LL GET TO THE BOTTOM OF THIS.
MY BROTHER AND I PROMISE WE'LL HELP YOU.
"ME?" YOU'RE GOING TO HELP "ME"?
HOW CAN YOU DO THAT, WHEN, AFTER EVERYTHING THAT HAS HAPPENED --

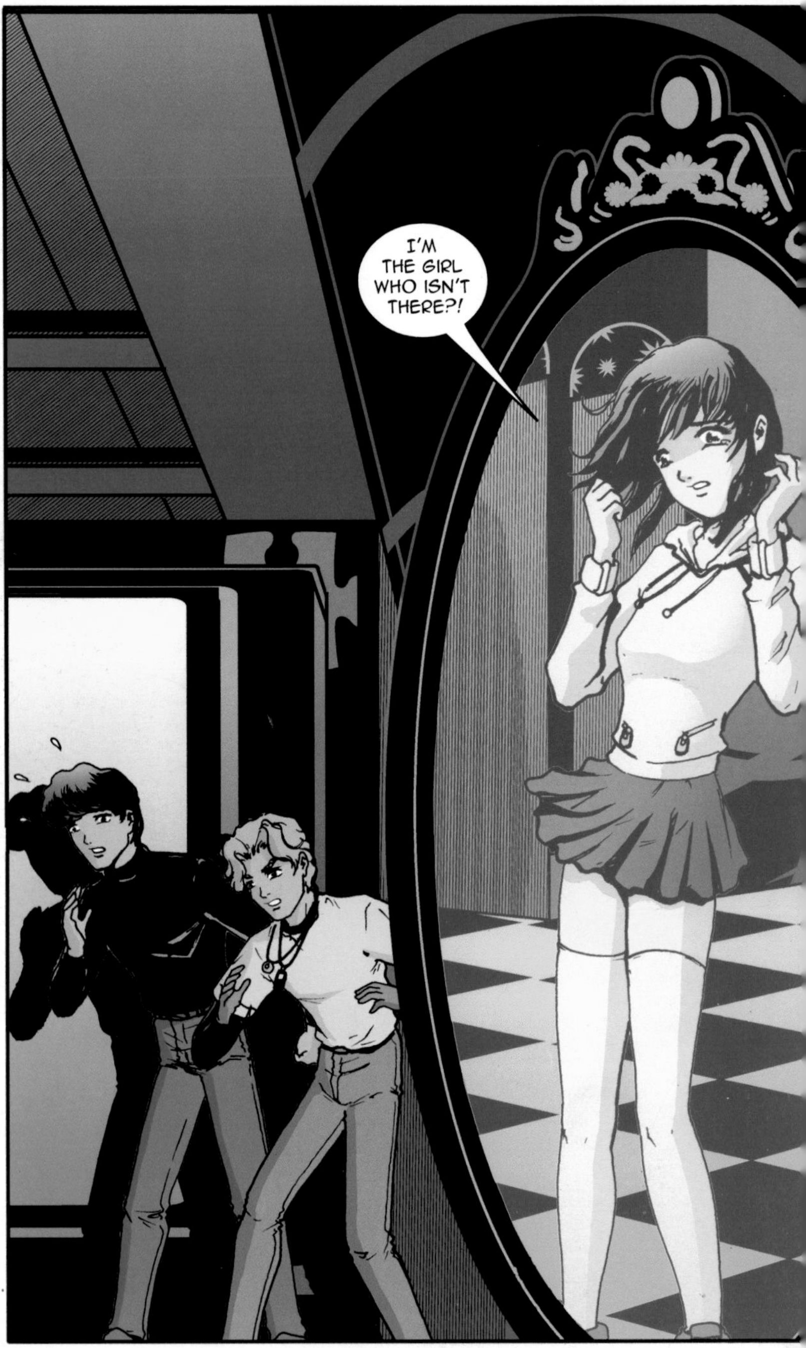
I'M THE GIRL WHO ISN'T THERE?!

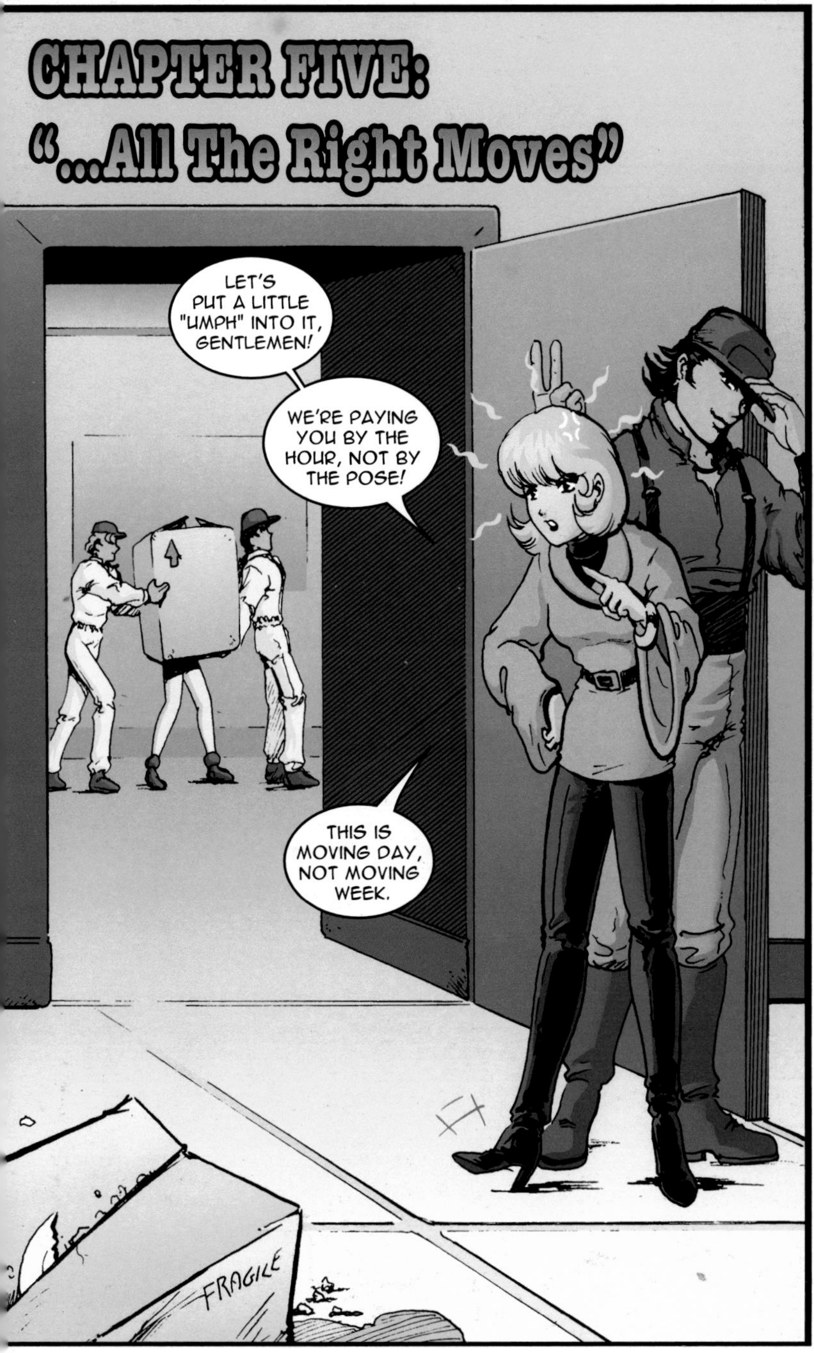
CHAPTER FIVE:
"...All The Right Moves"
LET'S PUT A LITTLE "UMPH" INTO IT, GENTLEMEN!
WE'RE PAYING YOU BY THE HOUR, NOT BY THE POSE!
THIS IS MOVING DAY, NOT MOVING WEEK.
FRAGILE

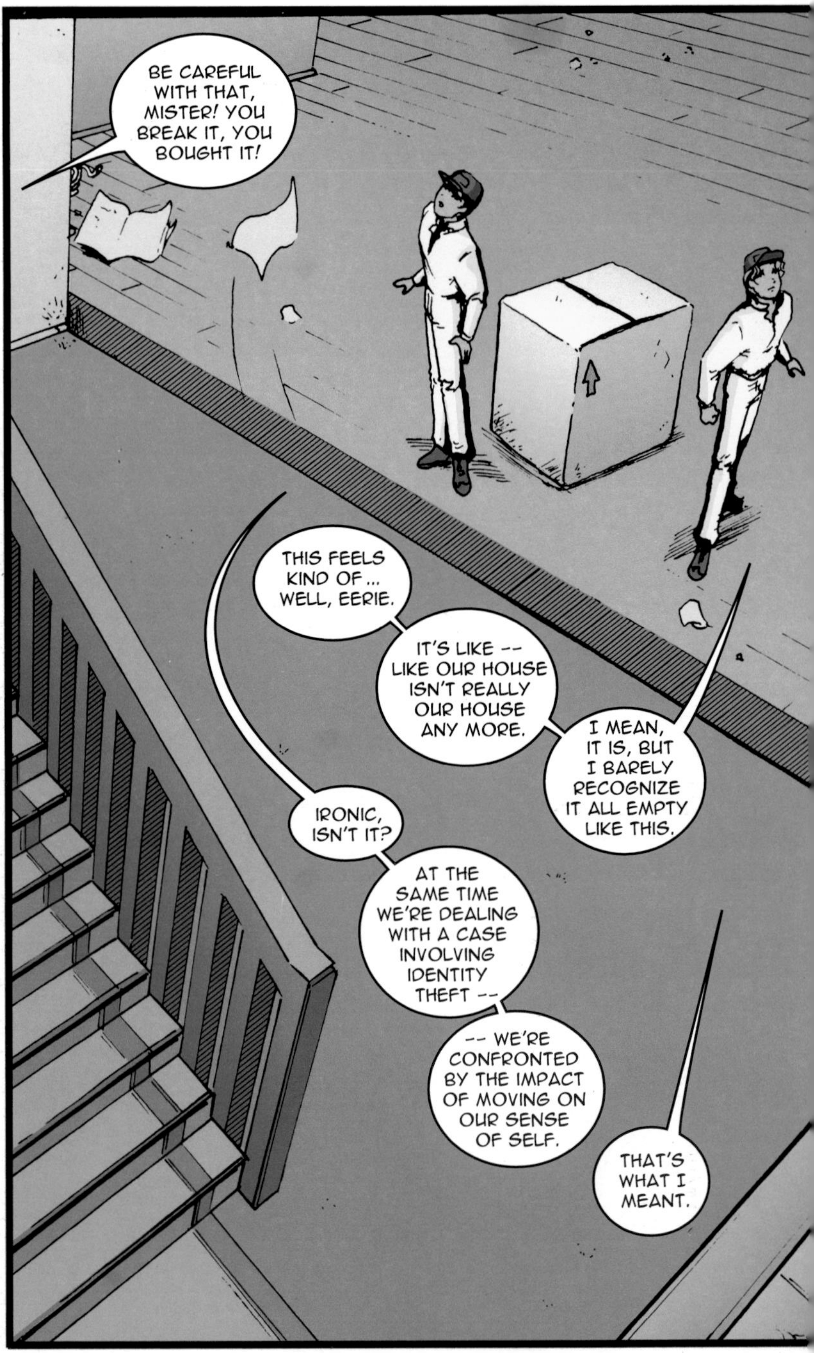
BE CAREFUL WITH THAT, MISTER! YOU BREAK IT, YOU BOUGHT IT!
THIS FEELS KIND OF ... WELL, EERIE.
IT'S LIKE -- LIKE OUR HOUSE ISN'T REALLY OUR HOUSE ANY MORE.
I MEAN, IT IS, BUT I BARELY RECOGNIZE IT ALL EMPTY LIKE THIS.
IRONIC, ISN'T IT?
AT THE SAME TIME WE'RE DEALING WITH A CASE INVOLVING IDENTITY THEFT --
-- WE'RE CONFRONTED BY THE IMPACT OF MOVING ON OUR SENSE OF SELF.
THAT'S WHAT I MEANT.

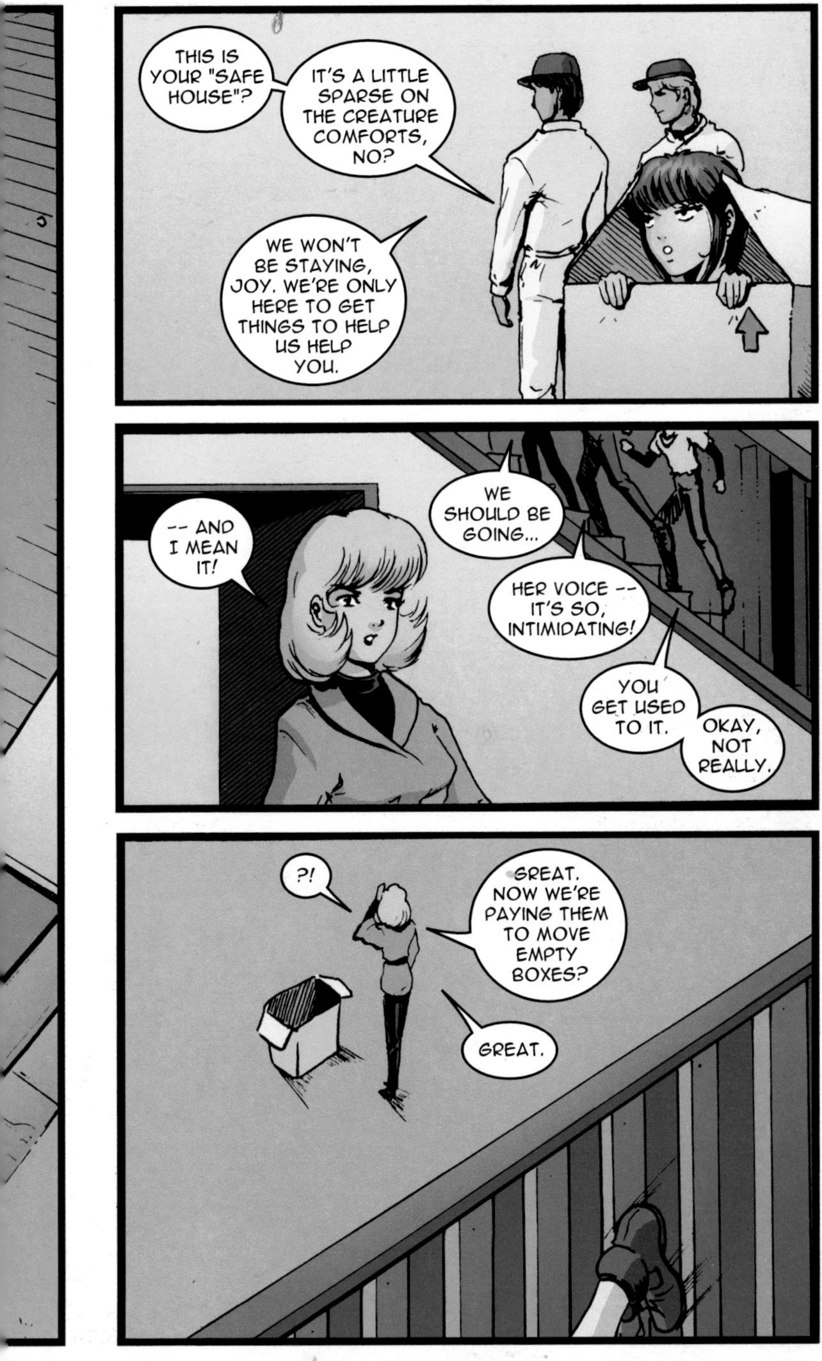
THIS IS YOUR "SAFE HOUSE"?
IT'S A LITTLE SPARSE ON THE CREATURE COMFORTS, NO?
WE WON'T BE STAYING, JOY. WE'RE ONLY HERE TO GET THINGS TO HELP US HELP YOU.
-- AND I MEAN IT!
WE SHOULD BE GOING...
HER VOICE -- IT'S SO, INTIMIDATING!
YOU GET USED TO IT.
OKAY, NOT REALLY.
?!
GREAT. NOW WE'RE PAYING THEM TO MOVE EMPTY BOXES?
GREAT.

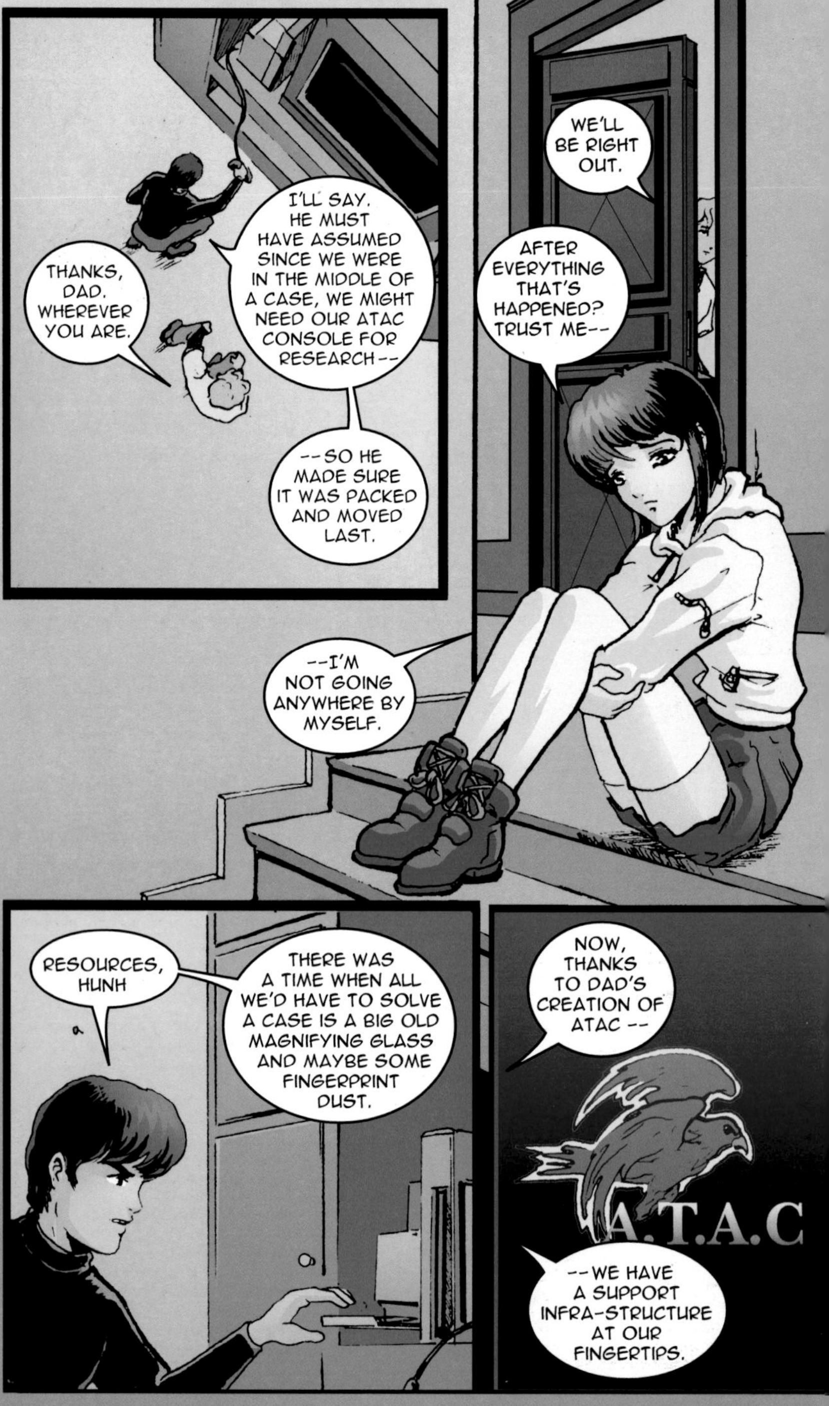
THANKS, DAD. WHEREVER YOU ARE.
I'LL SAY. HE MUST HAVE ASSUMED SINCE WE WERE IN THE MIDDLE OF A CASE, WE MIGHT NEED OUR ATAC CONSOLE FOR RESEARCH --
-- SO HE MADE SURE IT WAS PACKED AND MOVED LAST.
WE'LL BE RIGHT OUT.
AFTER EVERYTHING THAT'S HAPPENED? TRUST ME--
--I'M NOT GOING ANYWHERE BY MYSELF.
RESOURCES, HUNH
THERE WAS A TIME WHEN ALL WE'D HAVE TO SOLVE A CASE IS A BIG OLD MAGNIFYING GLASS AND MAYBE SOME FINGERPRINT DUST.
NOW, THANKS TO DAD'S CREATION OF ATAC --
A.T.A.C
--WE HAVE A SUPPORT INFRA-STRUCTURE AT OUR FINGERTIPS.

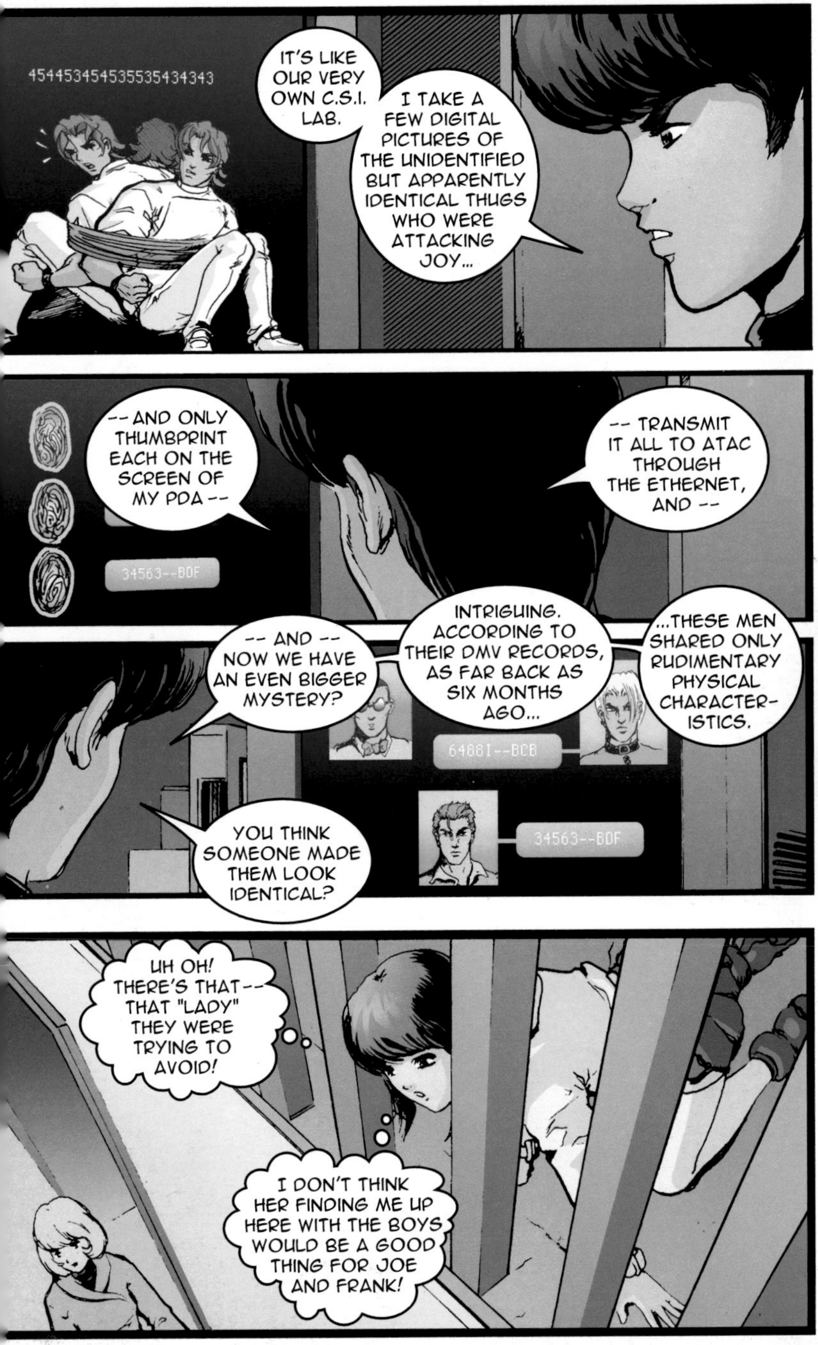
454453454535535434343
IT'S LIKE OUR VERY OWN C.S.I. LAB.
I TAKE A FEW DIGITAL PICTURES OF THE UNIDENTIFIED BUT APPARENTLY IDENTICAL THUGS WHO WERE ATTACKING JOY...
--AND ONLY THUMBPRINT EACH ON THE SCREEN OF MY PDA --
-- TRANSMIT IT ALL TO ATAC THROUGH THE ETHERNET, AND --
34563--BDF
-- AND -- NOW WE HAVE AN EVEN BIGGER MYSTERY?
INTRIGUING. ACCORDING TO THEIR DMV RECORDS, AS FAR BACK AS SIX MONTHS AGO...
...THESE MEN SHARED ONLY RUDIMENTARY PHYSICAL CHARACTER-ISTICS.
6488I--BCB
YOU THINK SOMEONE MADE THEM LOOK IDENTICAL?
34563--BDF
UH OH! THERE'S THAT-- THAT "LADY" THEY WERE TRYING TO AVOID!
I DON'T THINK HER FINDING ME UP HERE WITH THE BOYS WOULD BE A GOOD THING FOR JOE AND FRANK!

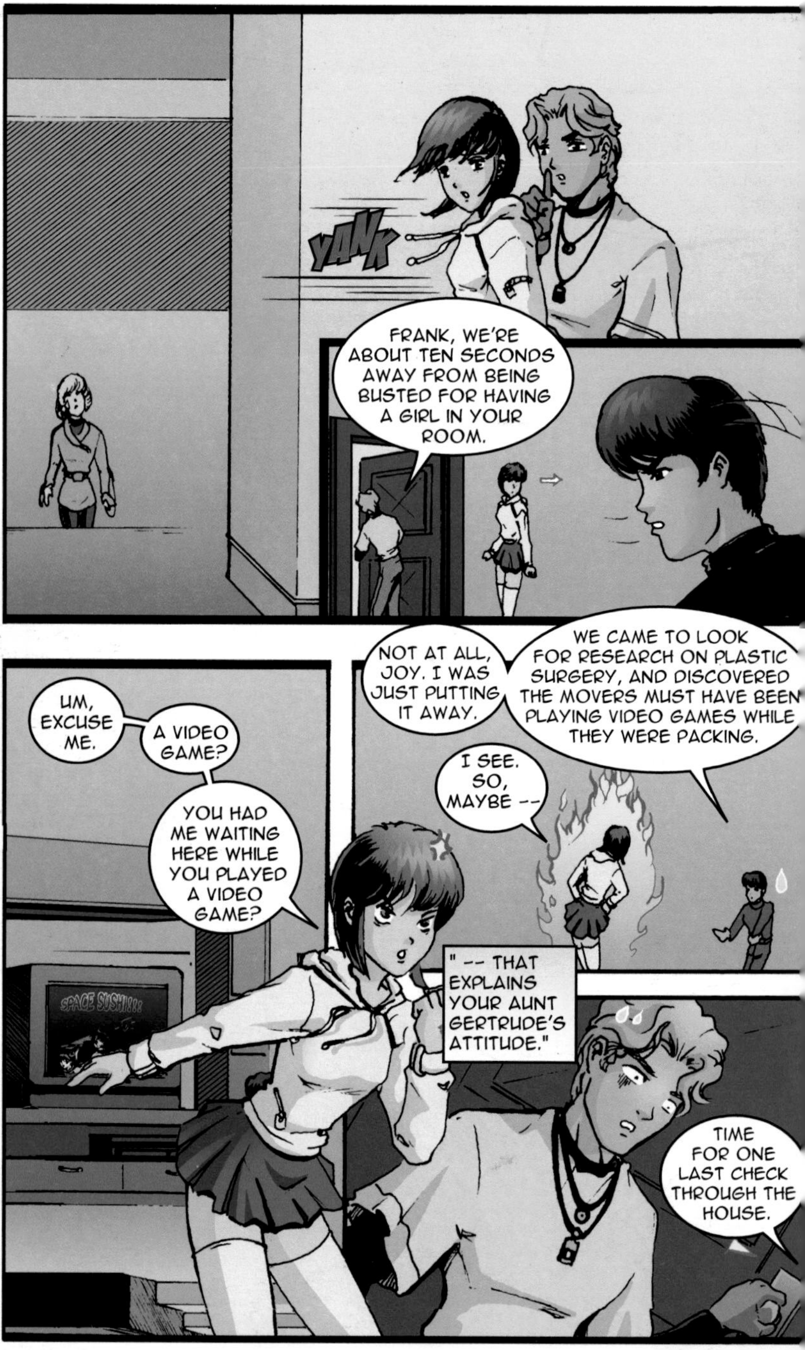
YANK
FRANK, WE'RE ABOUT TEN SECONDS AWAY FROM BEING BUSTED FOR HAVING A GIRL IN YOUR ROOM.
NOT AT ALL, JOY. I WAS JUST PUTTING IT AWAY.
WE CAME TO LOOK FOR RESEARCH ON PLASTIC SURGERY, AND DISCOVERED THE MOVERS MUST HAVE BEEN PLAYING VIDEO GAMES WHILE THEY WERE PACKING.
I SEE. SO, MAYBE --
UM, EXCUSE ME.
A VIDEO GAME?
YOU HAD ME WAITING HERE WHILE YOU PLAYED A VIDEO GAME?
SPACE SUSHI!!!
" -- THAT EXPLAINS YOUR AUNT GERTRUDE'S ATTITUDE."
TIME FOR ONE LAST CHECK THROUGH THE HOUSE.

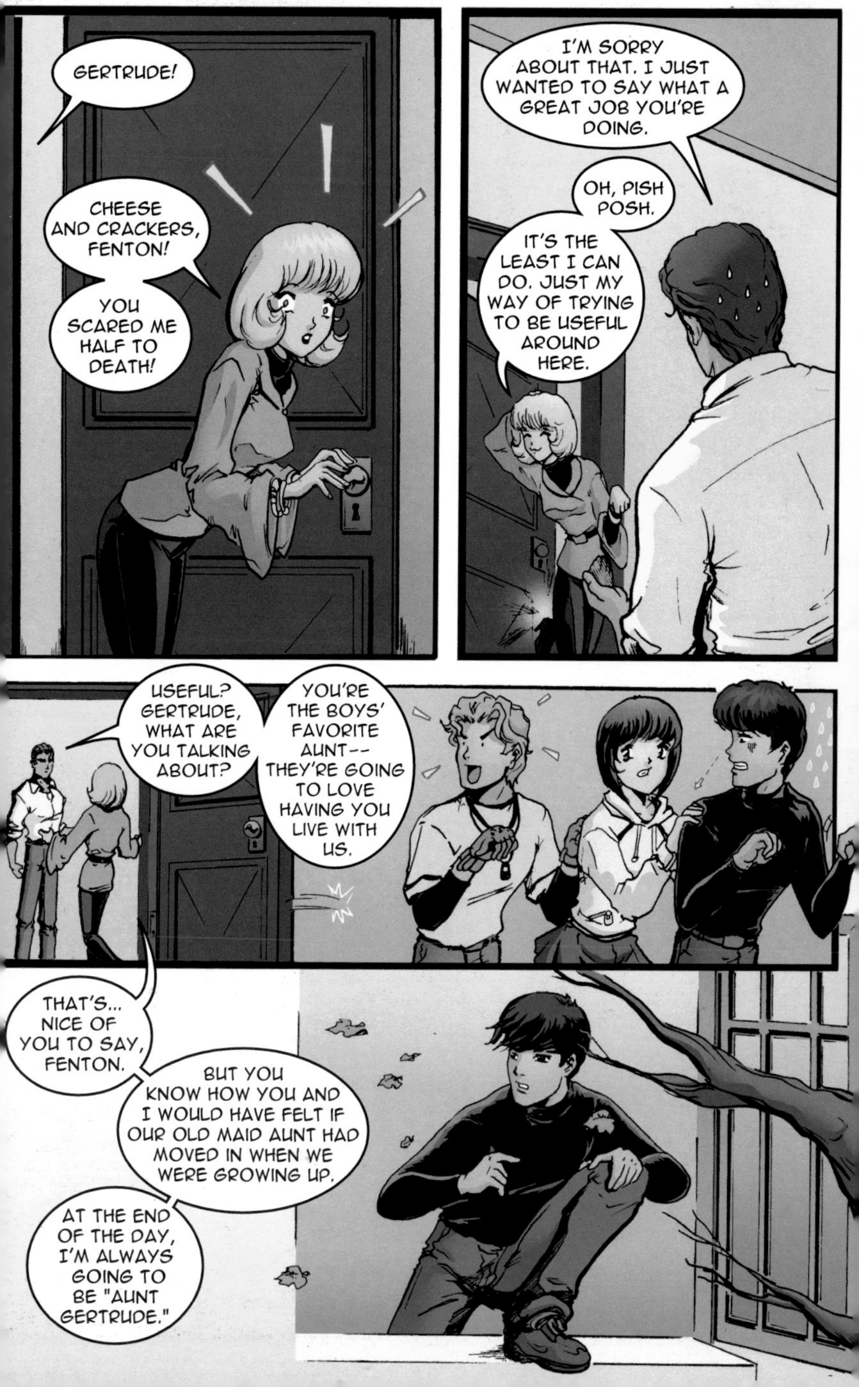
GERTRUDE!
CHEESE AND CRACKERS, FENTON!
YOU SCARED ME HALF TO DEATH!
I'M SORRY ABOUT THAT. I JUST WANTED TO SAY WHAT A GREAT JOB YOU'RE DOING.
OH, PISH POSH.
IT'S THE LEAST I CAN DO. JUST MY WAY OF TRYING TO BE USEFUL AROUND HERE.
USEFUL? GERTRUDE, WHAT ARE YOU TALKING ABOUT?
YOU'RE THE BOYS' FAVORITE AUNT-- THEY'RE GOING TO LOVE HAVING YOU LIVE WITH US.
THAT'S... NICE OF YOU TO SAY, FENTON.
BUT YOU KNOW HOW YOU AND I WOULD HAVE FELT IF OUR OLD MAID AUNT HAD MOVED IN WHEN WE WERE GROWING UP.
AT THE END OF THE DAY, I'M ALWAYS GOING TO BE "AUNT GERTRUDE."

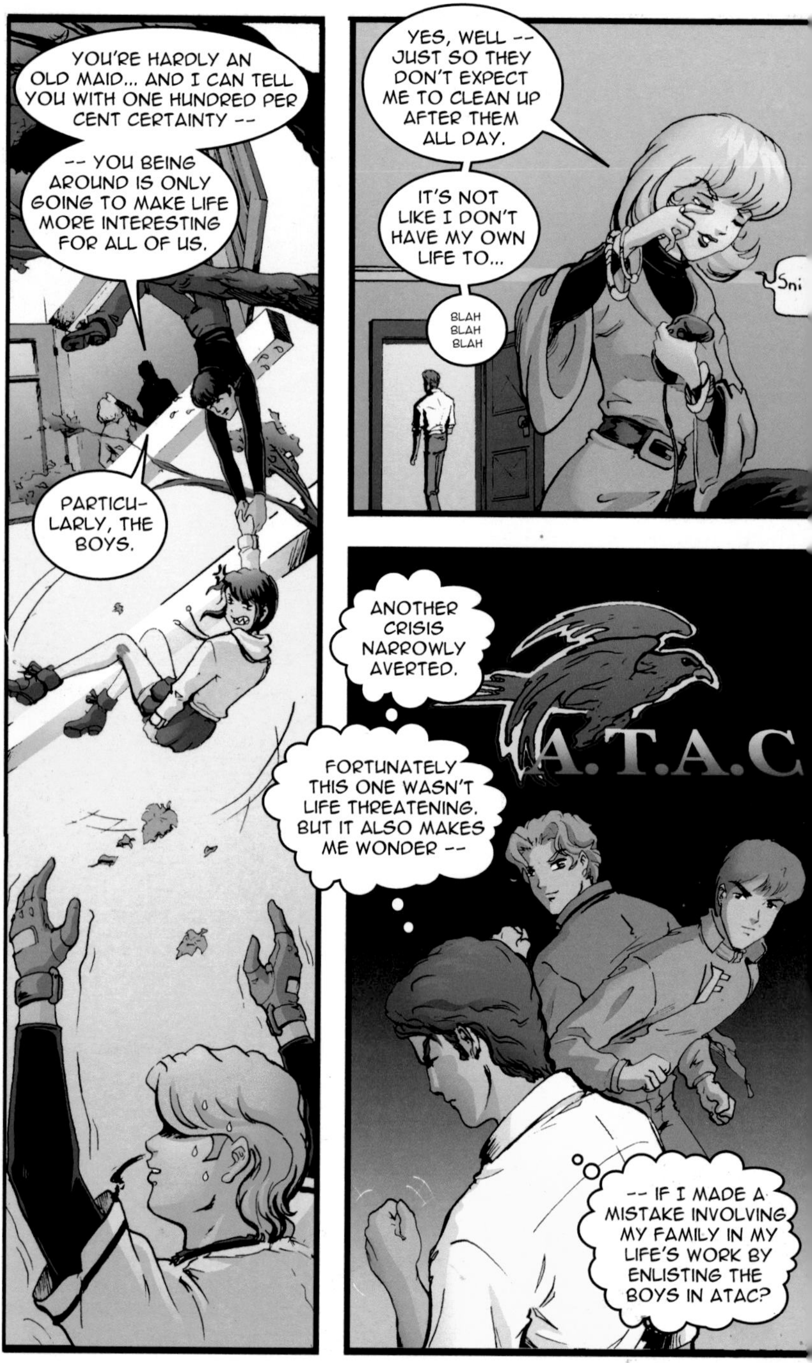
YOU'RE HARDLY AN OLD MAID... AND I CAN TELL YOU WITH ONE HUNDRED PER CENT CERTAINTY --
-- YOU BEING AROUND IS ONLY GOING TO MAKE LIFE MORE INTERESTING FOR ALL OF US.
PARTICU-LARLY, THE BOYS.
YES, WELL -- JUST SO THEY DON'T EXPECT ME TO CLEAN UP AFTER THEM ALL DAY.
IT'S NOT LIKE I DON'T HAVE MY OWN LIFE TO...
BLAH BLAH BLAH
Sni
ANOTHER CRISIS NARROWLY AVERTED.
A.T.A.C
FORTUNATELY THIS ONE WASN'T LIFE THREATENING. BUT IT ALSO MAKES ME WONDER --
-- IF I MADE A MISTAKE INVOLVING MY FAMILY IN MY LIFE'S WORK BY ENLISTING THE BOYS IN ATAC?

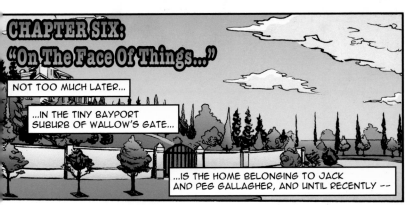

CHAPTER SIX: "On The Face Of Things..."

NOT TOO MUCH LATER...

...IN THE TINY BAYPORT SUBURB OF WALLOW'S GATE...

...IS THE HOME BELONGING TO JACK AND PEG GALLAGHER, AND UNTIL RECENTLY --

-- THEIR DAUGHTER, JOY!

TAP
TAP
PING
TA
PING

THE CODE IS "M.R. S.N.U.G.G.L.E.S" AFTER MY DOG.

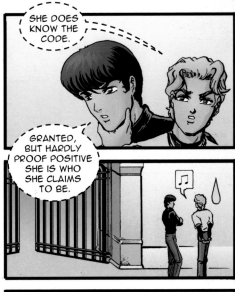

SHE DOES KNOW THE CODE.

GRANTED, BUT HARDLY PROOF POSITIVE SHE IS WHO SHE CLAIMS TO BE.

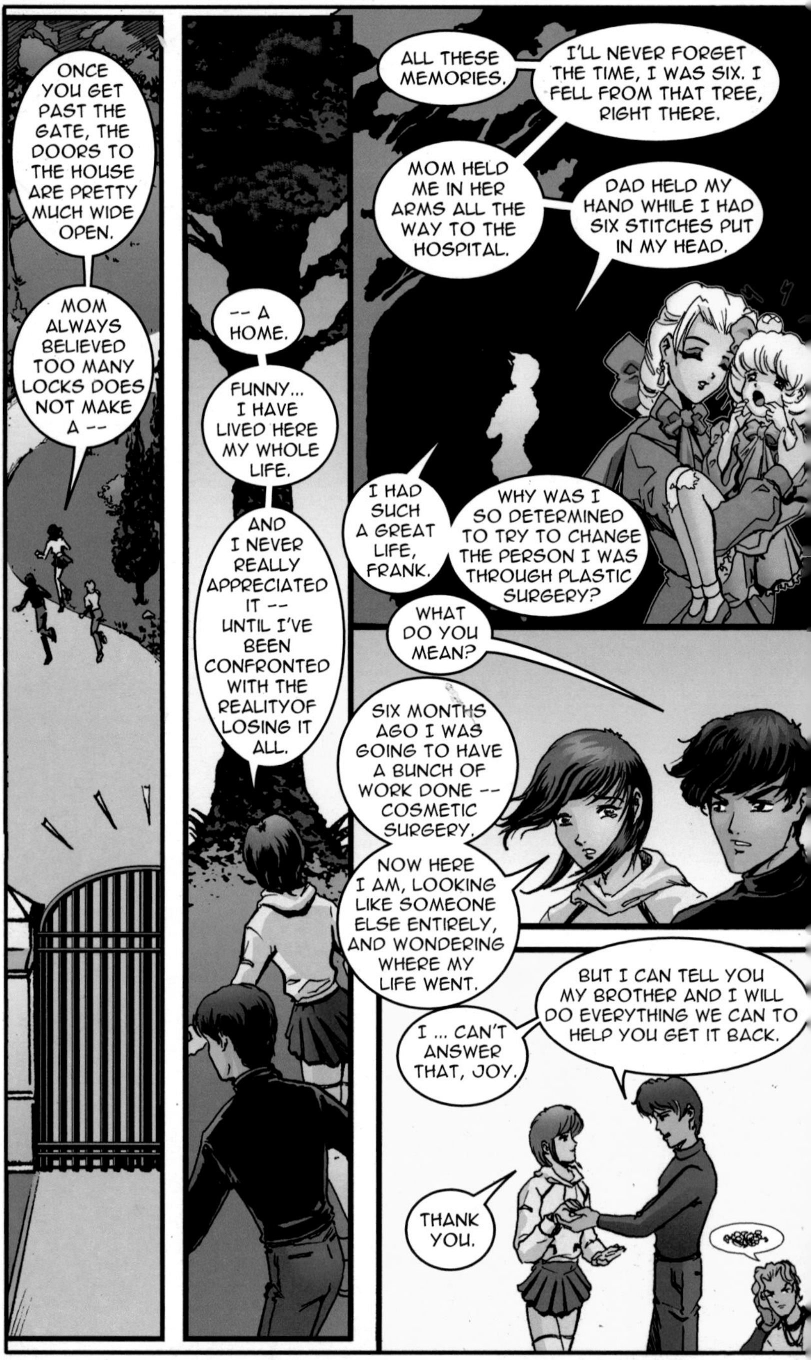
ONCE YOU GET PAST THE GATE, THE DOORS TO THE HOUSE ARE PRETTY MUCH WIDE OPEN.
MOM ALWAYS BELIEVED TOO MANY LOCKS DOES NOT MAKE A --
-- A HOME.
FUNNY... I HAVE LIVED HERE MY WHOLE LIFE.
AND I NEVER REALLY APPRECIATED IT --
UNTIL I'VE BEEN CONFRONTED WITH THE REALITYOF LOSING IT ALL.
ALL THESE MEMORIES.
I'LL NEVER FORGET THE TIME, I WAS SIX. I FELL FROM THAT TREE, RIGHT THERE.
MOM HELD ME IN HER ARMS ALL THE WAY TO THE HOSPITAL.
DAD HELD MY HAND WHILE I HAD SIX STITCHES PUT IN MY HEAD.
I HAD SUCH A GREAT LIFE, FRANK.
WHY WAS I SO DETERMINED TO TRY TO CHANGE THE PERSON I WAS THROUGH PLASTIC SURGERY?
WHAT DO YOU MEAN?
SIX MONTHS AGO I WAS GOING TO HAVE A BUNCH OF WORK DONE -- COSMETIC SURGERY.
NOW HERE I AM, LOOKING LIKE SOMEONE ELSE ENTIRELY, AND WONDERING WHERE MY LIFE WENT.
I ... CAN'T ANSWER THAT, JOY.
BUT I CAN TELL YOU MY BROTHER AND I WILL DO EVERYTHING WE CAN TO HELP YOU GET IT BACK.
THANK YOU.

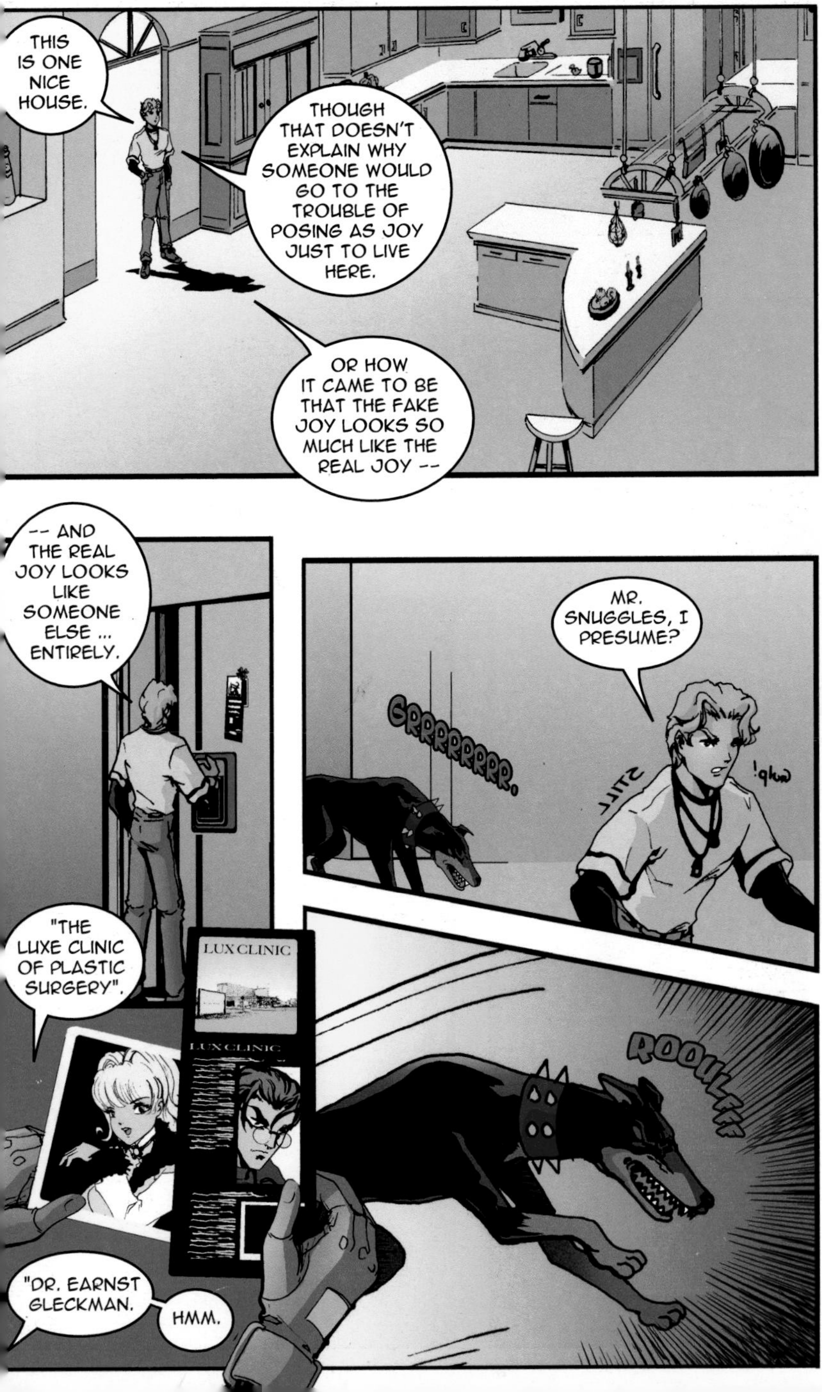
THIS IS ONE NICE HOUSE.
THOUGH THAT DOESN'T EXPLAIN WHY SOMEONE WOULD GO TO THE TROUBLE OF POSING AS JOY JUST TO LIVE HERE.
OR HOW IT CAME TO BE THAT THE FAKE JOY LOOKS SO MUCH LIKE THE REAL JOY --
-- AND THE REAL JOY LOOKS LIKE SOMEONE ELSE ... ENTIRELY.
MR. SNUGGLES, I PRESUME?
GRRRRRRRR.
"THE LUXE CLINIC OF PLASTIC SURGERY".
LUX CLINIC
LUX CLINIC
"DR. EARNST GLECKMAN.
HMM.
ROOWLFFF

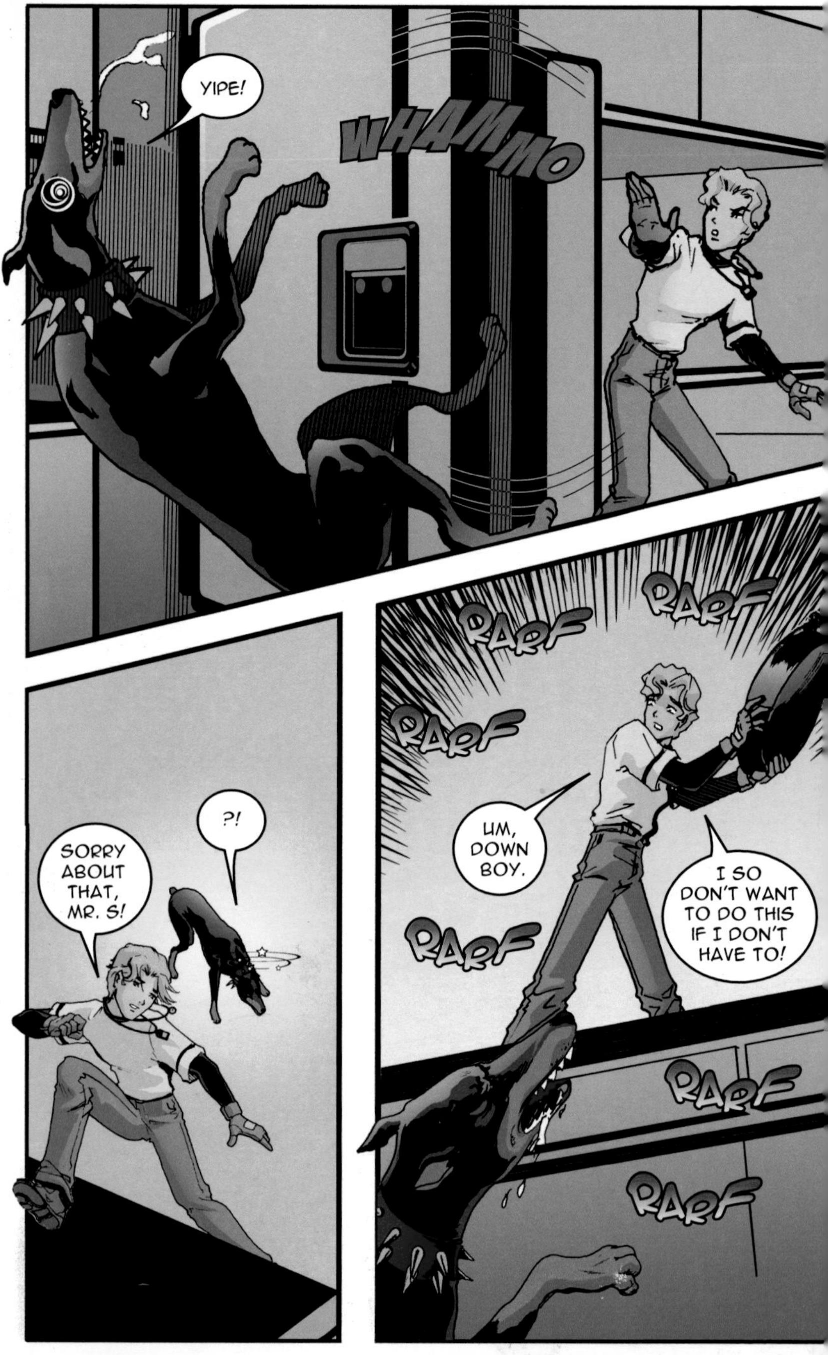

YIPE!
WHAMMO
RARF
RARF
RARF
RARF
RARF
RARF
UM, DOWN BOY.
I SO DON'T WANT TO DO THIS IF I DON'T HAVE TO!
?!
SORRY ABOUT THAT, MR. S!

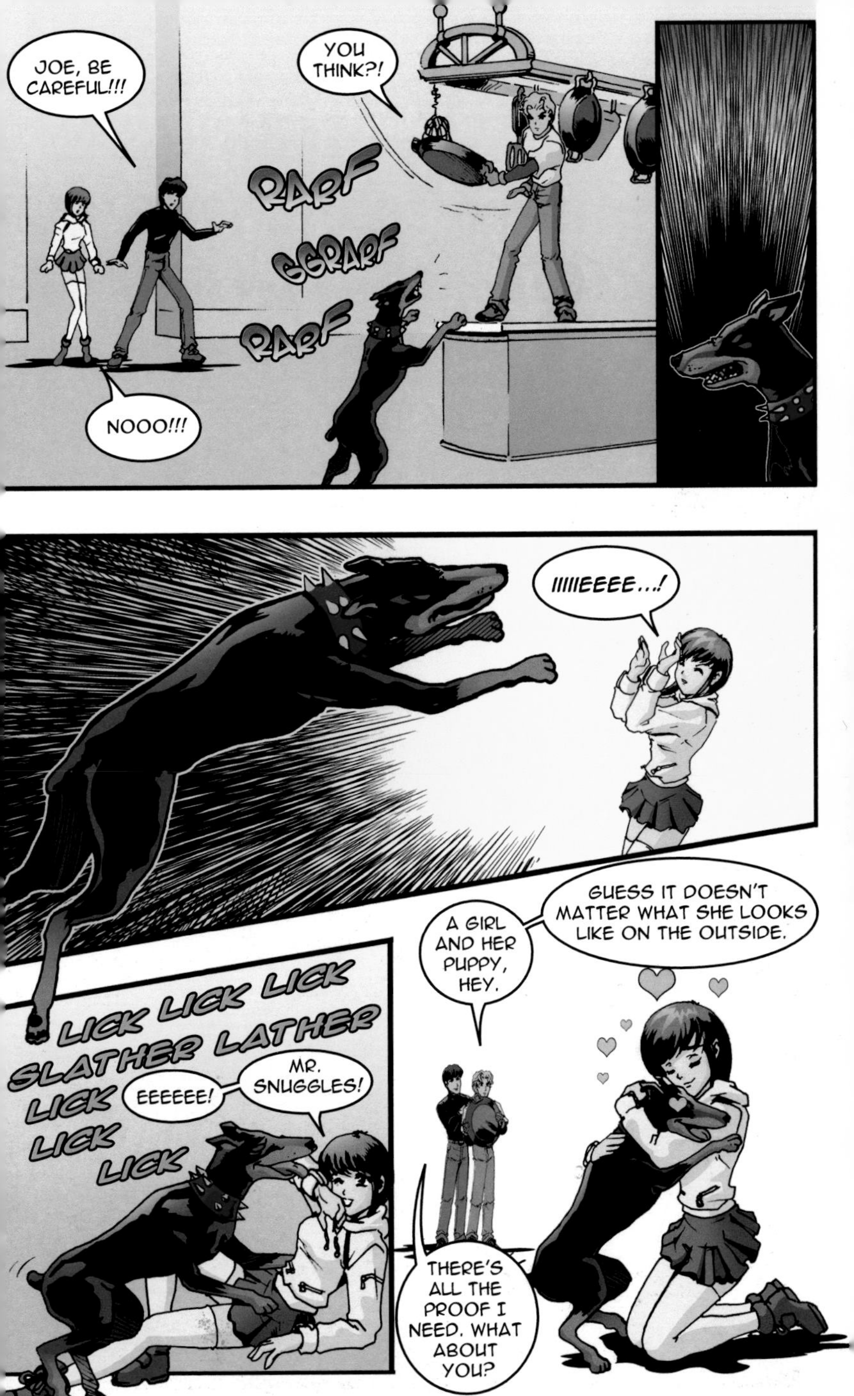
JOE, BE CAREFUL!!!
YOU THINK?!
RARF
GGRARF
RARF
NOOO!!!
IIIIIEEEE...!
LICK LICK LICK
SLATHER LATHER
LICK
EEEEEE!
MR. SNUGGLES!
LICK
LICK
A GIRL AND HER PUPPY, HEY.
GUESS IT DOESN'T MATTER WHAT SHE LOOKS LIKE ON THE OUTSIDE.
THERE'S ALL THE PROOF I NEED. WHAT ABOUT YOU?

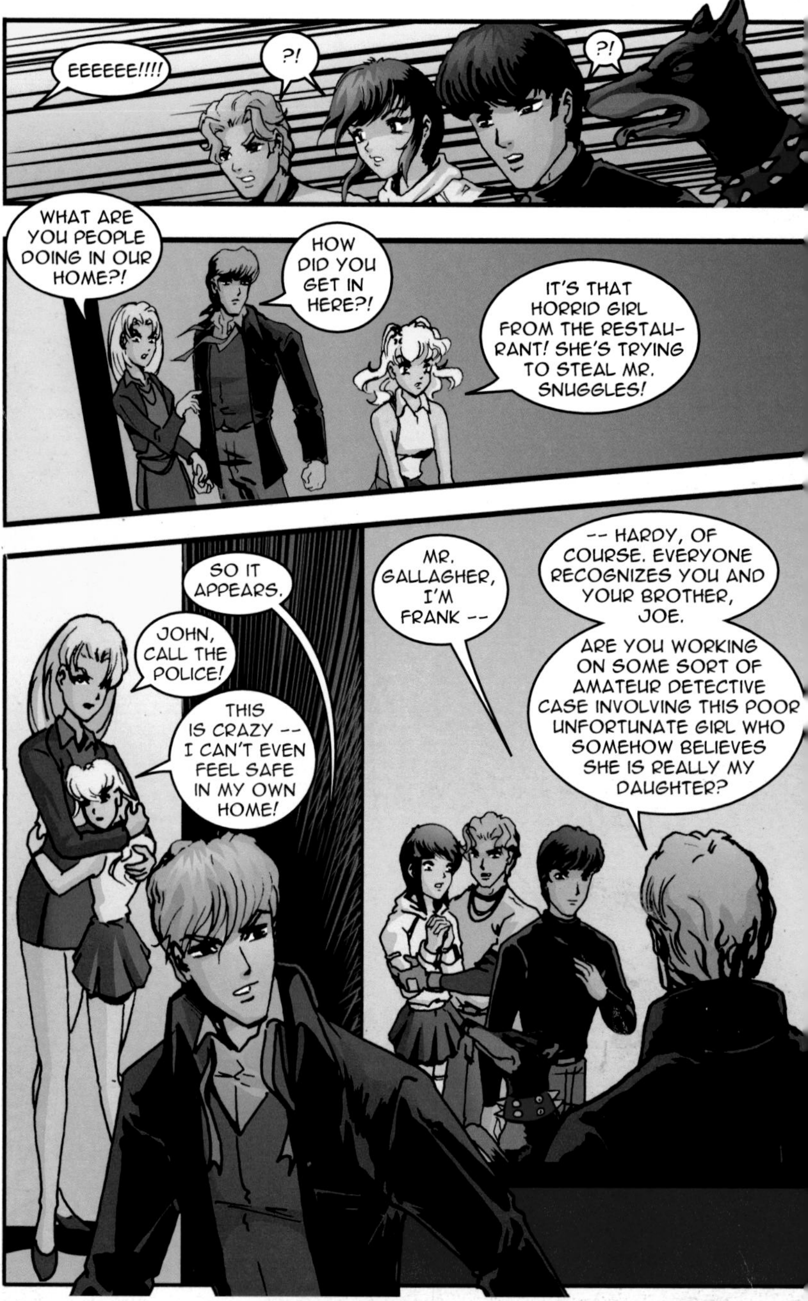
EEEEEE!!!!
?!
?!
WHAT ARE YOU PEOPLE DOING IN OUR HOME?!
HOW DID YOU GET IN HERE?!
IT'S THAT HORRID GIRL FROM THE RESTAU-RANT! SHE'S TRYING TO STEAL MR. SNUGGLES!
JOHN, CALL THE POLICE!
THIS IS CRAZY -- I CAN'T EVEN FEEL SAFE IN MY OWN HOME!
SO IT APPEARS.
MR. GALLAGHER, I'M FRANK --
-- HARDY, OF COURSE. EVERYONE RECOGNIZES YOU AND YOUR BROTHER, JOE.
ARE YOU WORKING ON SOME SORT OF AMATEUR DETECTIVE CASE INVOLVING THIS POOR UNFORTUNATE GIRL WHO SOMEHOW BELIEVES SHE IS REALLY MY DAUGHTER?

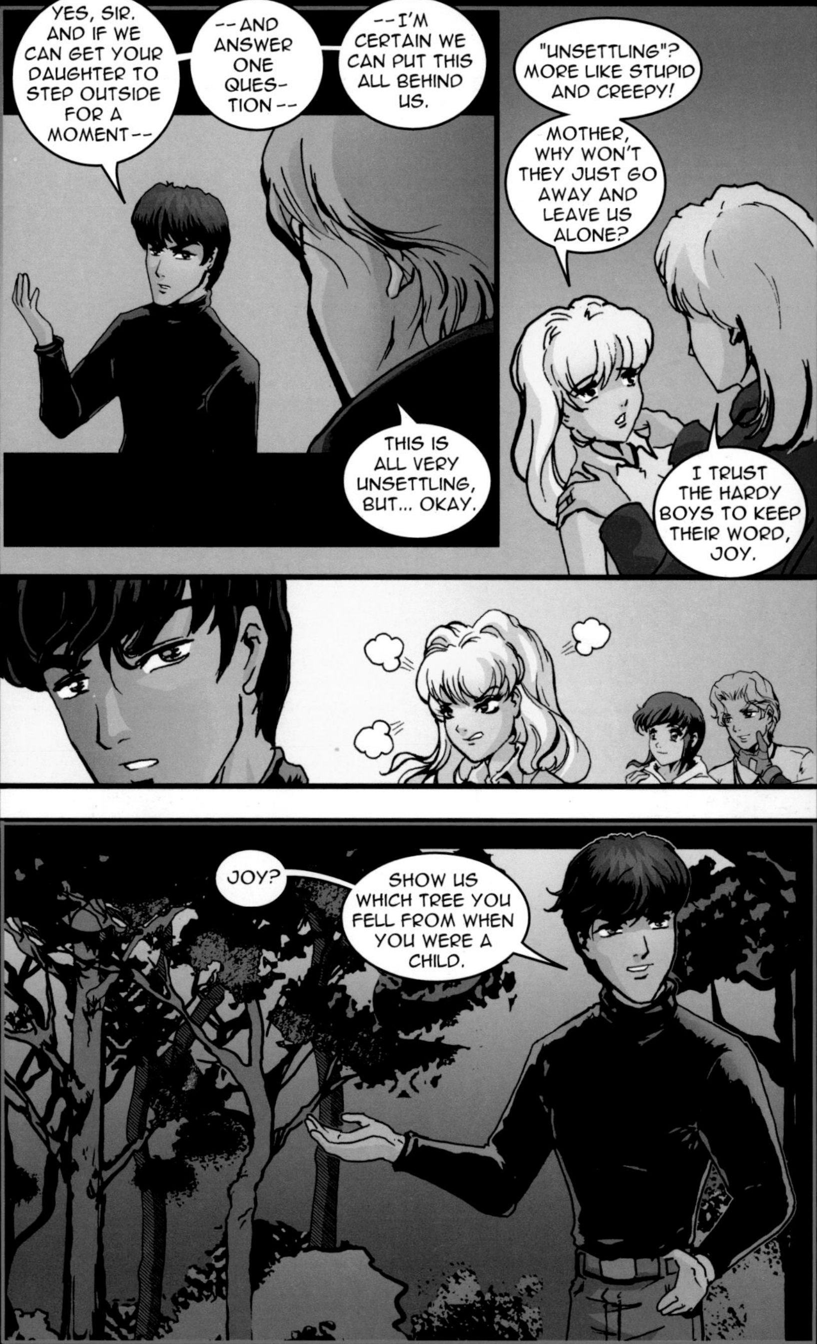
YES, SIR. AND IF WE CAN GET YOUR DAUGHTER TO STEP OUTSIDE FOR A MOMENT--
--AND ANSWER ONE QUES- TION--
--I'M CERTAIN WE CAN PUT THIS ALL BEHIND US.
THIS IS ALL VERY UNSETTLING, BUT... OKAY.
"UNSETTLING"? MORE LIKE STUPID AND CREEPY!
MOTHER, WHY WON'T THEY JUST GO AWAY AND LEAVE US ALONE?
I TRUST THE HARDY BOYS TO KEEP THEIR WORD, JOY.
JOY?
SHOW US WHICH TREE YOU FELL FROM WHEN YOU WERE A CHILD.

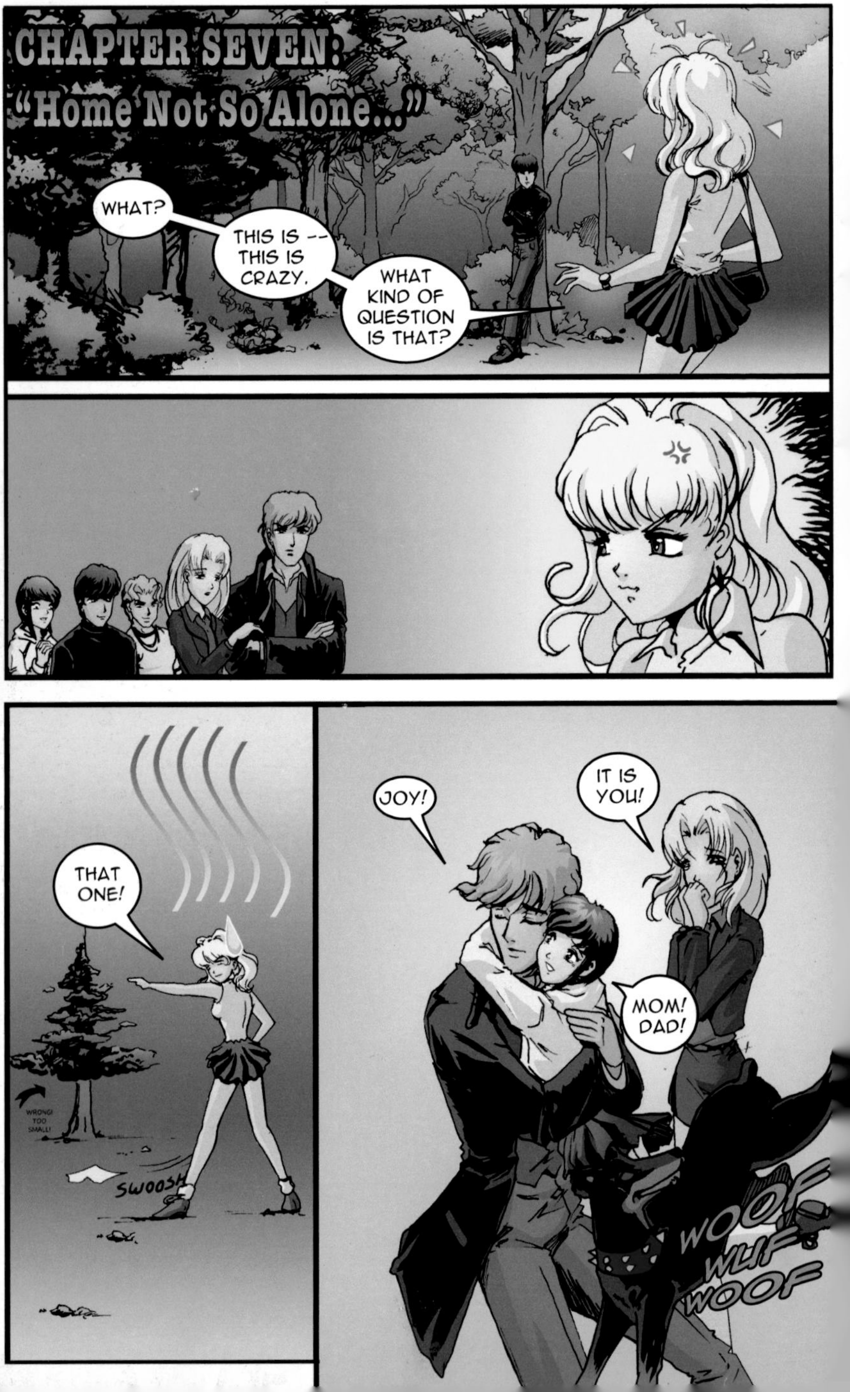
CHAPTER SEVEN:
"Home Not So Alone..."
WHAT?
THIS IS -- THIS IS CRAZY.
WHAT KIND OF QUESTION IS THAT?
THAT ONE!
WRONG! TOO SMALL!
SWOOSH
JOY!
IT IS YOU!
MOM! DAD!
WOOF WLIF WOOF

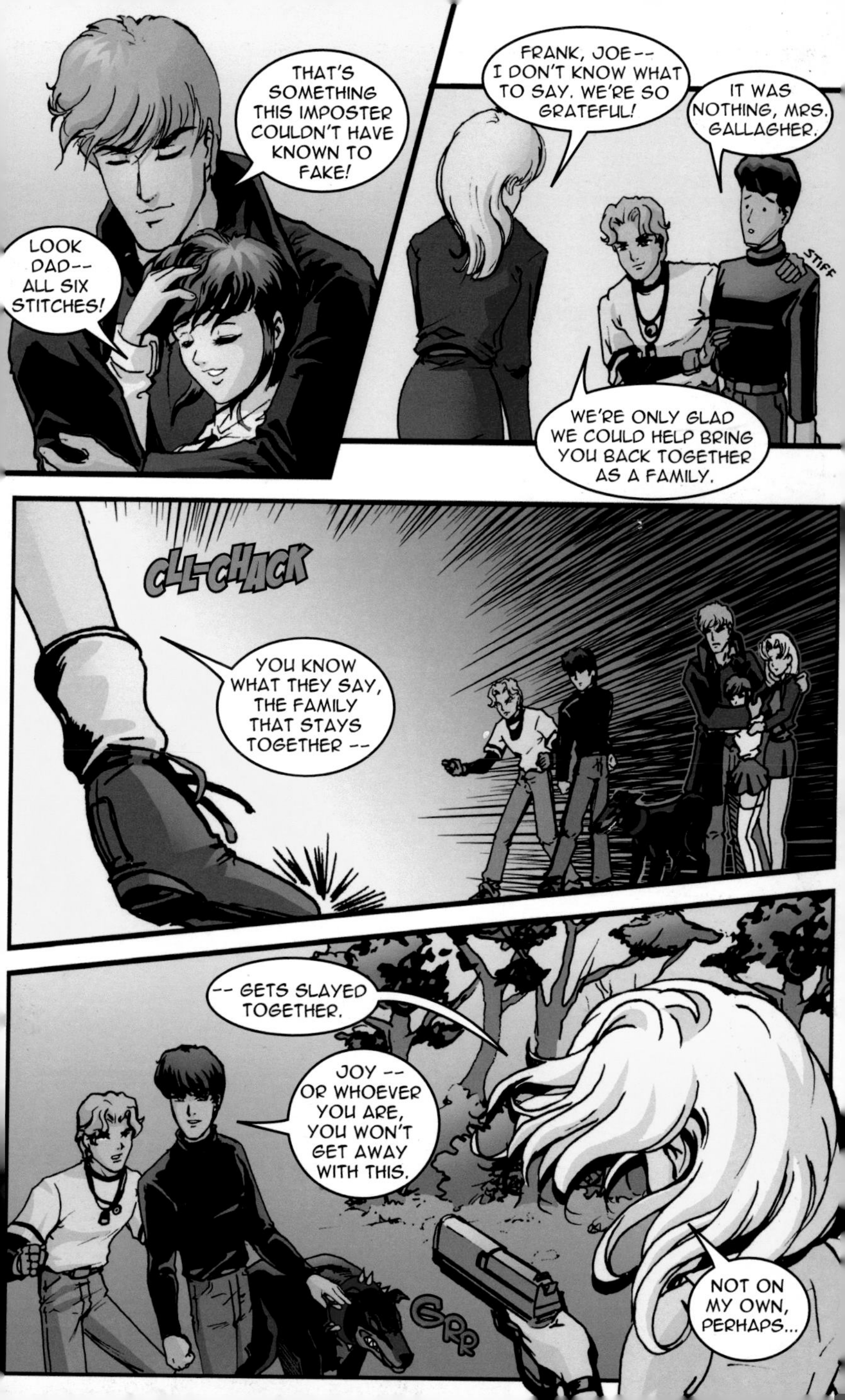
THAT'S SOMETHING THIS IMPOSTER COULDN'T HAVE KNOWN TO FAKE!
LOOK DAD-- ALL SIX STITCHES!
FRANK, JOE-- I DON'T KNOW WHAT TO SAY. WE'RE SO GRATEFUL!
IT WAS NOTHING, MRS. GALLAGHER.
STIFF
WE'RE ONLY GLAD WE COULD HELP BRING YOU BACK TOGETHER AS A FAMILY.
CLL-CHACK
YOU KNOW WHAT THEY SAY, THE FAMILY THAT STAYS TOGETHER --
-- GETS SLAYED TOGETHER.
JOY -- OR WHOEVER YOU ARE, YOU WON'T GET AWAY WITH THIS.
NOT ON MY OWN, PERHAPS...
GRR

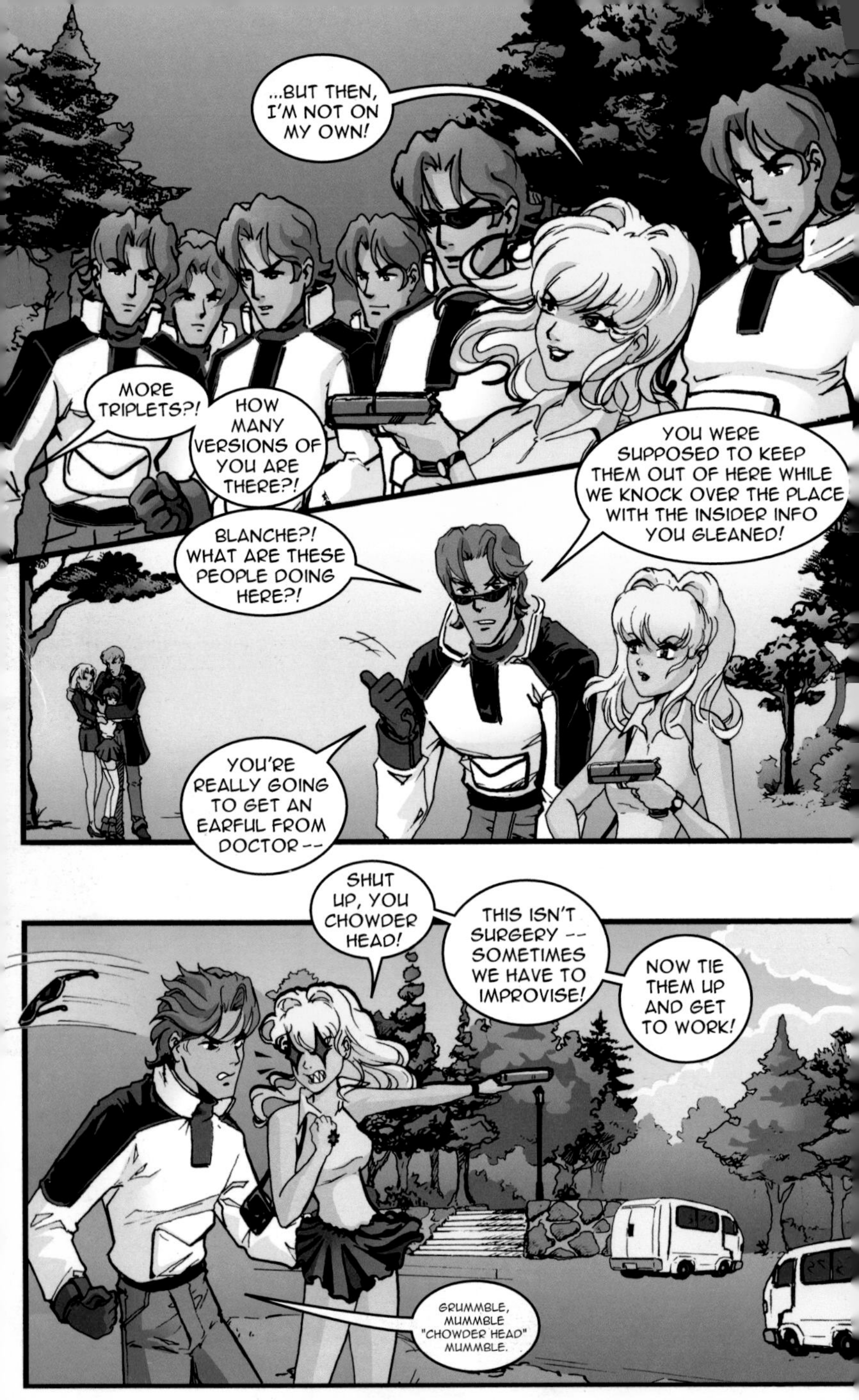
...BUT THEN, I'M NOT ON MY OWN!
MORE TRIPLETS?!
HOW MANY VERSIONS OF YOU ARE THERE?!
BLANCHE?! WHAT ARE THESE PEOPLE DOING HERE?!
YOU WERE SUPPOSED TO KEEP THEM OUT OF HERE WHILE WE KNOCK OVER THE PLACE WITH THE INSIDER INFO YOU GLEANED!
YOU'RE REALLY GOING TO GET AN EARFUL FROM DOCTOR --
SHUT UP, YOU CHOWDER HEAD!
THIS ISN'T SURGERY -- SOMETIMES WE HAVE TO IMPROVISE!
NOW TIE THEM UP AND GET TO WORK!
GRUMMBLE, MUMMBLE "CHOWDER HEAD" MUMMBLE.

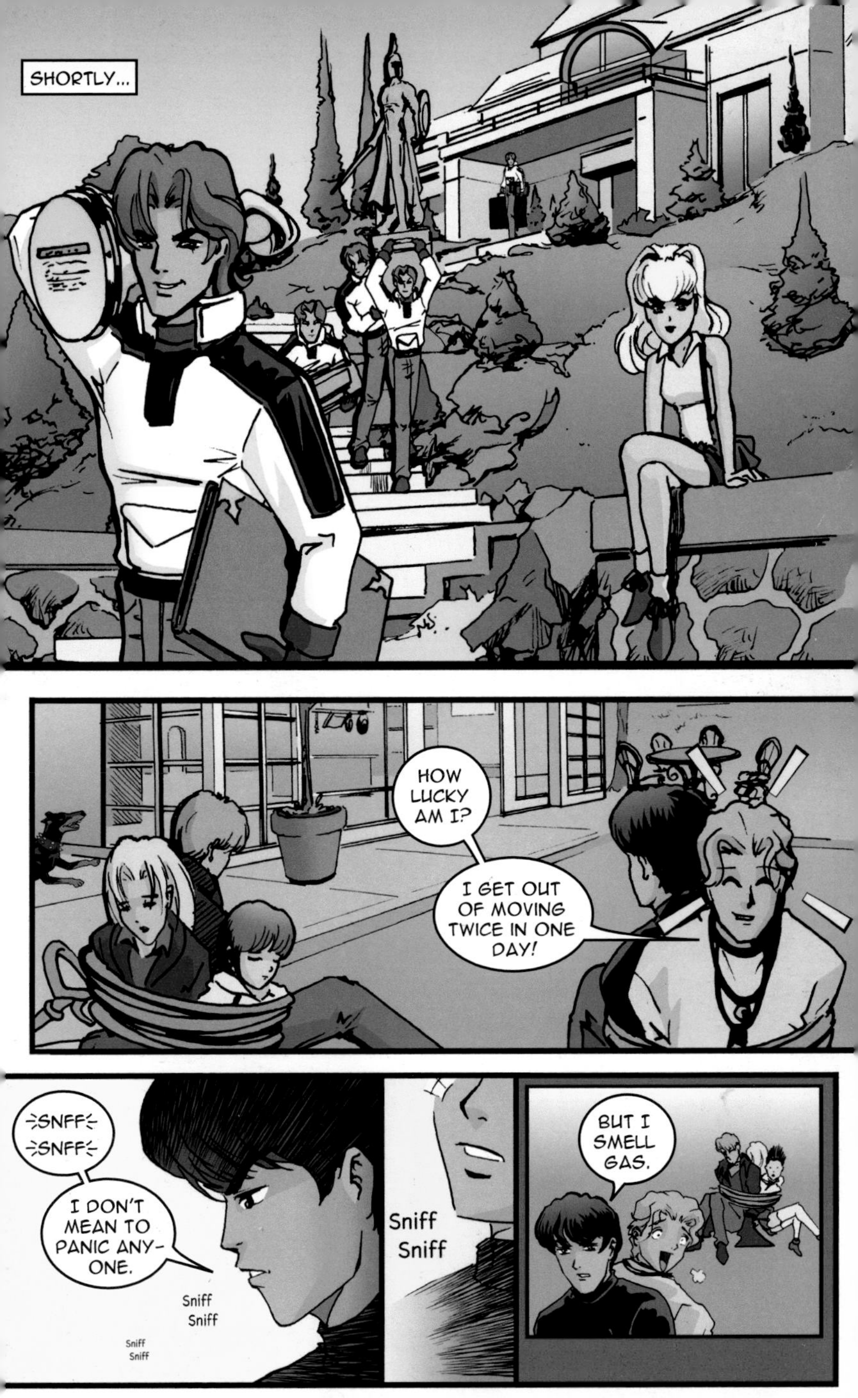

SHORTLY...
HOW LUCKY AM I?
I GET OUT OF MOVING TWICE IN ONE DAY!
=SNFF=
=SNFF=
I DON'T MEAN TO PANIC ANY-ONE.
Sniff
Sniff
Sniff
Sniff
Sniff
Sniff
BUT I SMELL GAS.

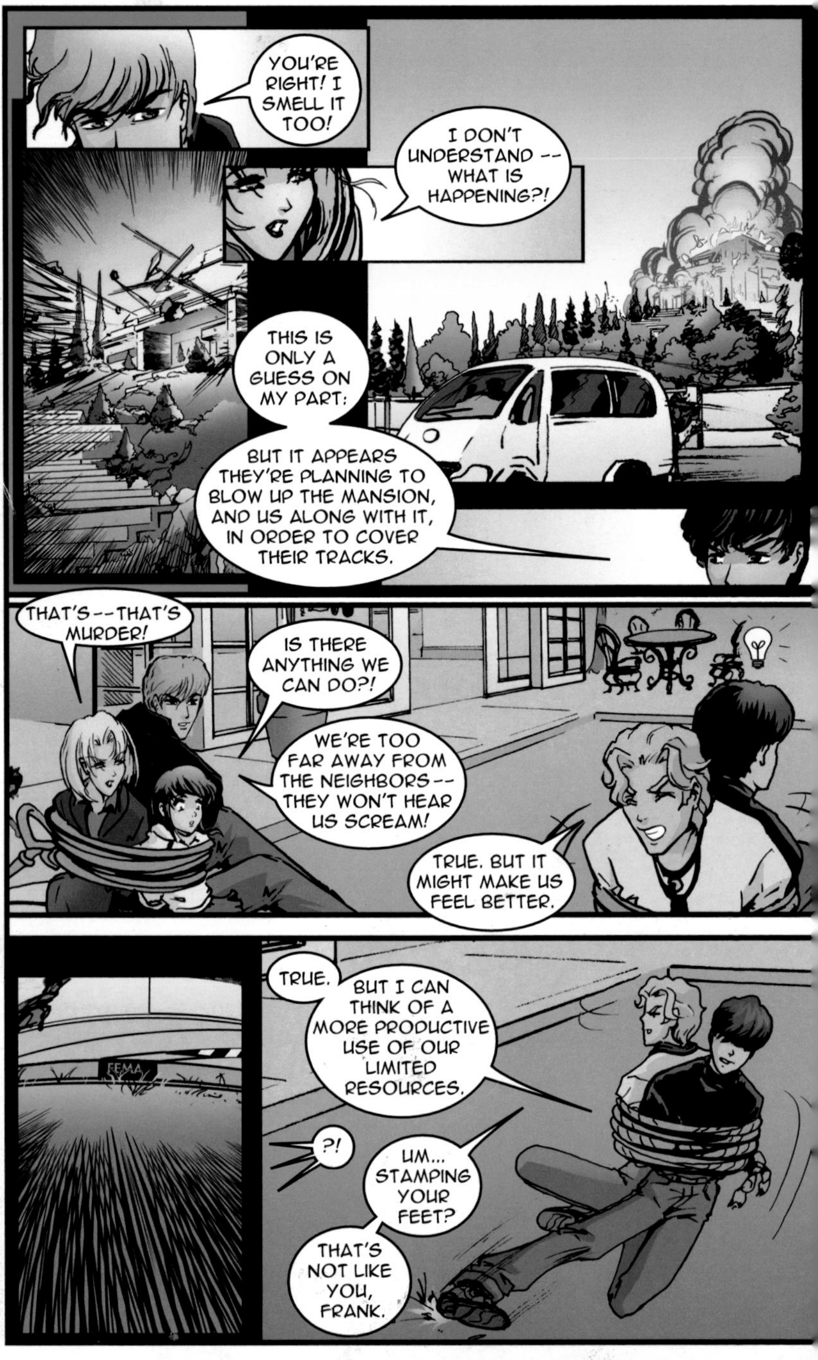
YOU'RE RIGHT! I SMELL IT TOO!
I DON'T UNDERSTAND -- WHAT IS HAPPENING?!
THIS IS ONLY A GUESS ON MY PART:
BUT IT APPEARS THEY'RE PLANNING TO BLOW UP THE MANSION, AND US ALONG WITH IT, IN ORDER TO COVER THEIR TRACKS.
THAT'S--THAT'S MURDER!
IS THERE ANYTHING WE CAN DO?!
WE'RE TOO FAR AWAY FROM THE NEIGHBORS-- THEY WON'T HEAR US SCREAM!
TRUE. BUT IT MIGHT MAKE US FEEL BETTER.
FEMA
TRUE.
BUT I CAN THINK OF A MORE PRODUCTIVE USE OF OUR LIMITED RESOURCES.
?!
UM... STAMPING YOUR FEET?
THAT'S NOT LIKE YOU, FRANK.

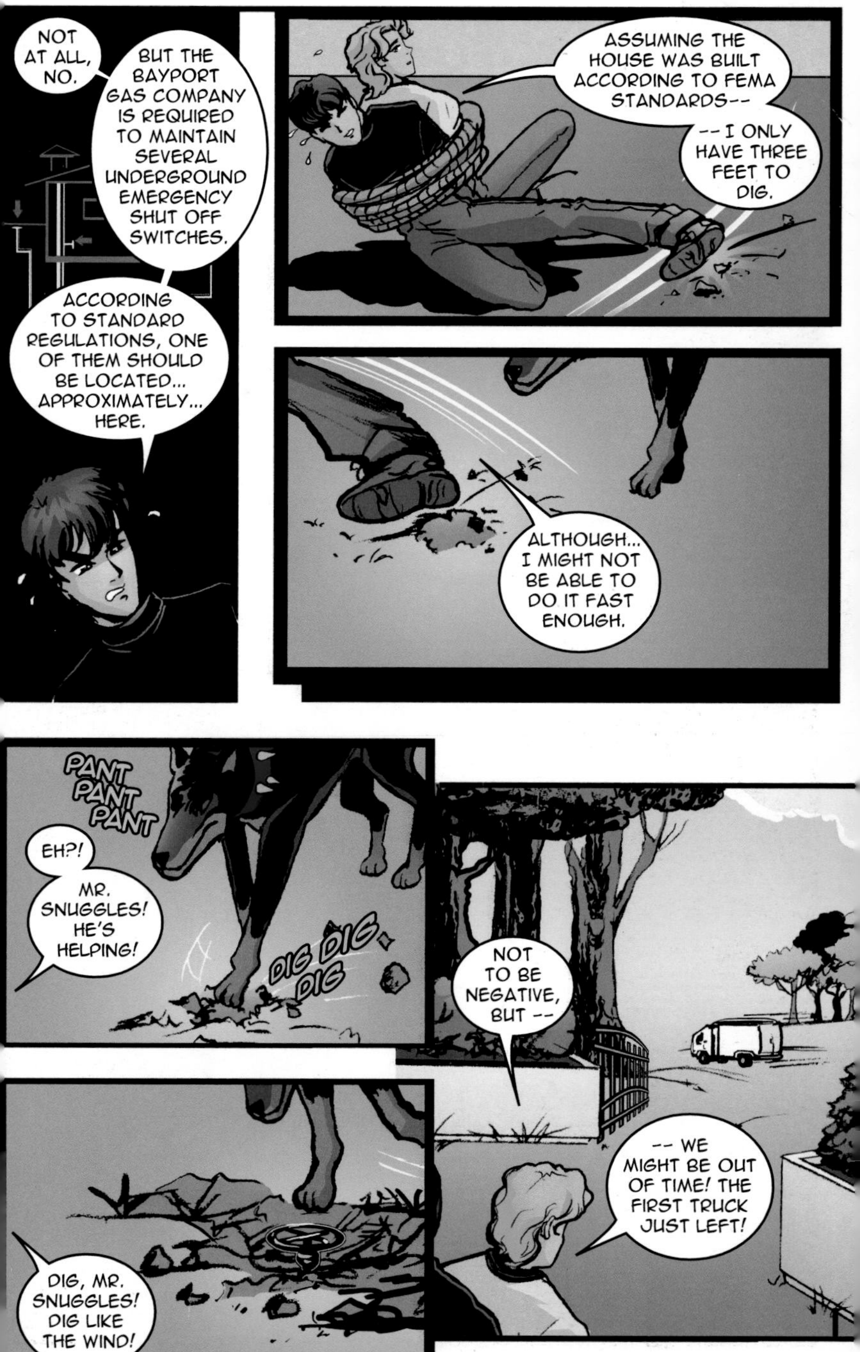
NOT AT ALL, NO.
BUT THE BAYPORT GAS COMPANY IS REQUIRED TO MAINTAIN SEVERAL UNDERGROUND EMERGENCY SHUT OFF SWITCHES.
ACCORDING TO STANDARD REGULATIONS, ONE OF THEM SHOULD BE LOCATED... APPROXIMATELY... HERE.
ASSUMING THE HOUSE WAS BUILT ACCORDING TO FEMA STANDARDS--
-- I ONLY HAVE THREE FEET TO DIG.
ALTHOUGH... I MIGHT NOT BE ABLE TO DO IT FAST ENOUGH.
PANT PANT PANT
EH?!
MR. SNUGGLES! HE'S HELPING!
DIG DIG DIG
DIG, MR. SNUGGLES! DIG LIKE THE WIND!
NOT TO BE NEGATIVE, BUT --
-- WE MIGHT BE OUT OF TIME! THE FIRST TRUCK JUST LEFT!

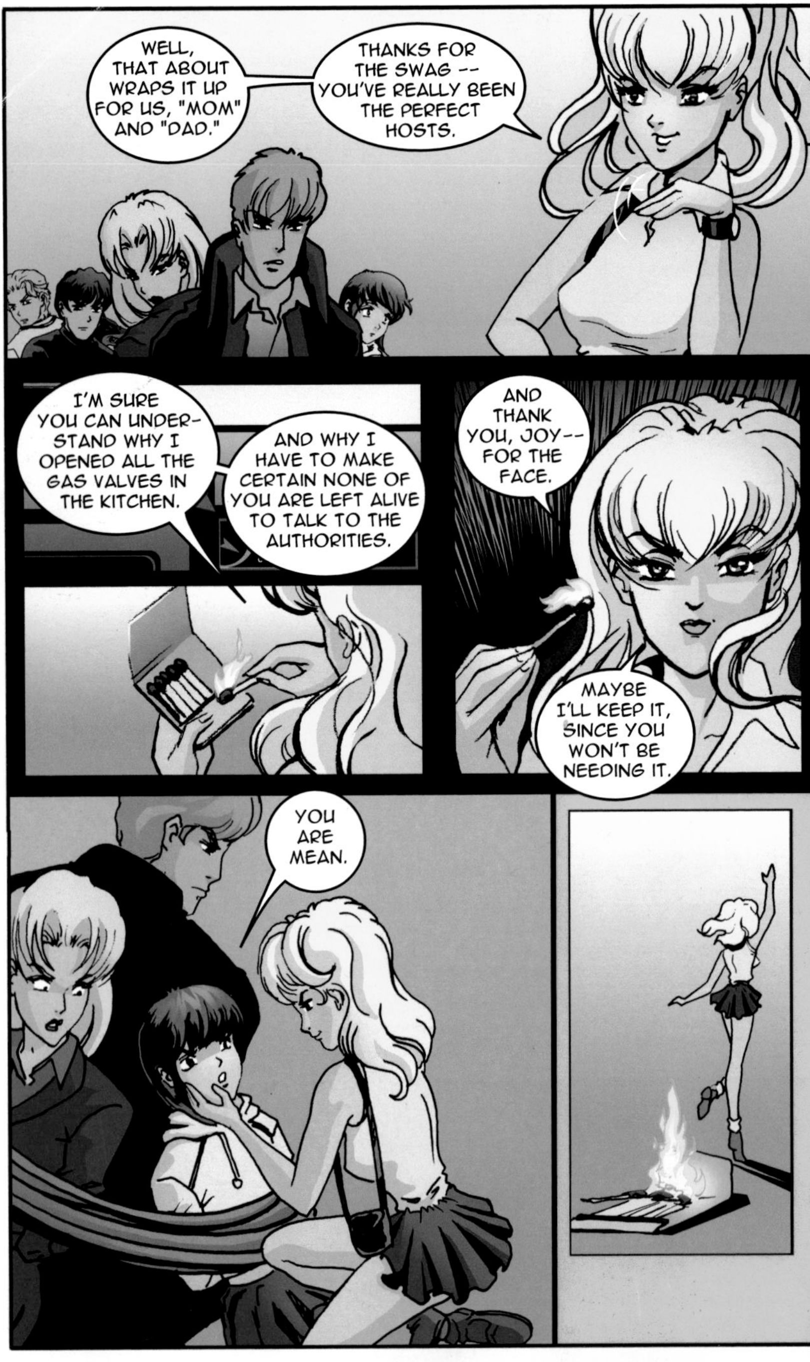
WELL, THAT ABOUT WRAPS IT UP FOR US, "MOM" AND "DAD."
THANKS FOR THE SWAG -- YOU'VE REALLY BEEN THE PERFECT HOSTS.
I'M SURE YOU CAN UNDER-STAND WHY I OPENED ALL THE GAS VALVES IN THE KITCHEN.
AND WHY I HAVE TO MAKE CERTAIN NONE OF YOU ARE LEFT ALIVE TO TALK TO THE AUTHORITIES.
AND THANK YOU, JOY-- FOR THE FACE.
MAYBE I'LL KEEP IT, SINCE YOU WON'T BE NEEDING IT.
YOU ARE MEAN.

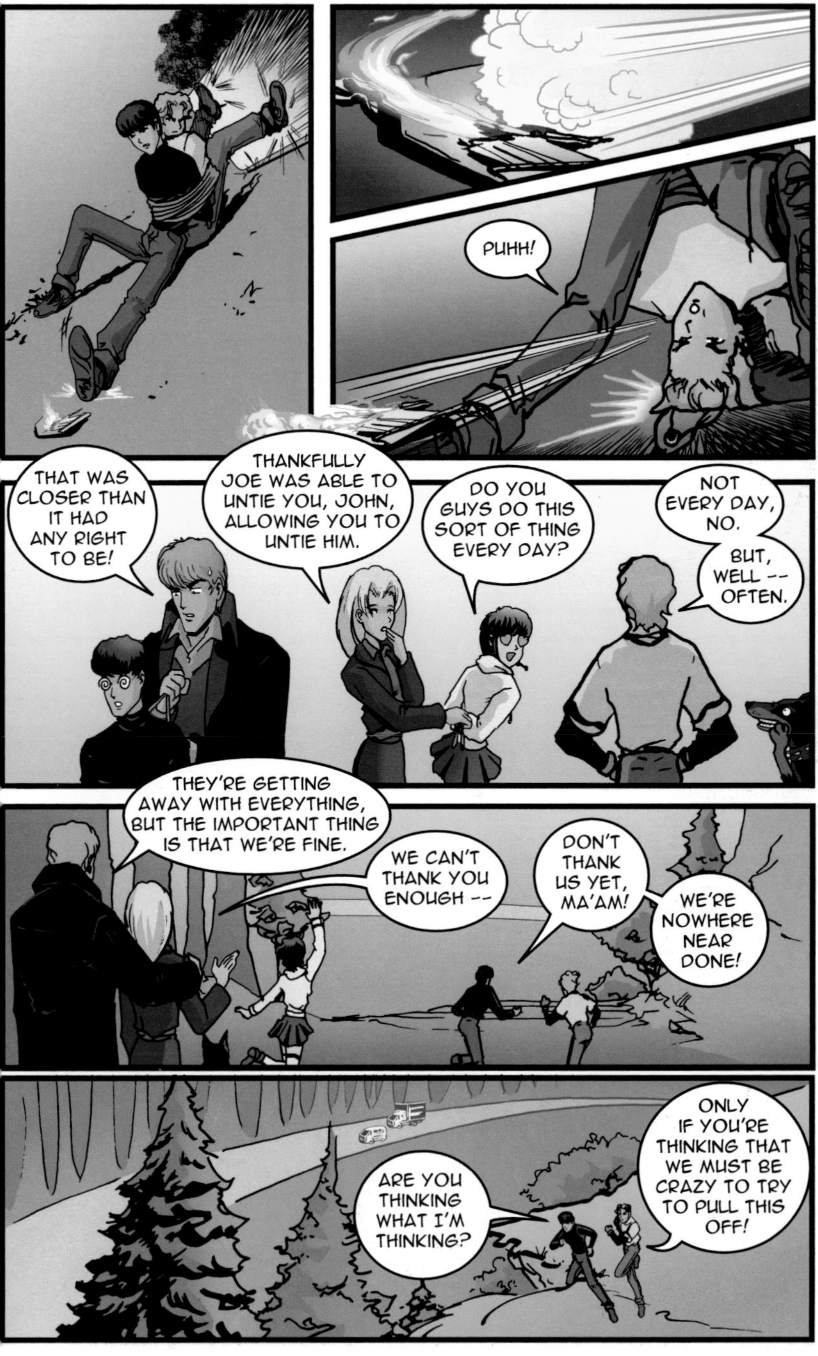
PUHH!
THAT WAS CLOSER THAN IT HAD ANY RIGHT TO BE!
THANKFULLY JOE WAS ABLE TO UNTIE YOU, JOHN, ALLOWING YOU TO UNTIE HIM.
DO YOU GUYS DO THIS SORT OF THING EVERY DAY?
NOT EVERY DAY, NO.
BUT, WELL -- OFTEN.
THEY'RE GETTING AWAY WITH EVERYTHING, BUT THE IMPORTANT THING IS THAT WE'RE FINE.
WE CAN'T THANK YOU ENOUGH --
DON'T THANK US YET, MA'AM!
WE'RE NOWHERE NEAR DONE!
ARE YOU THINKING WHAT I'M THINKING?
ONLY IF YOU'RE THINKING THAT WE MUST BE CRAZY TO TRY TO PULL THIS OFF!

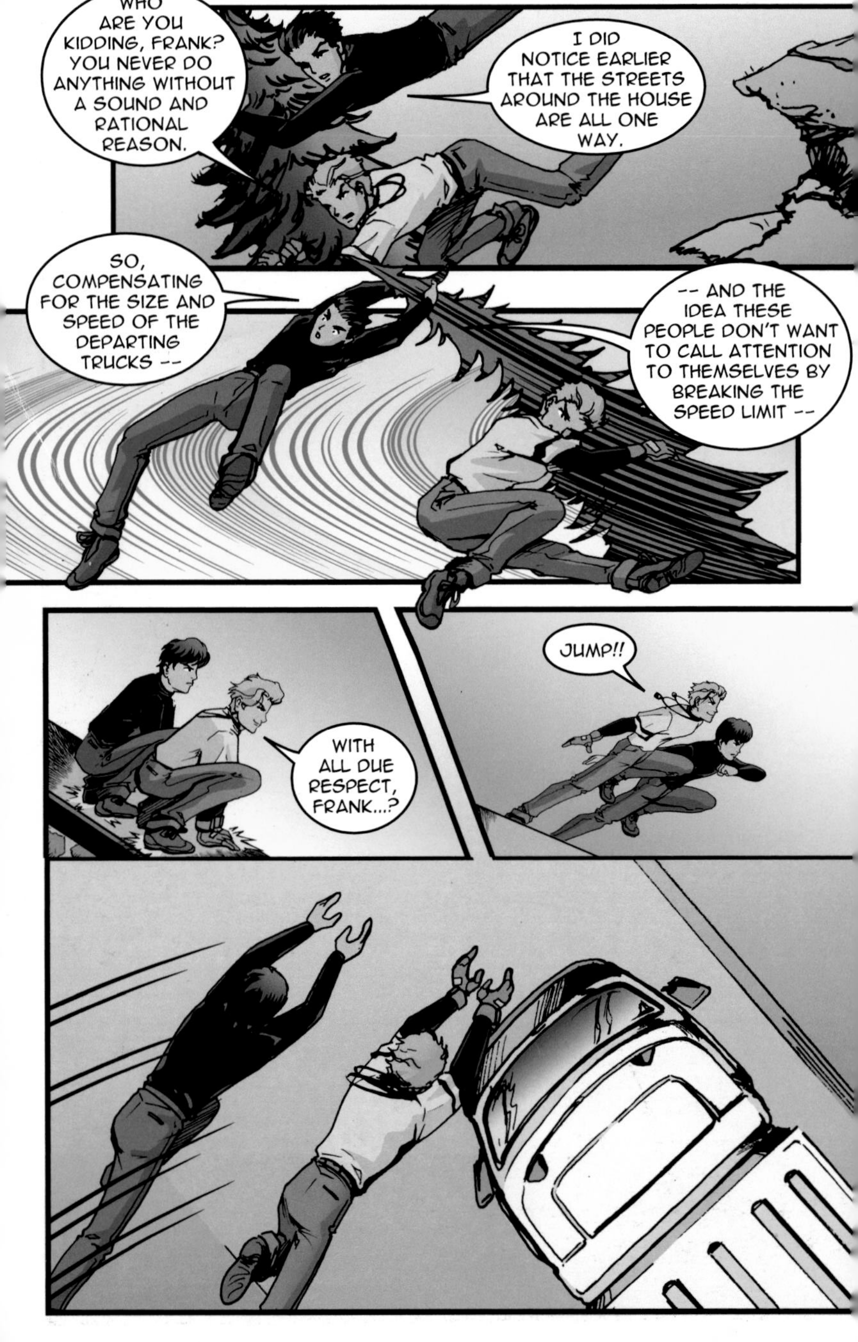
WHO ARE YOU KIDDING, FRANK? YOU NEVER DO ANYTHING WITHOUT A SOUND AND RATIONAL REASON.
I DID NOTICE EARLIER THAT THE STREETS AROUND THE HOUSE ARE ALL ONE WAY.
SO, COMPENSATING FOR THE SIZE AND SPEED OF THE DEPARTING TRUCKS --
-- AND THE IDEA THESE PEOPLE DON'T WANT TO CALL ATTENTION TO THEMSELVES BY BREAKING THE SPEED LIMIT --
WITH ALL DUE RESPECT, FRANK...?
JUMP!!

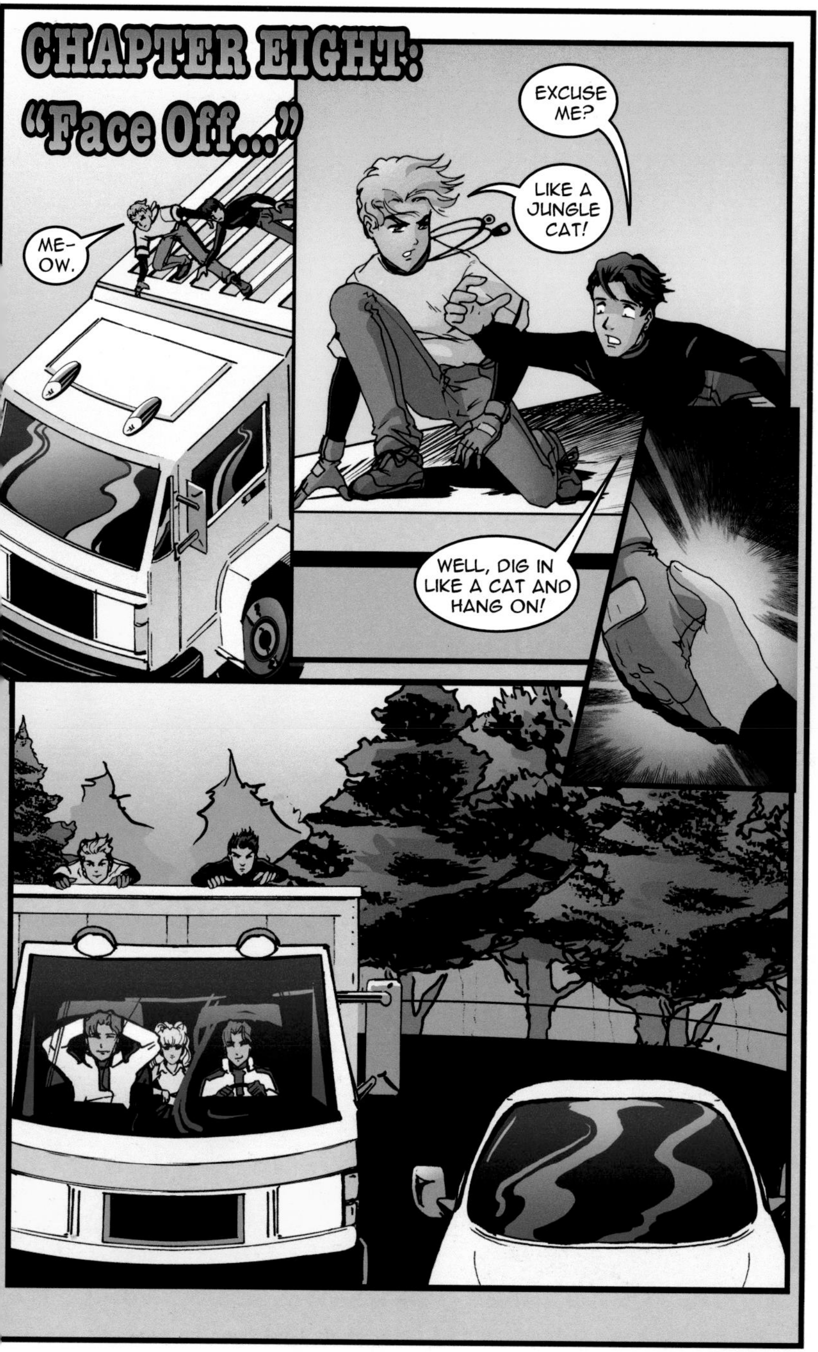

CHAPTER EIGHT:
"Face Off..."
ME-OW.
EXCUSE ME?
LIKE A JUNGLE CAT!
WELL, DIG IN LIKE A CAT AND HANG ON!

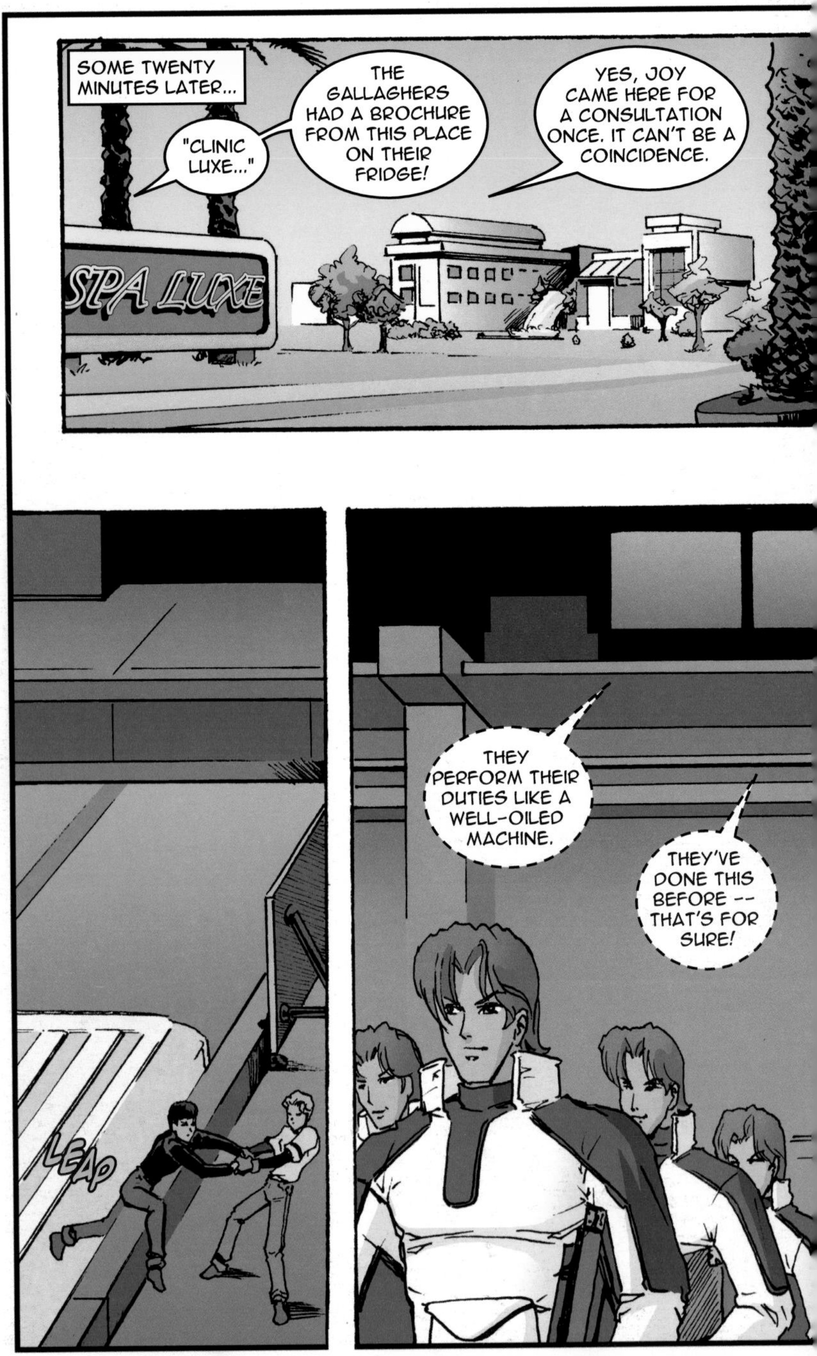
SOME TWENTY MINUTES LATER...
"CLINIC LUXE..."
THE GALLAGHERS HAD A BROCHURE FROM THIS PLACE ON THEIR FRIDGE!
YES, JOY CAME HERE FOR A CONSULTATION ONCE. IT CAN'T BE A COINCIDENCE.
SPA LUXE
LEAP
THEY PERFORM THEIR DUTIES LIKE A WELL-OILED MACHINE.
THEY'VE DONE THIS BEFORE -- THAT'S FOR SURE!

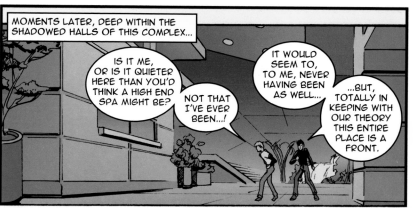

MOMENTS LATER, DEEP WITHIN THE SHADOWED HALLS OF THIS COMPLEX...

IS IT ME, OR IS IT QUIETER HERE THAN YOU'D THINK A HIGH END SPA MIGHT BE?

NOT THAT I'VE EVER BEEN...!

IT WOULD SEEM TO, TO ME, NEVER HAVING BEEN AS WELL...

...BUT, TOTALLY IN KEEPING WITH OUR THEORY THIS ENTIRE PLACE IS A FRONT.

IT FEELS LIKE MORE OF A CROSS BETWEEN A WAREHOUSE AND A HOSPITAL THAN A SPA.

DOCTOR GLECKMAN 1A
DOCTOR A. BEL... 2C
DOCTOR KMAN 1A
DOCTOR R. STRAUS
DOCTOR R. CORNW
DOCTOR S. BIGPIC
TOR D. SMALL

ONCE WE'VE QUESTIONED DR. GLECKMAN, THE MAN BEHIND ALL OF THIS, WE'LL HAVE OUR ANSWERS.

ACCORDING TO THAT DIRECTORY, HIS OFFICE SHOULD BE RIGHT DOWN THIS HALL.

IT ALWAYS AMAZES ME WHEN WE ENCOUNTER SUCH SMART PEOPLE--

--WHO USE THEIR TALENTS FOR CRIME INSTEAD OF GOOD.

WHAT DO YOU THINK MAKES A PERSON DO THAT?

I DON'T KNOW. BUT HERE'S YOUR CHANCE TO ASK DR. GLECKMAN YOURSELF.

GLECKMAN

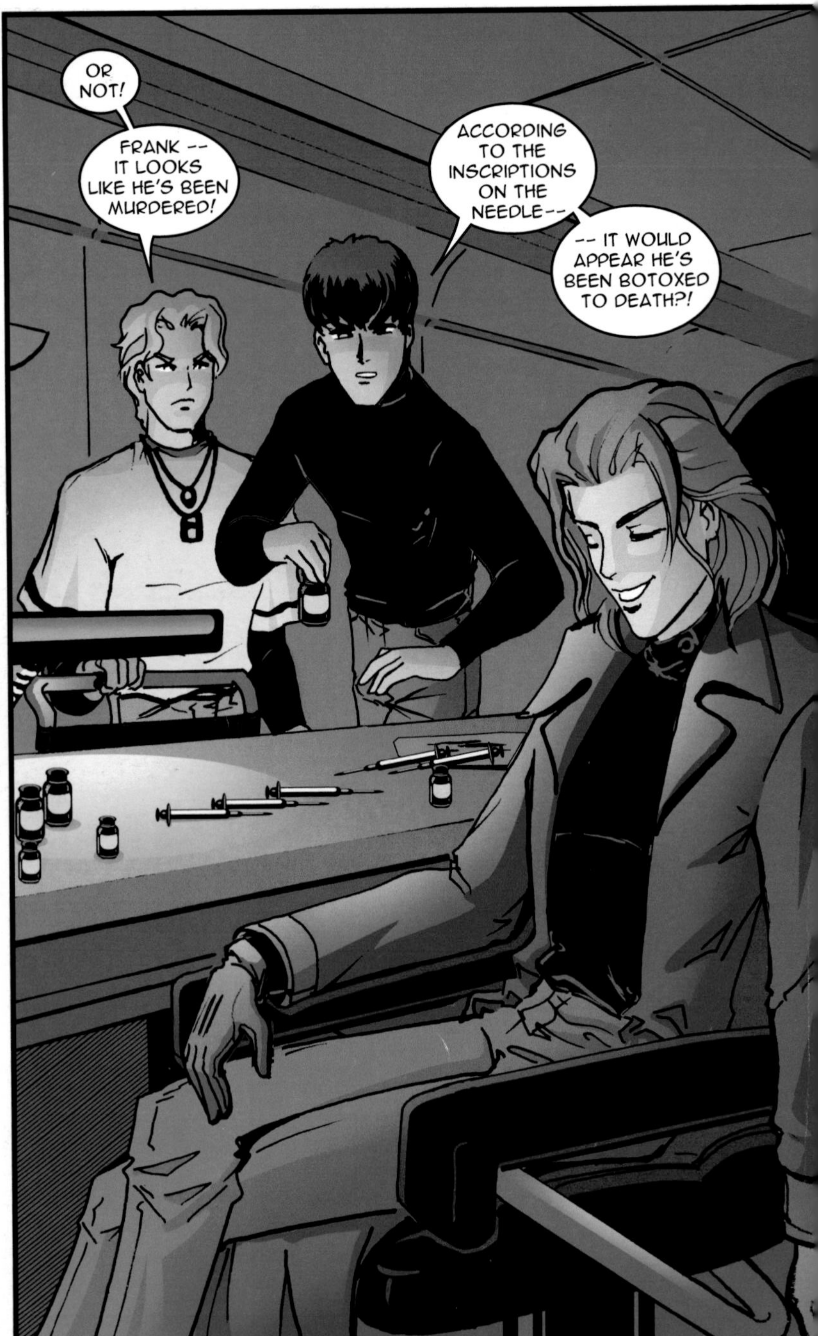
OR NOT!
FRANK -- IT LOOKS LIKE HE'S BEEN MURDERED!
ACCORDING TO THE INSCRIPTIONS ON THE NEEDLE--
-- IT WOULD APPEAR HE'S BEEN BOTOXED TO DEATH?!

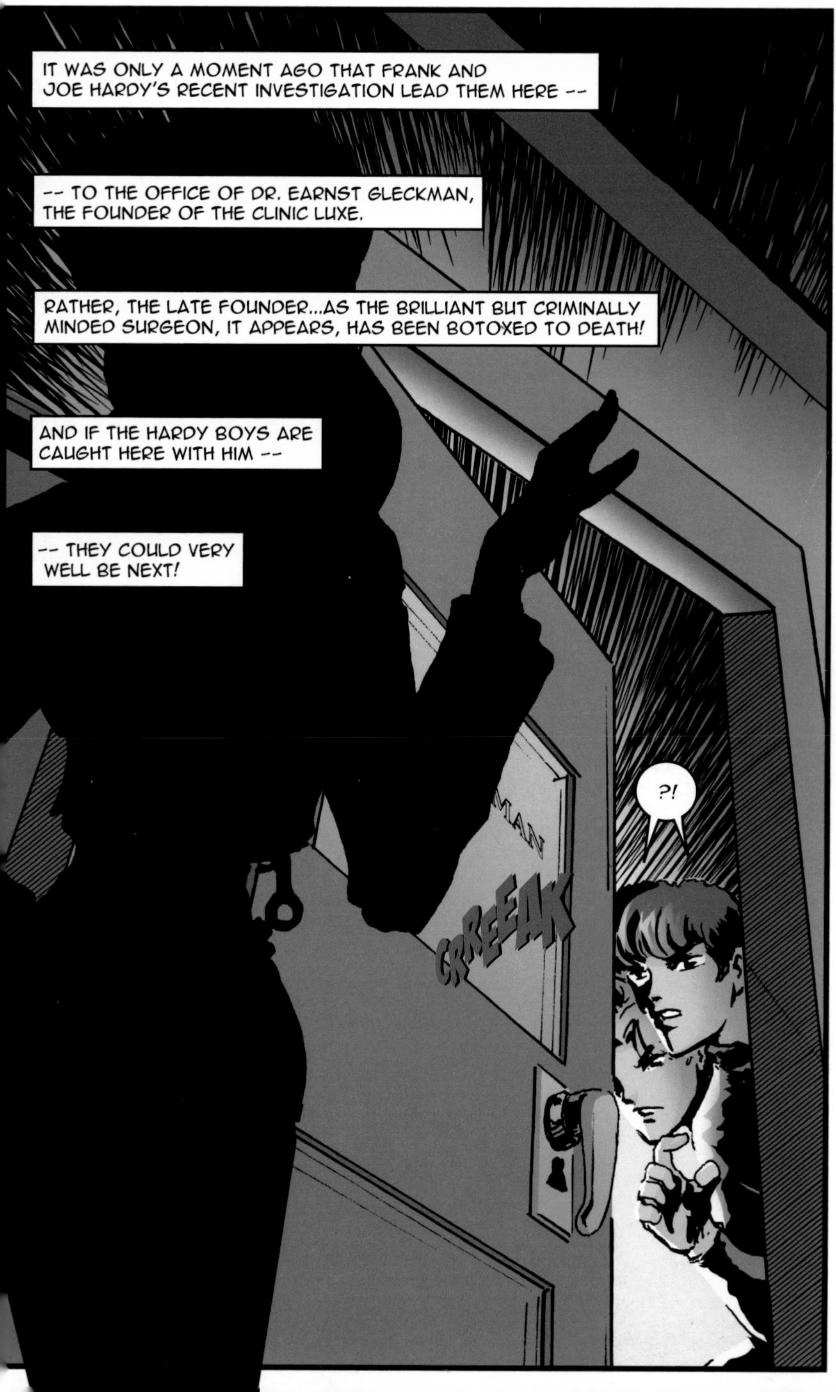
IT WAS ONLY A MOMENT AGO THAT FRANK AND JOE HARDY'S RECENT INVESTIGATION LEAD THEM HERE --
-- TO THE OFFICE OF DR. EARNST GLECKMAN, THE FOUNDER OF THE CLINIC LUXE.
RATHER, THE LATE FOUNDER...AS THE BRILLIANT BUT CRIMINALLY MINDED SURGEON, IT APPEARS, HAS BEEN BOTOXED TO DEATH!
AND IF THE HARDY BOYS ARE CAUGHT HERE WITH HIM --
-- THEY COULD VERY WELL BE NEXT!
?!
CRREEAK

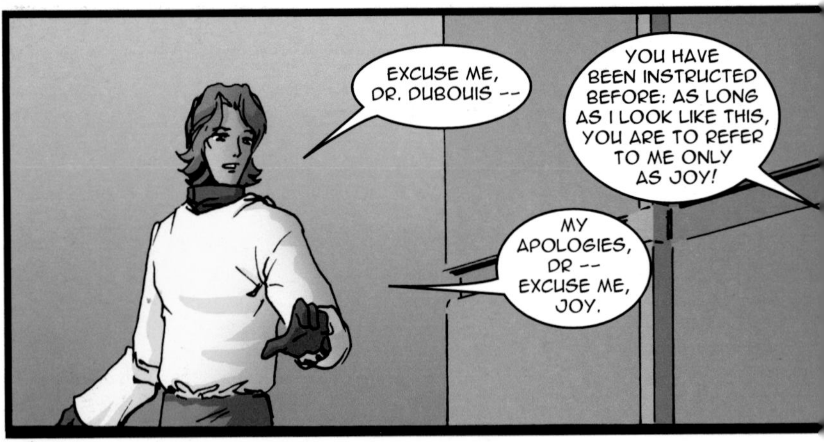
EXCUSE ME, DR. DUBOUIS --
YOU HAVE BEEN INSTRUCTED BEFORE: AS LONG AS I LOOK LIKE THIS, YOU ARE TO REFER TO ME ONLY AS JOY!
MY APOLOGIES, DR -- EXCUSE ME, JOY.

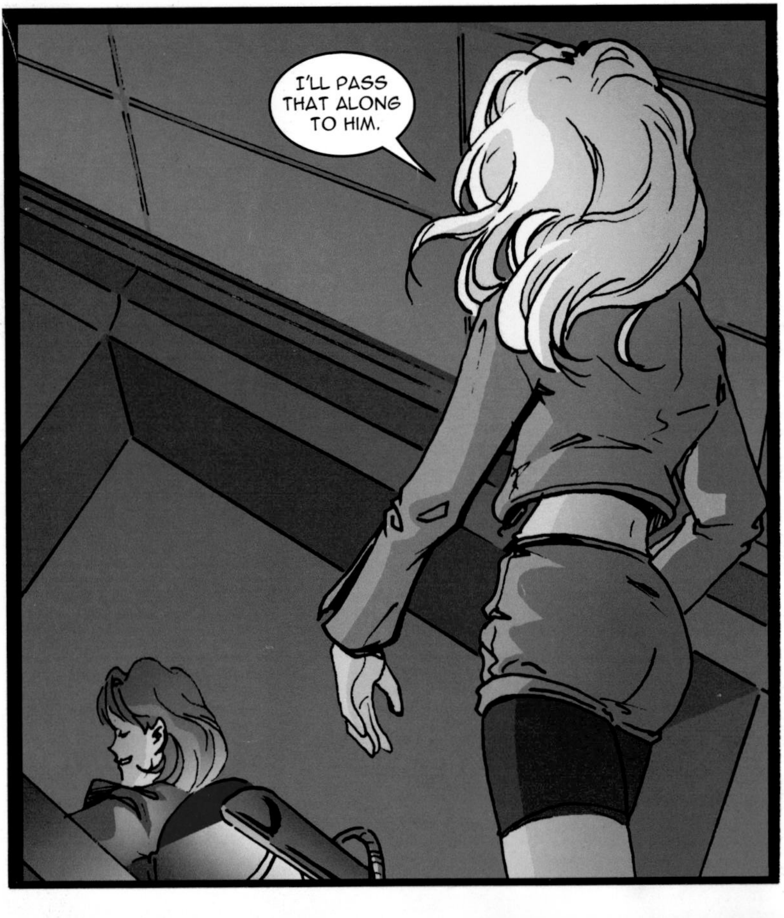
I'LL PASS THAT ALONG TO HIM.

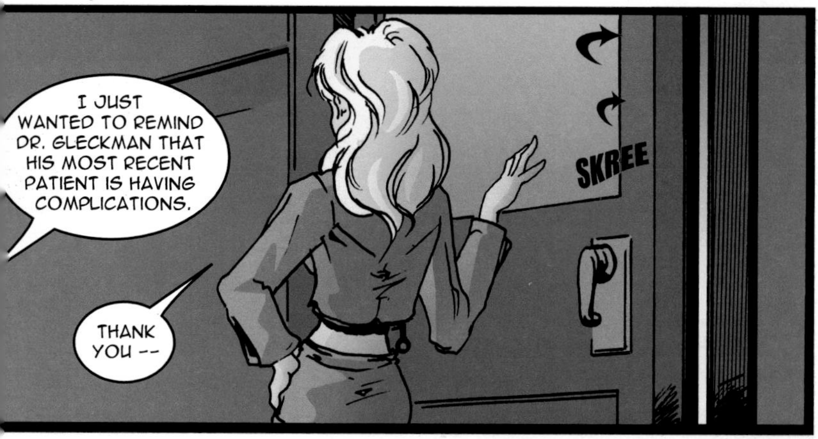
I JUST WANTED TO REMIND DR. GLECKMAN THAT HIS MOST RECENT PATIENT IS HAVING COMPLICATIONS.
SKREE
THANK YOU --

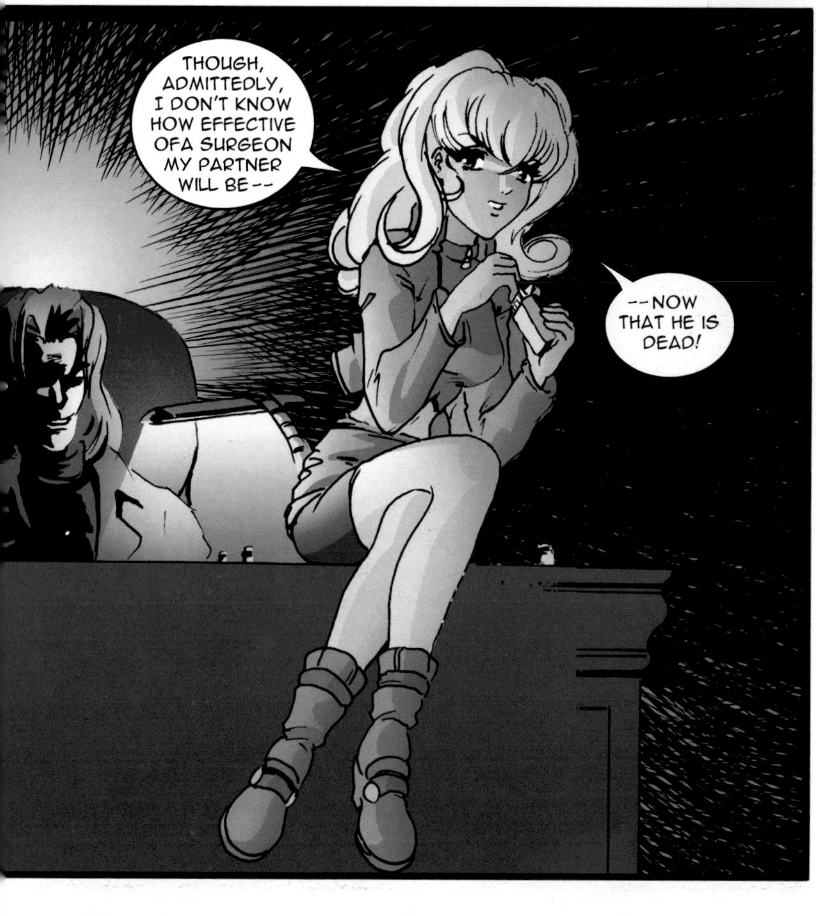
THOUGH, ADMITTEDLY, I DON'T KNOW HOW EFFECTIVE OFA SURGEON MY PARTNER WILL BE--
--NOW THAT HE IS DEAD!

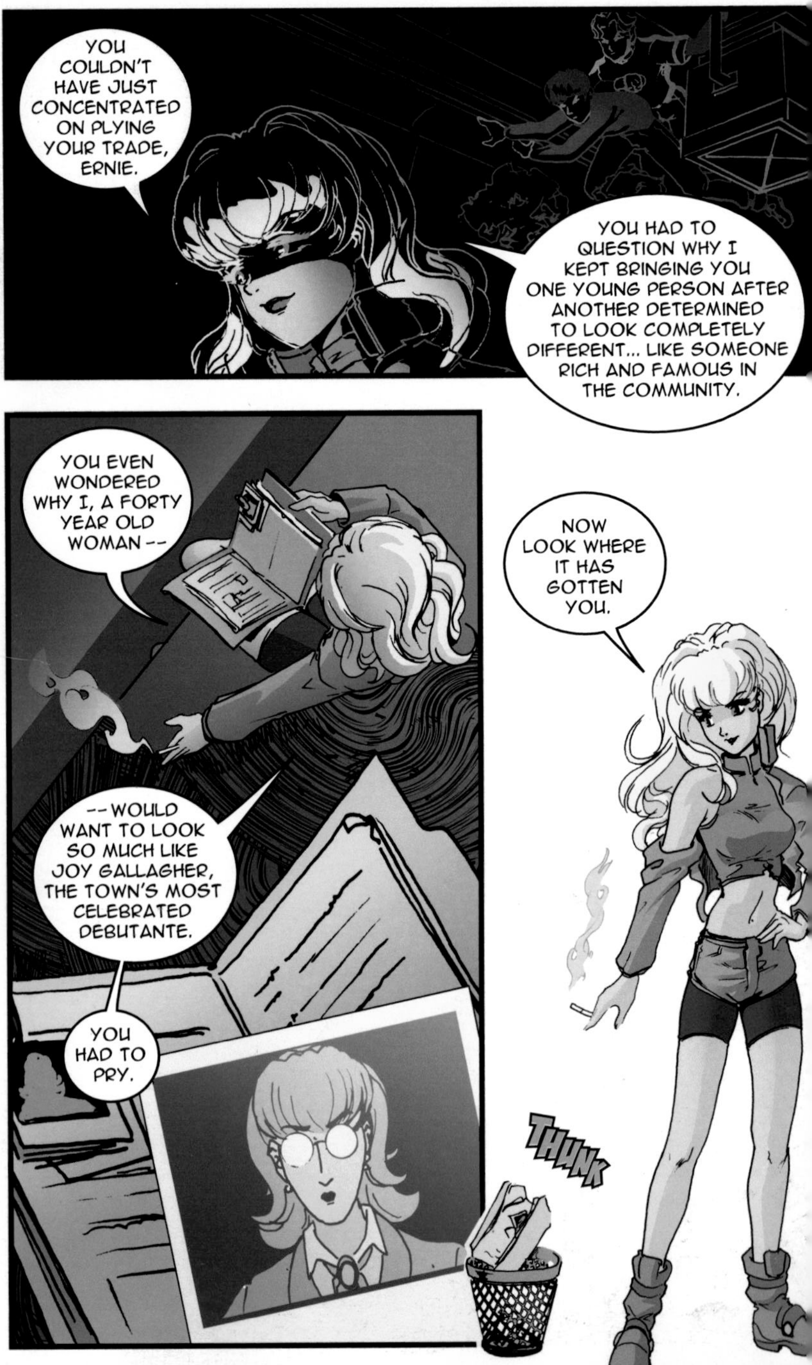
YOU COULDN'T HAVE JUST CONCENTRATED ON PLYING YOUR TRADE, ERNIE.
YOU HAD TO QUESTION WHY I KEPT BRINGING YOU ONE YOUNG PERSON AFTER ANOTHER DETERMINED TO LOOK COMPLETELY DIFFERENT... LIKE SOMEONE RICH AND FAMOUS IN THE COMMUNITY.
YOU EVEN WONDERED WHY I, A FORTY YEAR OLD WOMAN --
--WOULD WANT TO LOOK SO MUCH LIKE JOY GALLAGHER, THE TOWN'S MOST CELEBRATED DEBUTANTE.
YOU HAD TO PRY.
NOW LOOK WHERE IT HAS GOTTEN YOU.
THUNK

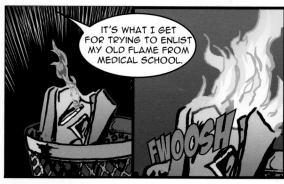
IT'S WHAT I GET FOR TRYING TO ENLIST MY OLD FLAME FROM MEDICAL SCHOOL.

FWOOSH

BUT THAT WOMAN IS DEAD, ERNIE.

AND THANKS TO THE MUSCLE PARALYSIS SHOT DIRECTLY INTO YOUR HEART--

--SO ARE YOU.

THUMP

SO MUCH INFORMATION TO DIGEST.

RIGHT AFTER WE PUT OUT THIS FIRE AND PRESERVE THIS EVIDENCE.

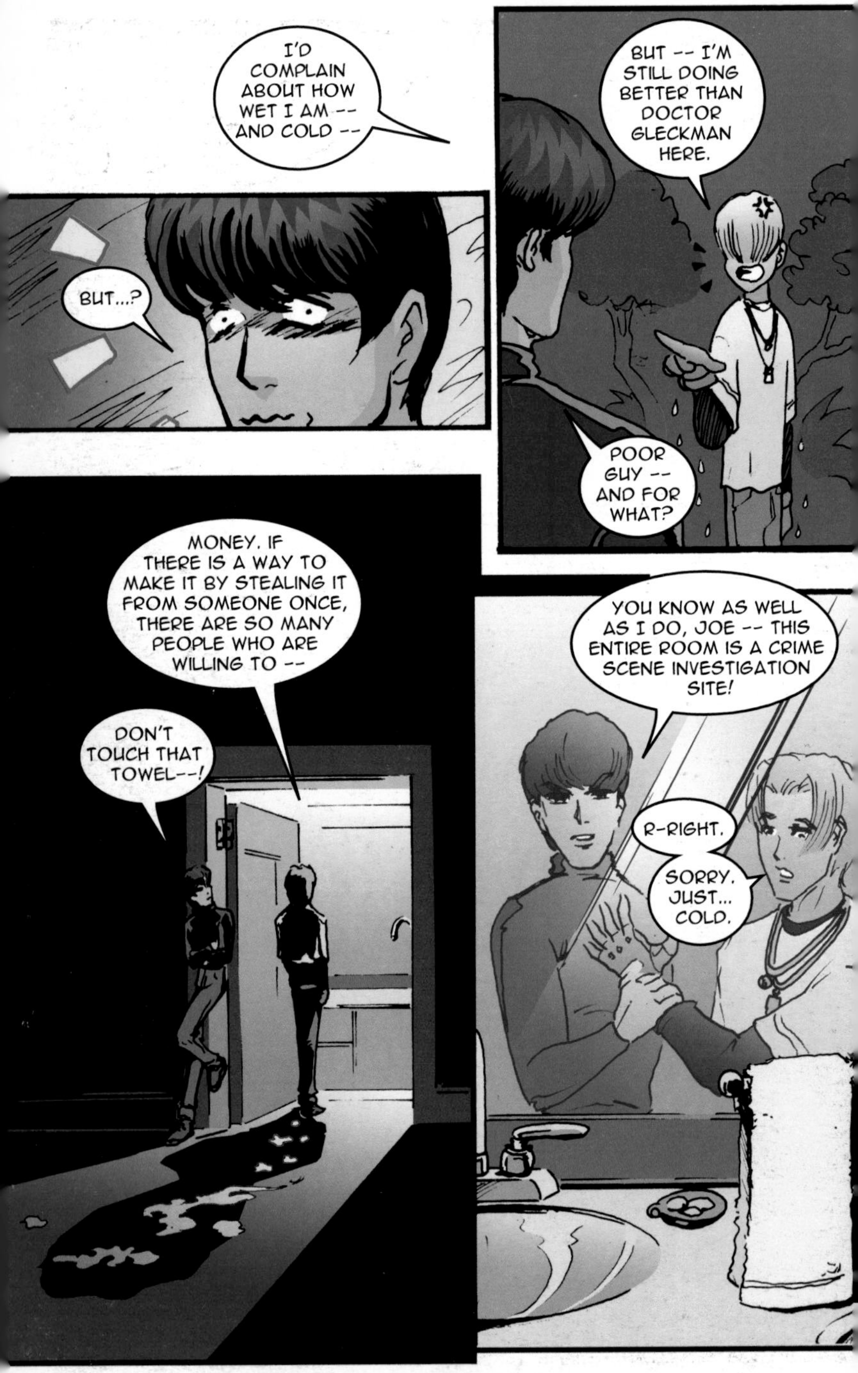
I'D COMPLAIN ABOUT HOW WET I AM -- AND COLD --
BUT -- I'M STILL DOING BETTER THAN DOCTOR GLECKMAN HERE.
BUT...?
POOR GUY -- AND FOR WHAT?
MONEY. IF THERE IS A WAY TO MAKE IT BY STEALING IT FROM SOMEONE ONCE, THERE ARE SO MANY PEOPLE WHO ARE WILLING TO --
DON'T TOUCH THAT TOWEL--!
YOU KNOW AS WELL AS I DO, JOE -- THIS ENTIRE ROOM IS A CRIME SCENE INVESTIGATION SITE!
R-RIGHT.
SORRY. JUST... COLD.

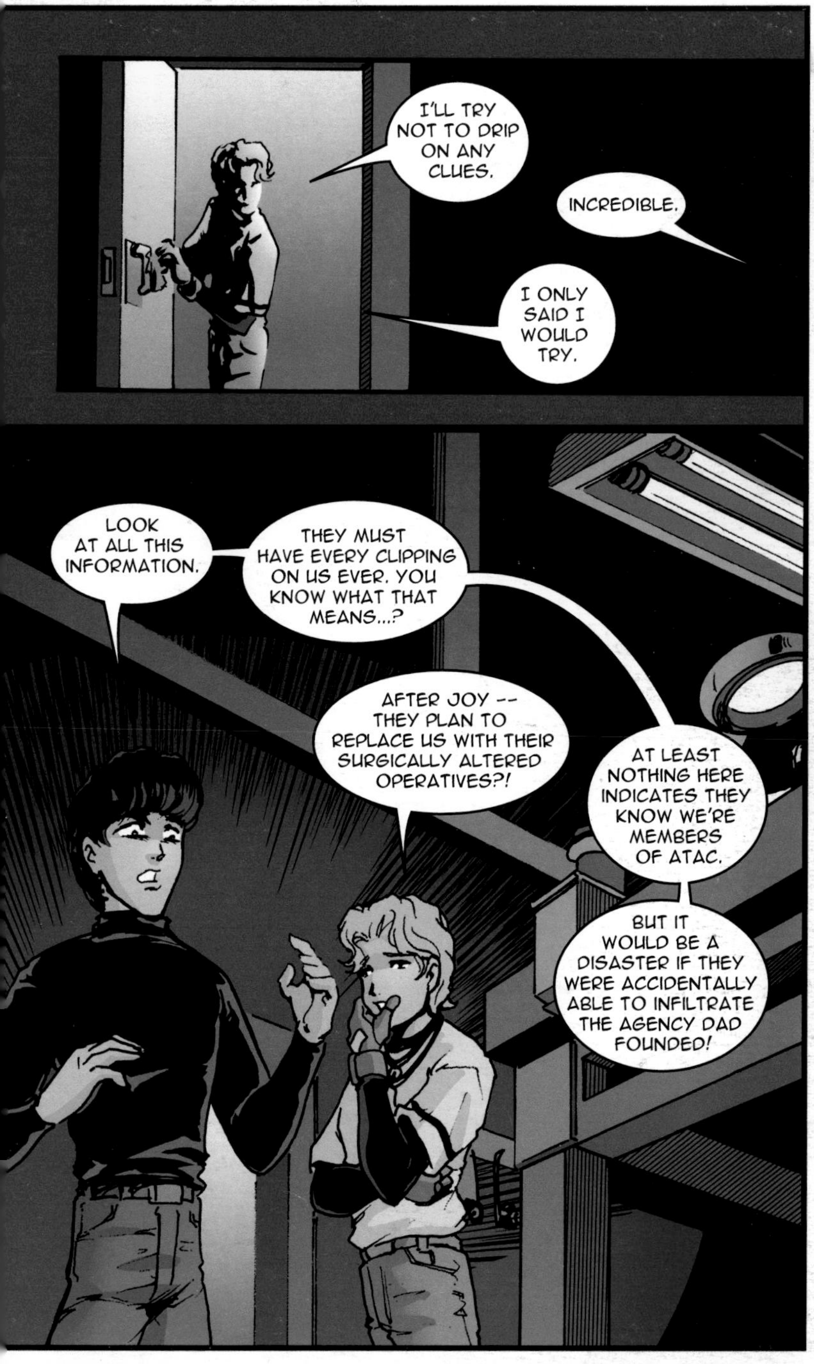
I'LL TRY NOT TO DRIP ON ANY CLUES.
INCREDIBLE.
I ONLY SAID I WOULD TRY.
LOOK AT ALL THIS INFORMATION.
THEY MUST HAVE EVERY CLIPPING ON US EVER. YOU KNOW WHAT THAT MEANS...?
AFTER JOY -- THEY PLAN TO REPLACE US WITH THEIR SURGICALLY ALTERED OPERATIVES?!
AT LEAST NOTHING HERE INDICATES THEY KNOW WE'RE MEMBERS OF ATAC.
BUT IT WOULD BE A DISASTER IF THEY WERE ACCIDENTALLY ABLE TO INFILTRATE THE AGENCY DAD FOUNDED!

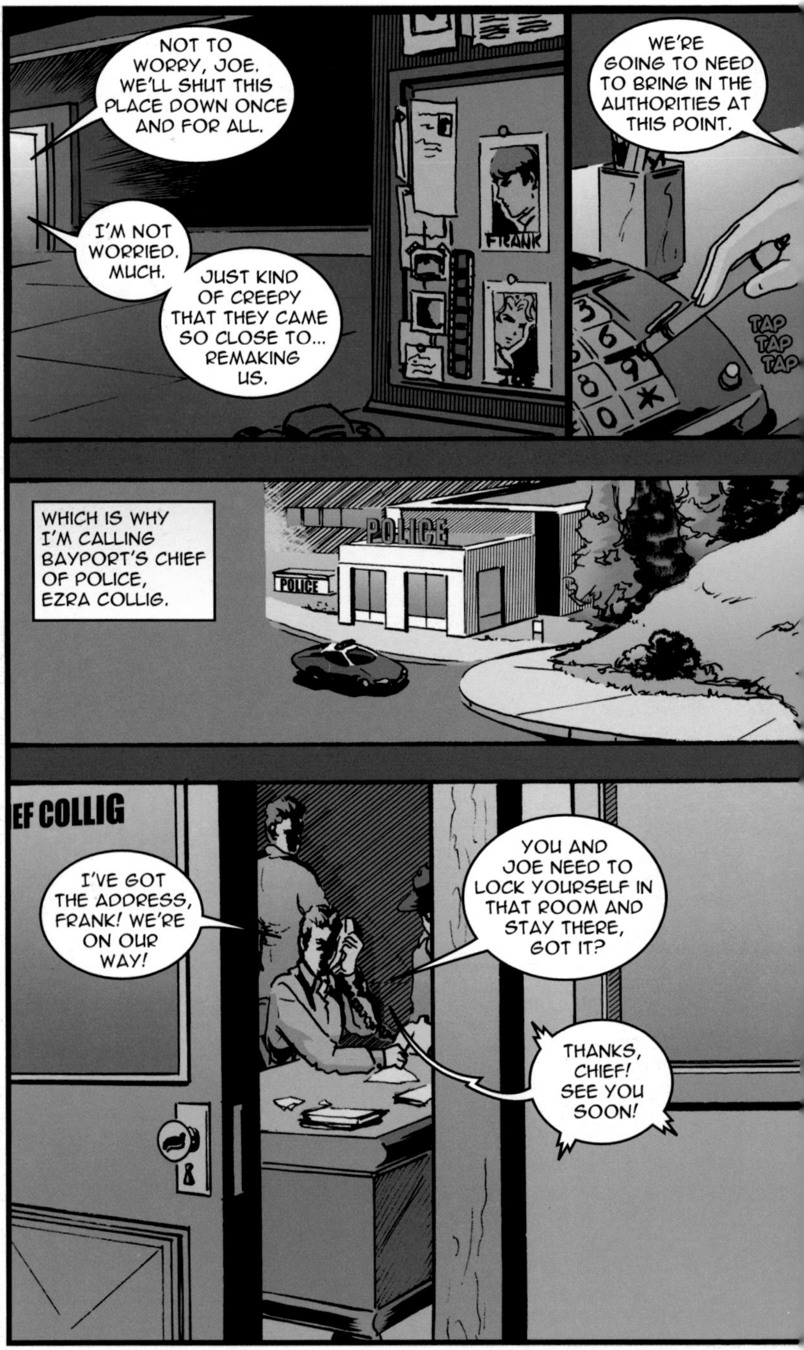
NOT TO WORRY, JOE. WE'LL SHUT THIS PLACE DOWN ONCE AND FOR ALL.
I'M NOT WORRIED. MUCH.
JUST KIND OF CREEPY THAT THEY CAME SO CLOSE TO... REMAKING US.
FRANK
WE'RE GOING TO NEED TO BRING IN THE AUTHORITIES AT THIS POINT.
TAP TAP TAP
WHICH IS WHY I'M CALLING BAYPORT'S CHIEF OF POLICE, EZRA COLLIG.
POLICE
POLICE
EF COLLIG
I'VE GOT THE ADDRESS, FRANK! WE'RE ON OUR WAY!
YOU AND JOE NEED TO LOCK YOURSELF IN THAT ROOM AND STAY THERE, GOT IT?
THANKS, CHIEF! SEE YOU SOON!

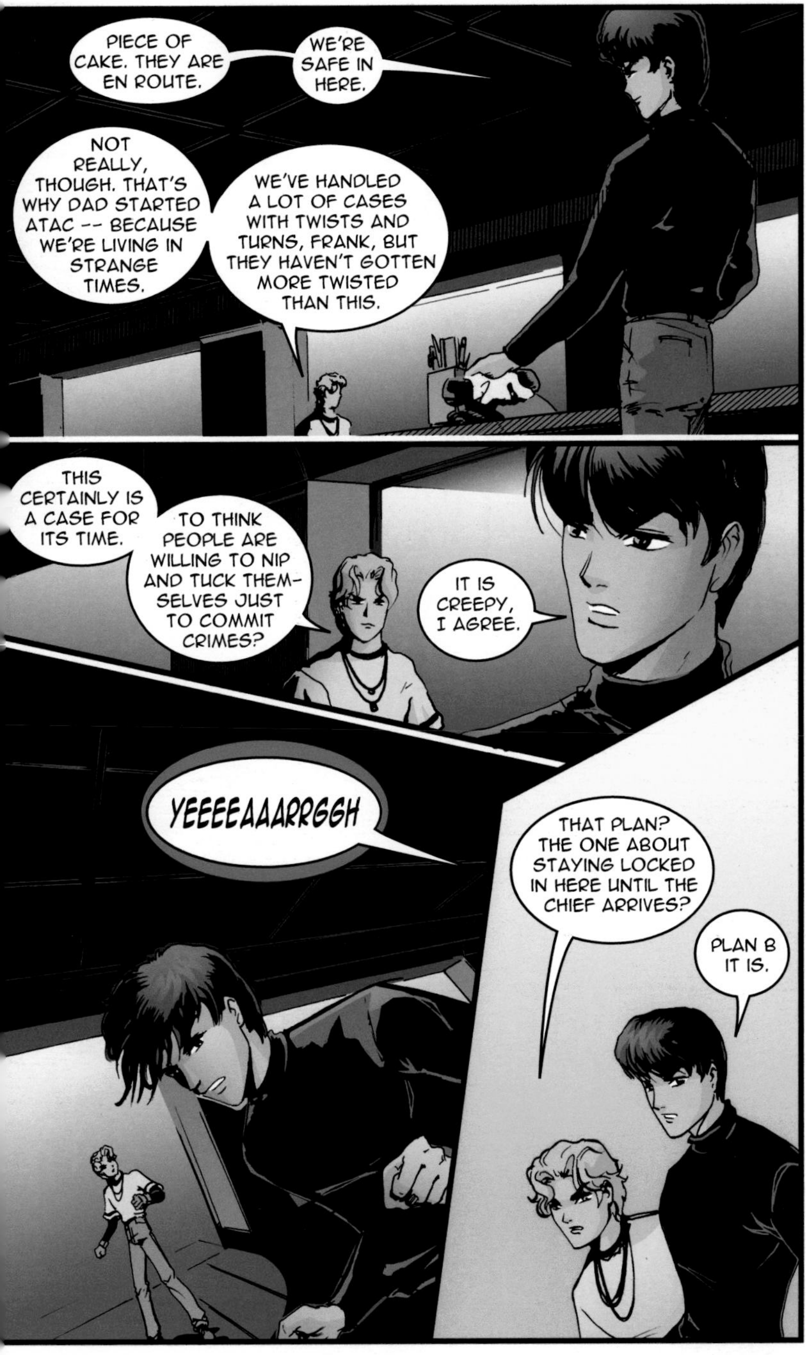
PIECE OF CAKE. THEY ARE EN ROUTE.
WE'RE SAFE IN HERE.
NOT REALLY, THOUGH. THAT'S WHY DAD STARTED ATAC -- BECAUSE WE'RE LIVING IN STRANGE TIMES.
WE'VE HANDLED A LOT OF CASES WITH TWISTS AND TURNS, FRANK, BUT THEY HAVEN'T GOTTEN MORE TWISTED THAN THIS.
THIS CERTAINLY IS A CASE FOR ITS TIME.
TO THINK PEOPLE ARE WILLING TO NIP AND TUCK THEMSELVES JUST TO COMMIT CRIMES?
IT IS CREEPY, I AGREE.
YEEEEAAARRGGH
THAT PLAN? THE ONE ABOUT STAYING LOCKED IN HERE UNTIL THE CHIEF ARRIVES?
PLAN B IT IS.

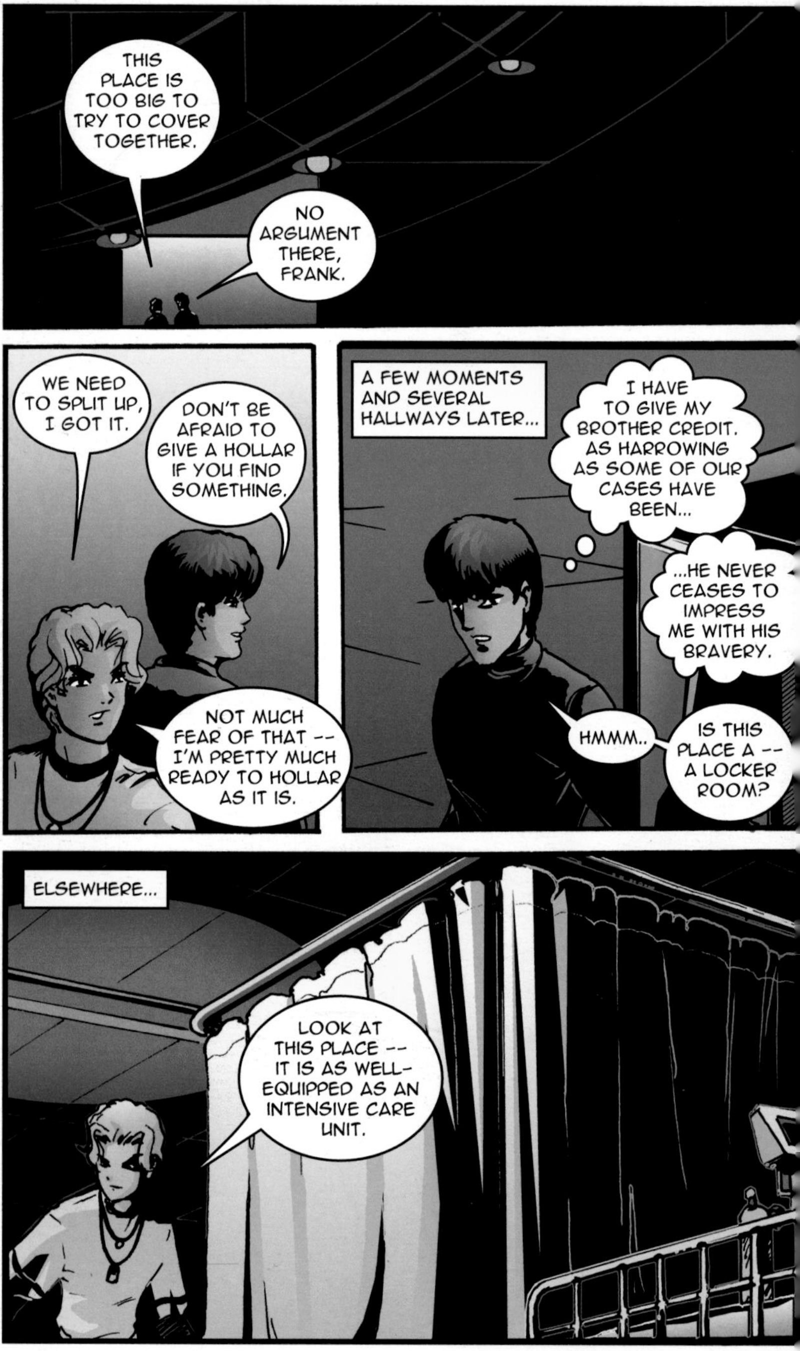
THIS PLACE IS TOO BIG TO TRY TO COVER TOGETHER.
NO ARGUMENT THERE, FRANK.
WE NEED TO SPLIT UP, I GOT IT.
DON'T BE AFRAID TO GIVE A HOLLAR IF YOU FIND SOMETHING.
NOT MUCH FEAR OF THAT -- I'M PRETTY MUCH READY TO HOLLAR AS IT IS.
A FEW MOMENTS AND SEVERAL HALLWAYS LATER...
I HAVE TO GIVE MY BROTHER CREDIT. AS HARROWING AS SOME OF OUR CASES HAVE BEEN...
...HE NEVER CEASES TO IMPRESS ME WITH HIS BRAVERY.
HMMM..
IS THIS PLACE A -- A LOCKER ROOM?
ELSEWHERE...
LOOK AT THIS PLACE -- IT IS AS WELL-EQUIPPED AS AN INTENSIVE CARE UNIT.

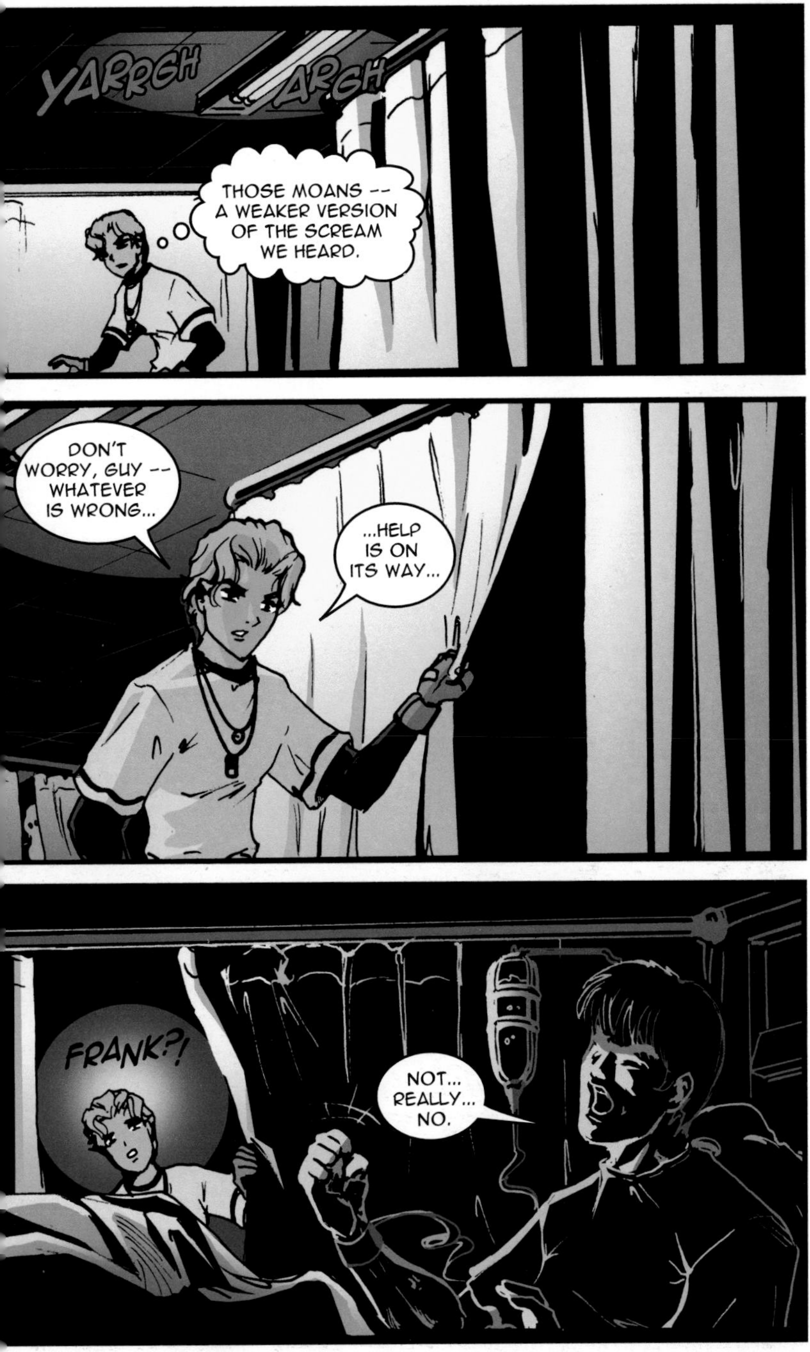
YARRGH
ARGH
THOSE MOANS -- A WEAKER VERSION OF THE SCREAM WE HEARD.
DON'T WORRY, GUY -- WHATEVER IS WRONG...
...HELP IS ON ITS WAY...
FRANK?!
NOT... REALLY... NO.

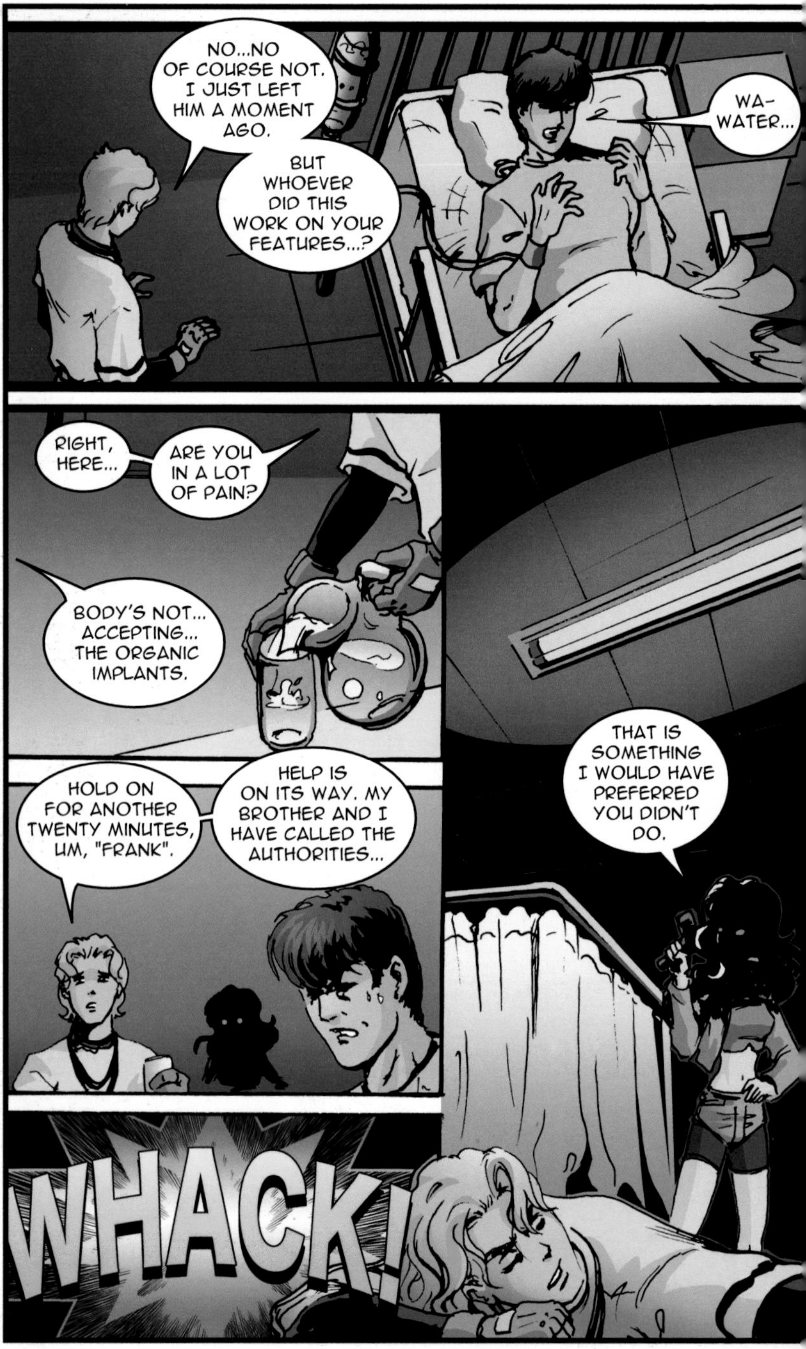
NO...NO OF COURSE NOT. I JUST LEFT HIM A MOMENT AGO.
BUT WHOEVER DID THIS WORK ON YOUR FEATURES...?
WA- WATER...
RIGHT, HERE...
ARE YOU IN A LOT OF PAIN?
BODY'S NOT... ACCEPTING... THE ORGANIC IMPLANTS.
HOLD ON FOR ANOTHER TWENTY MINUTES, UM, "FRANK".
HELP IS ON ITS WAY. MY BROTHER AND I HAVE CALLED THE AUTHORITIES...
THAT IS SOMETHING I WOULD HAVE PREFERRED YOU DIDN'T DO.
WHACK!

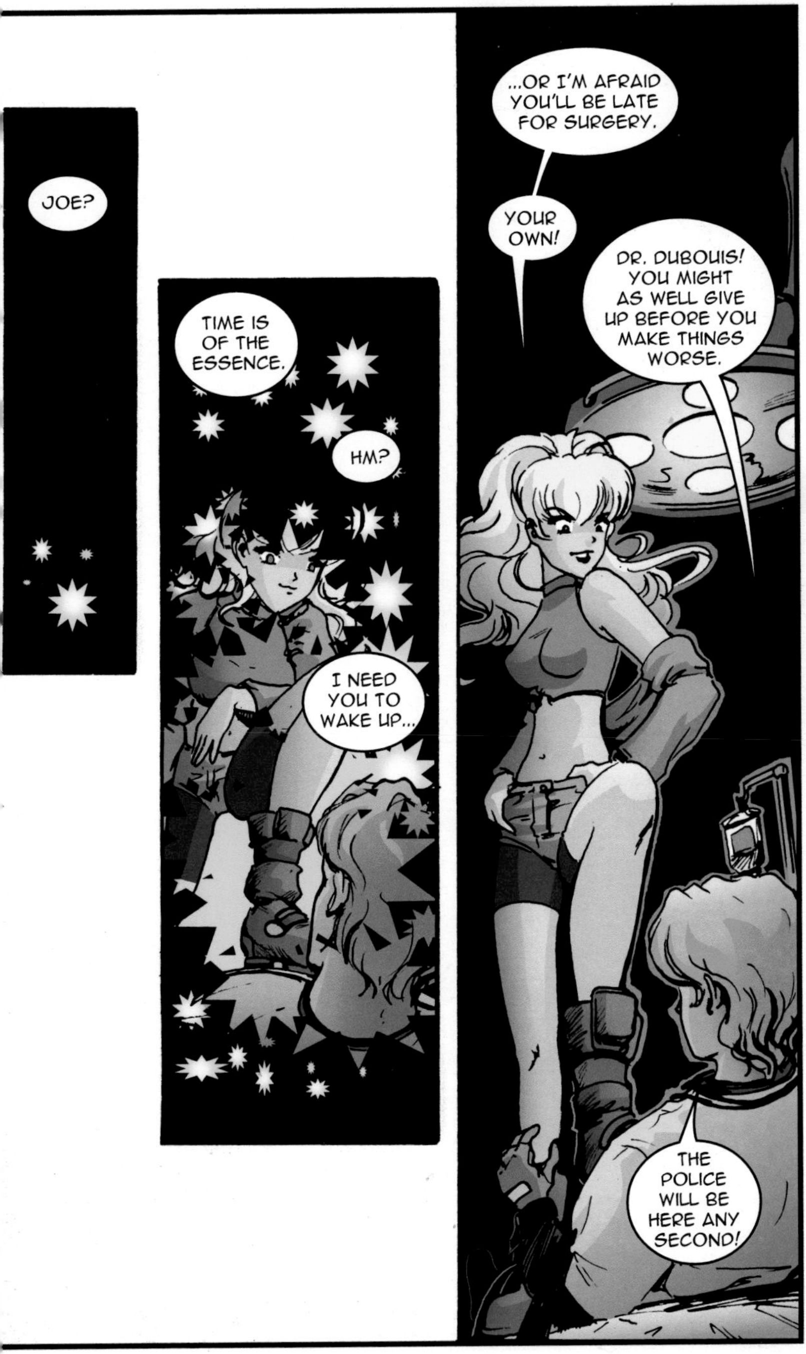

JOE?
TIME IS OF THE ESSENCE.
HM?
I NEED YOU TO WAKE UP...
...OR I'M AFRAID YOU'LL BE LATE FOR SURGERY.
YOUR OWN!
DR. DUBOUIS! YOU MIGHT AS WELL GIVE UP BEFORE YOU MAKE THINGS WORSE.
THE POLICE WILL BE HERE ANY SECOND!

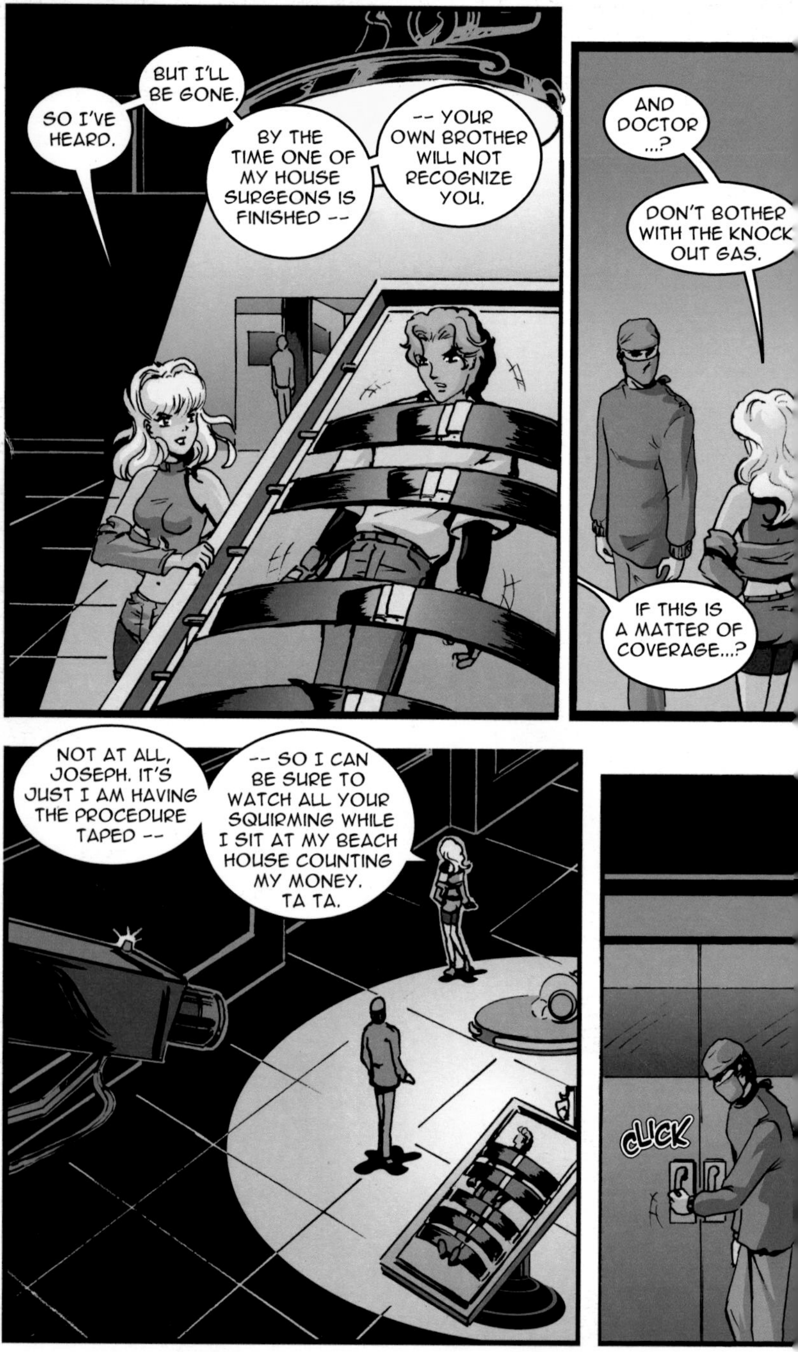
SO I'VE HEARD.
BUT I'LL BE GONE.
BY THE TIME ONE OF MY HOUSE SURGEONS IS FINISHED --
-- YOUR OWN BROTHER WILL NOT RECOGNIZE YOU.
AND DOCTOR ...?
DON'T BOTHER WITH THE KNOCK OUT GAS.
IF THIS IS A MATTER OF COVERAGE...?
NOT AT ALL, JOSEPH. IT'S JUST I AM HAVING THE PROCEDURE TAPED --
-- SO I CAN BE SURE TO WATCH ALL YOUR SQUIRMING WHILE I SIT AT MY BEACH HOUSE COUNTING MY MONEY. TA TA.
CLICK

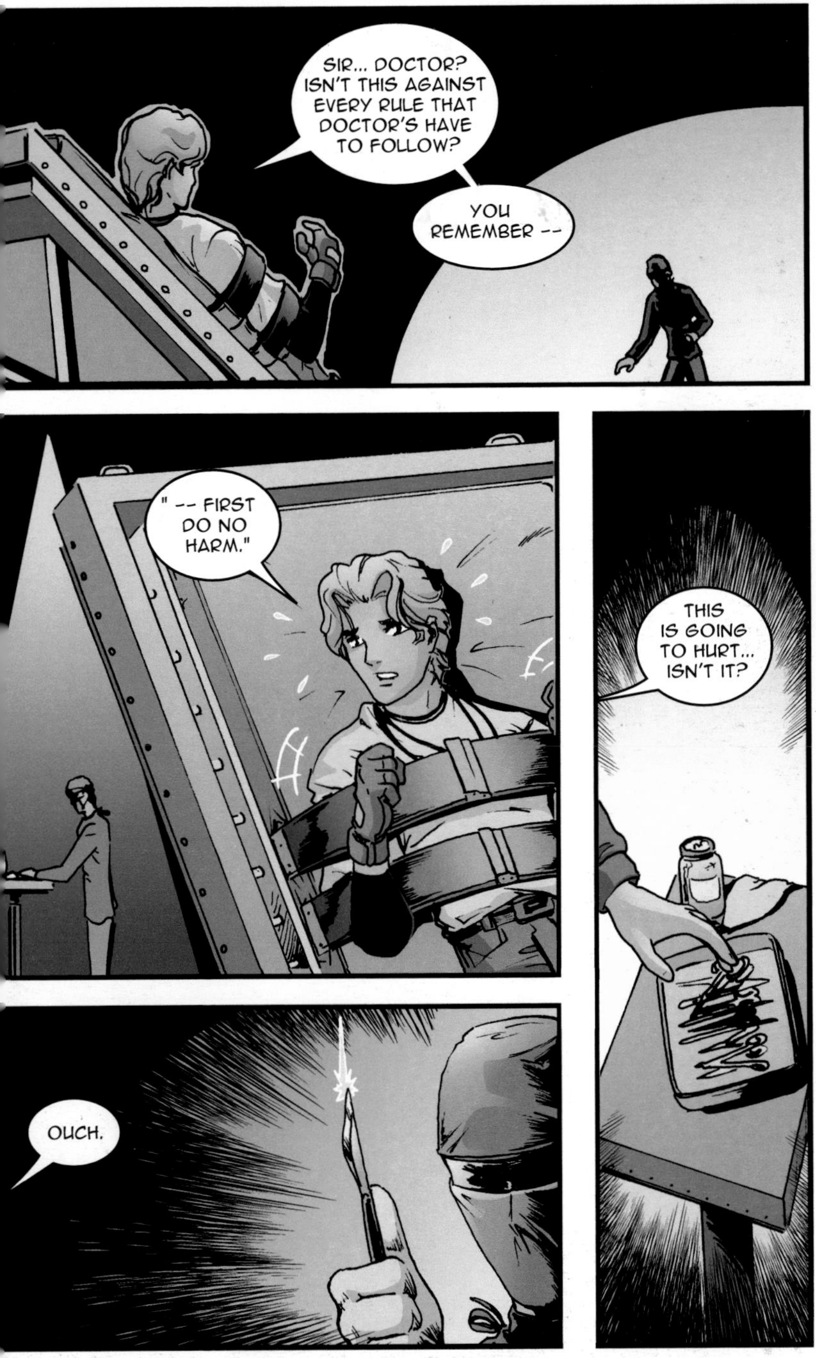
SIR... DOCTOR? ISN'T THIS AGAINST EVERY RULE THAT DOCTOR'S HAVE TO FOLLOW?
YOU REMEMBER --
" -- FIRST DO NO HARM."
THIS IS GOING TO HURT... ISN'T IT?
OUCH.

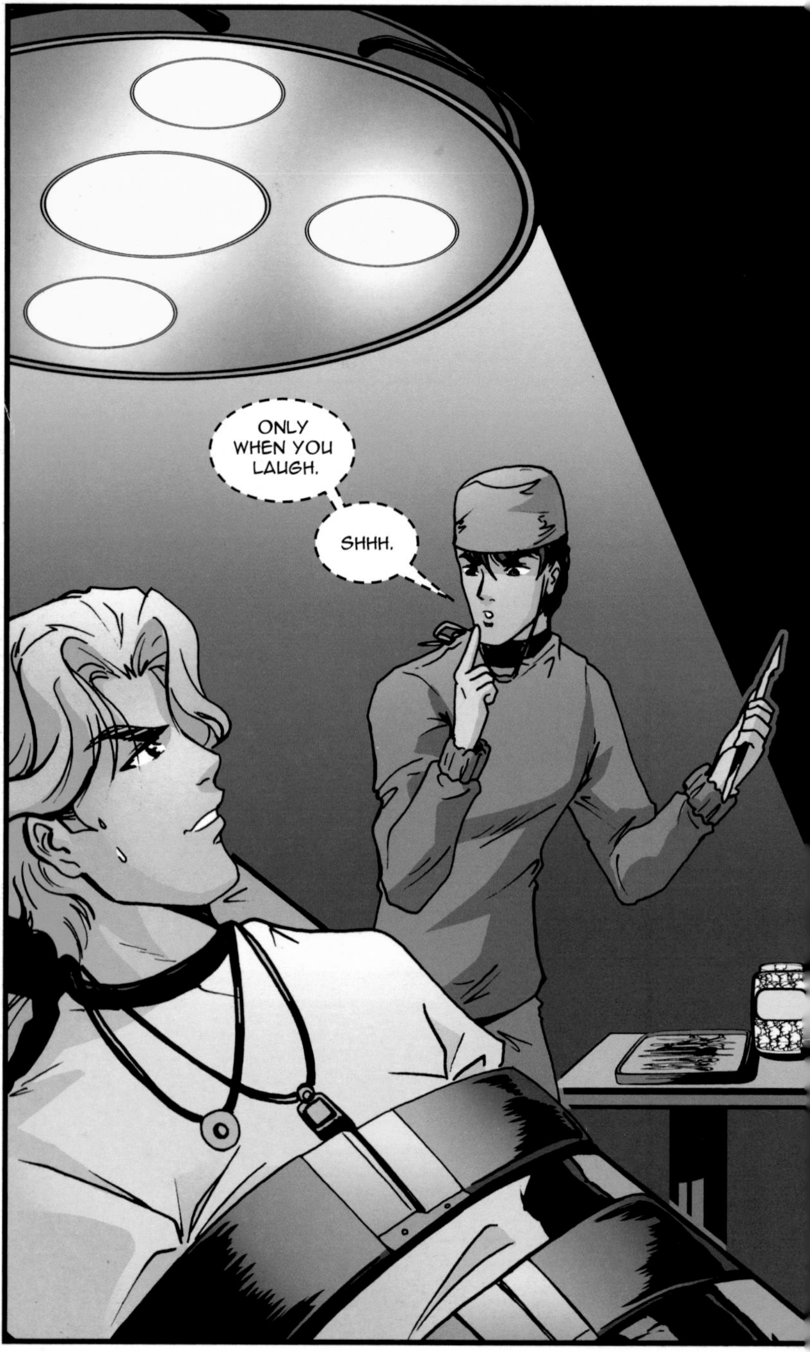
ONLY WHEN YOU LAUGH.
SHHH.

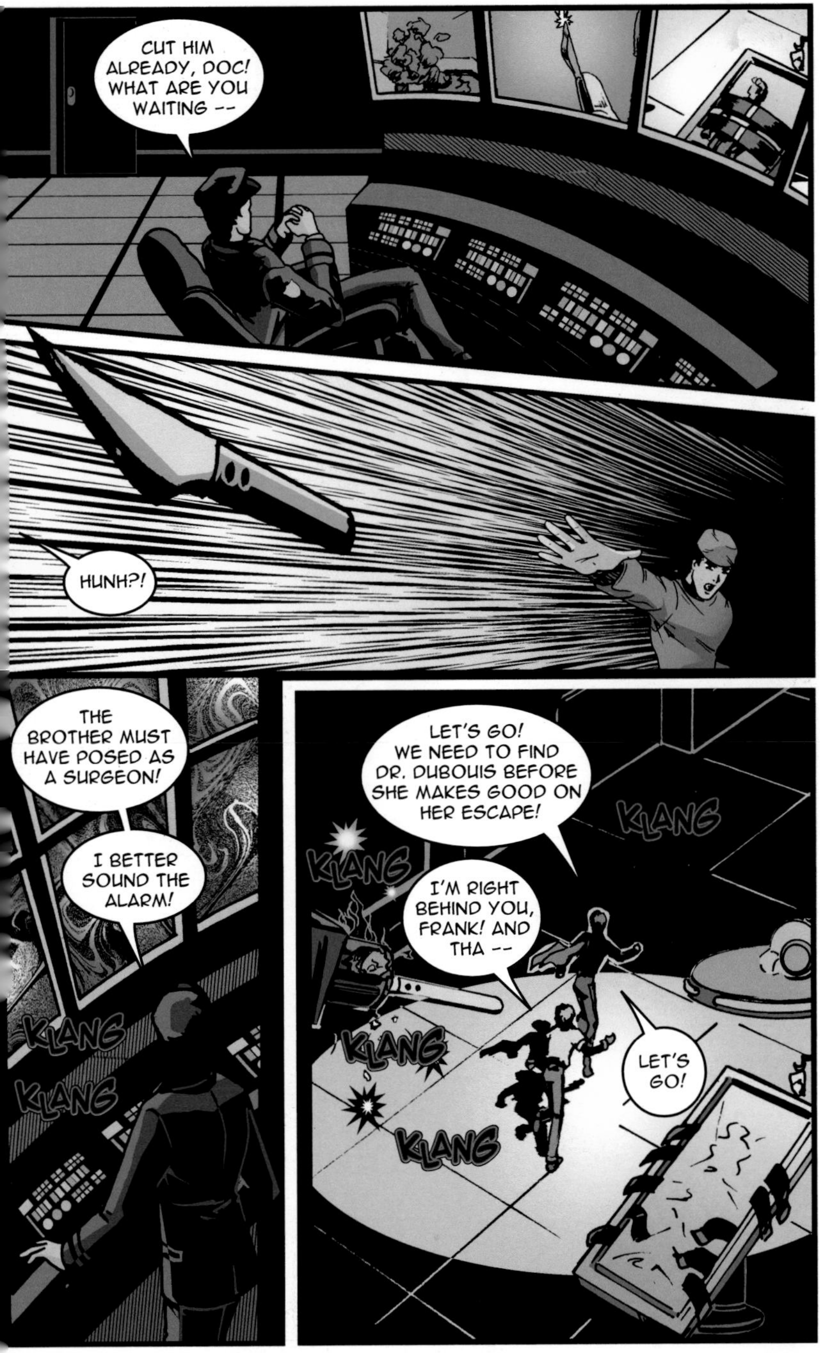
CUT HIM ALREADY, DOC! WHAT ARE YOU WAITING --
HUNH?!
THE BROTHER MUST HAVE POSED AS A SURGEON!
I BETTER SOUND THE ALARM!
KLANG
KLANG
LET'S GO! WE NEED TO FIND DR. DUBOUIS BEFORE SHE MAKES GOOD ON HER ESCAPE!
KLANG
KLANG
I'M RIGHT BEHIND YOU, FRANK! AND THA --
LET'S GO!
KLANG
KLANG

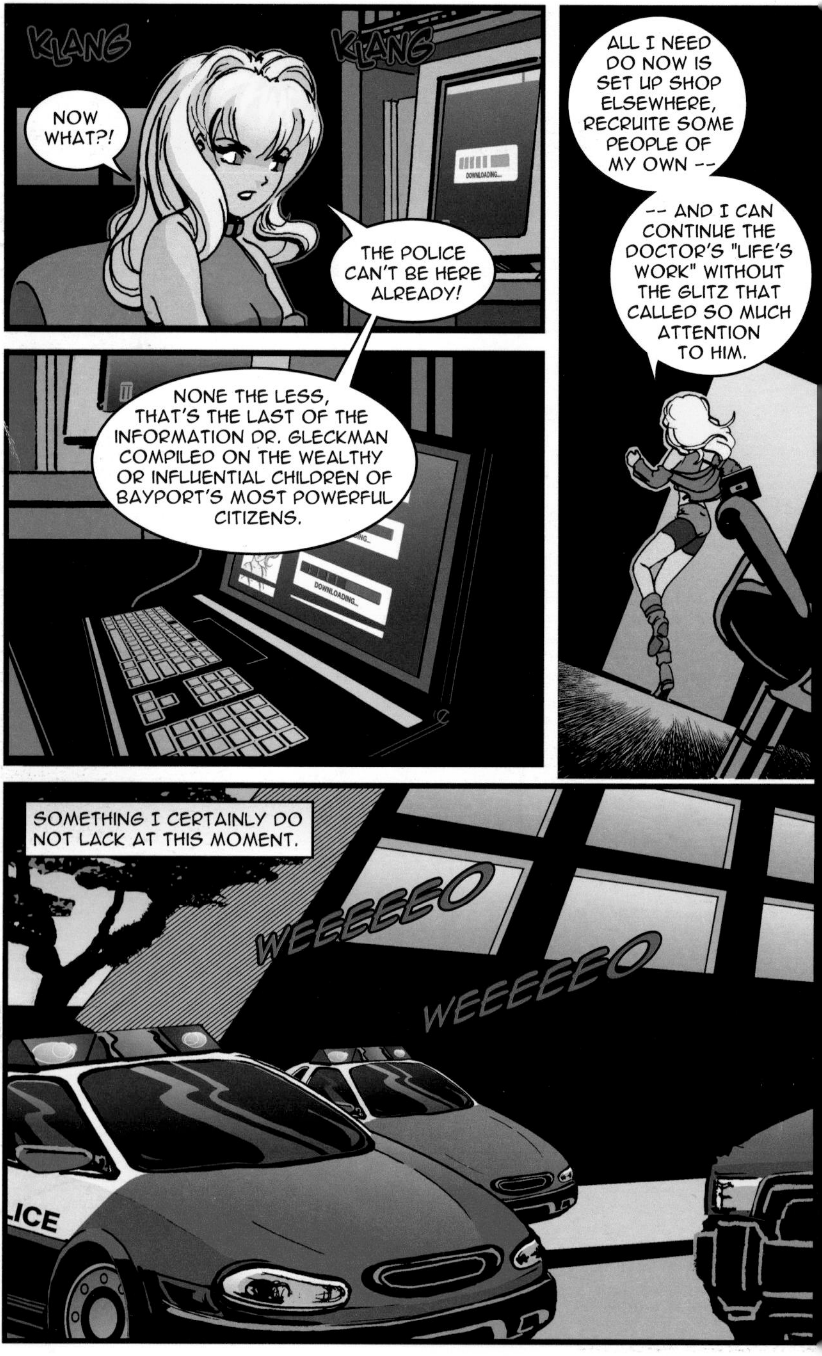
KLANG
KLANG
NOW WHAT?!
THE POLICE CAN'T BE HERE ALREADY!
DOWNLOADING...
NONE THE LESS, THAT'S THE LAST OF THE INFORMATION DR. GLECKMAN COMPILED ON THE WEALTHY OR INFLUENTIAL CHILDREN OF BAYPORT'S MOST POWERFUL CITIZENS.
DOWNLOADING...
ALL I NEED DO NOW IS SET UP SHOP ELSEWHERE, RECRUITE SOME PEOPLE OF MY OWN --
-- AND I CAN CONTINUE THE DOCTOR'S "LIFE'S WORK" WITHOUT THE GLITZ THAT CALLED SO MUCH ATTENTION TO HIM.
SOMETHING I CERTAINLY DO NOT LACK AT THIS MOMENT.
WEEEEEEO
WEEEEEEO
LICE

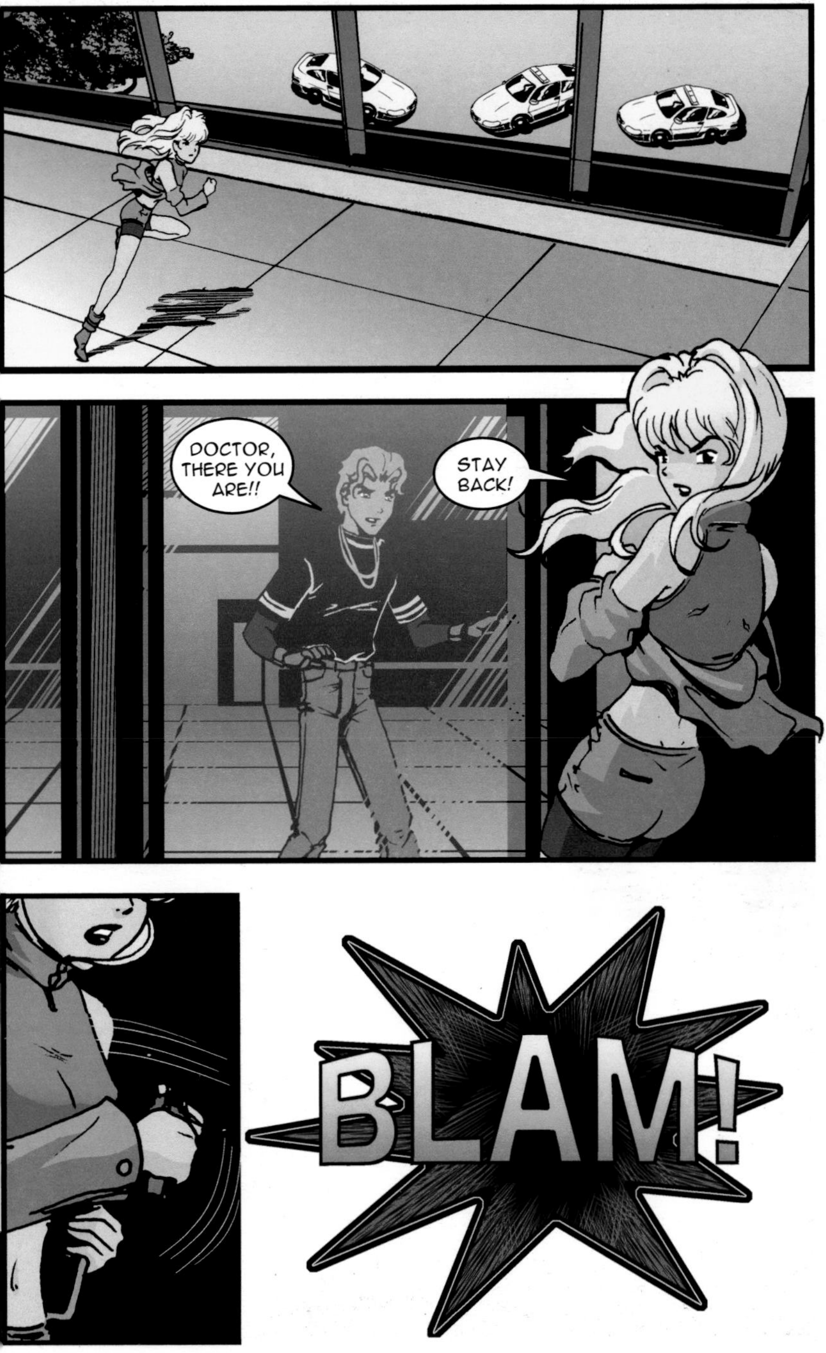
DOCTOR, THERE YOU ARE!!
STAY BACK!
BLAM!

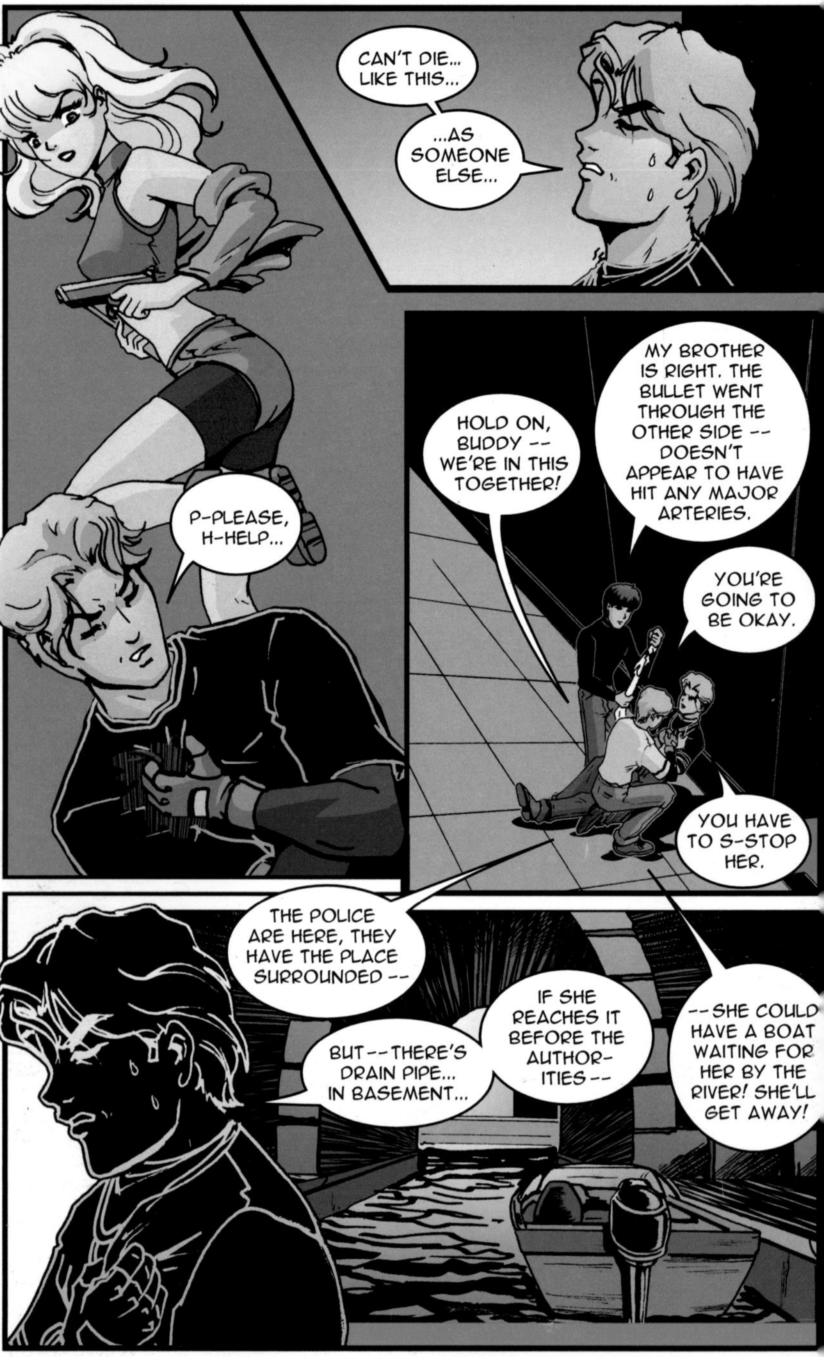
CAN'T DIE... LIKE THIS...
...AS SOMEONE ELSE...
P-PLEASE, H-HELP...
HOLD ON, BUDDY -- WE'RE IN THIS TOGETHER!
MY BROTHER IS RIGHT. THE BULLET WENT THROUGH THE OTHER SIDE -- DOESN'T APPEAR TO HAVE HIT ANY MAJOR ARTERIES.
YOU'RE GOING TO BE OKAY.
YOU HAVE TO S-STOP HER.
THE POLICE ARE HERE, THEY HAVE THE PLACE SURROUNDED --
BUT--THERE'S DRAIN PIPE... IN BASEMENT...
IF SHE REACHES IT BEFORE THE AUTHOR-ITIES --
--SHE COULD HAVE A BOAT WAITING FOR HER BY THE RIVER! SHE'LL GET AWAY!

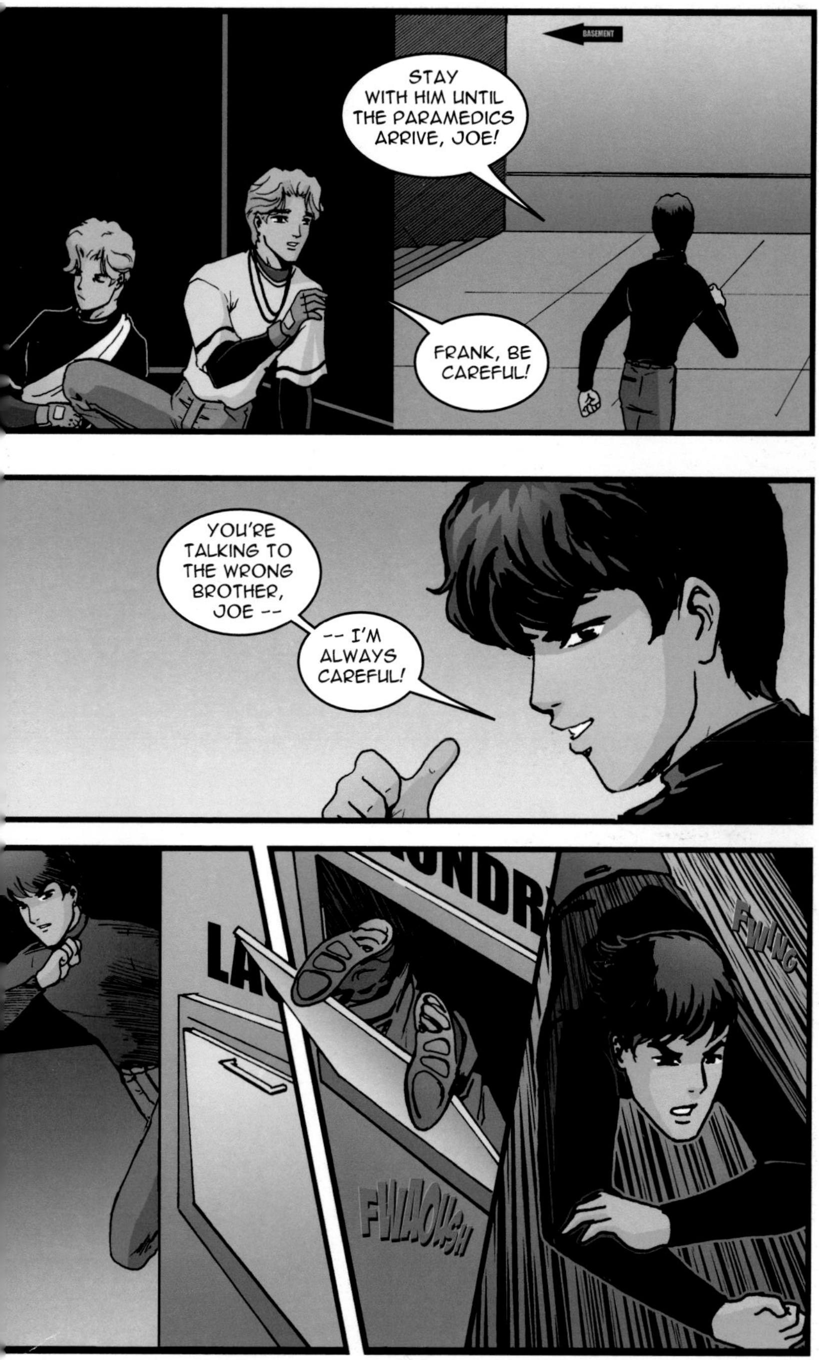
BASEMENT
STAY WITH HIM UNTIL THE PARAMEDICS ARRIVE, JOE!
FRANK, BE CAREFUL!
YOU'RE TALKING TO THE WRONG BROTHER, JOE --
-- I'M ALWAYS CAREFUL!
FWAOWSH
FWING

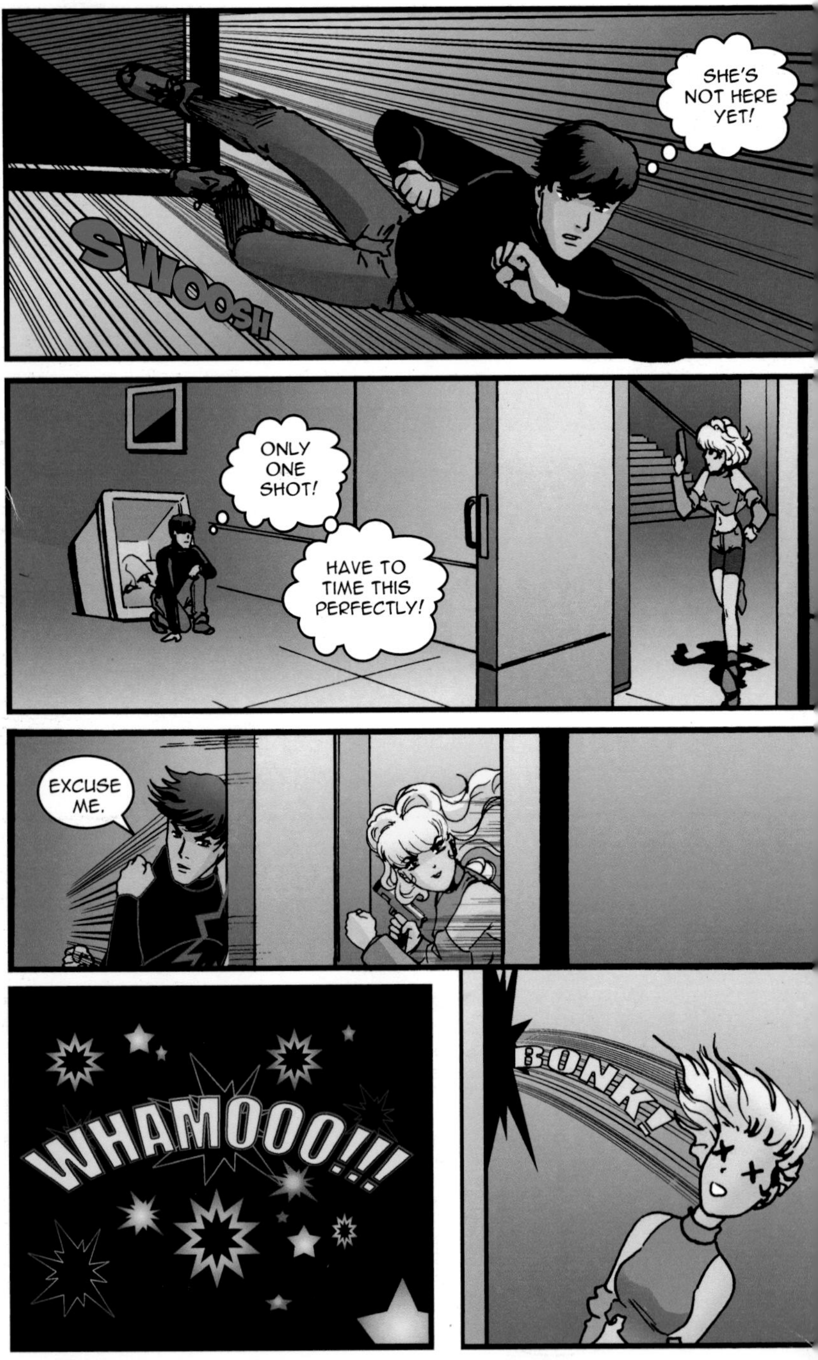
SHE'S NOT HERE YET!
SWOOSH
ONLY ONE SHOT!
HAVE TO TIME THIS PERFECTLY!
EXCUSE ME.
WHAMOOO!!!
BONK!

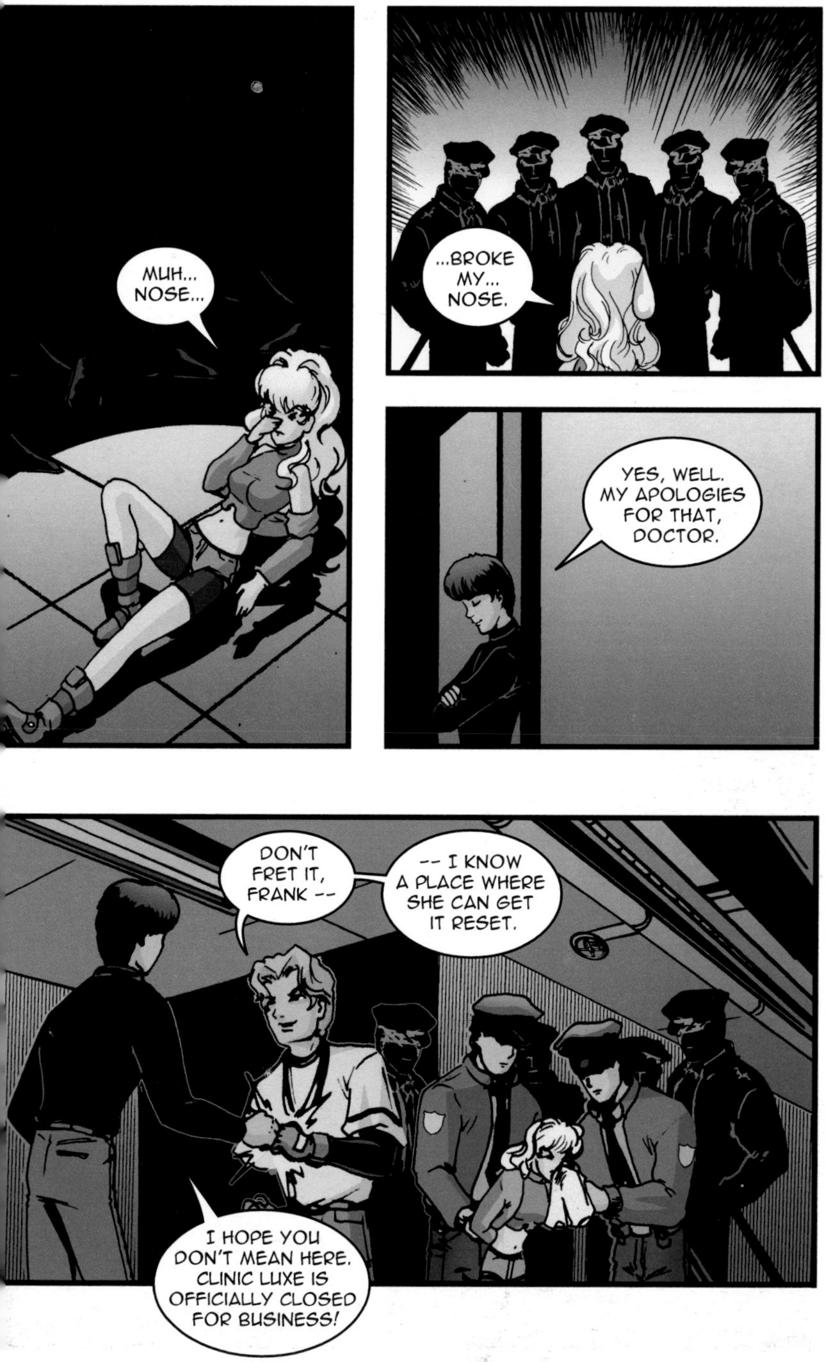
MUH... NOSE...
...BROKE MY... NOSE.
YES, WELL. MY APOLOGIES FOR THAT, DOCTOR.
DON'T FRET IT, FRANK --
-- I KNOW A PLACE WHERE SHE CAN GET IT RESET.
I HOPE YOU DON'T MEAN HERE. CLINIC LUXE IS OFFICIALLY CLOSED FOR BUSINESS!

CHAPTER TWELVE: "After All The Hubbub..."

SO, THIS IS IT --

-- THIS IS IT. THIS IS GOOD-BYE TO THE HOME THAT WE GREW UP IN.

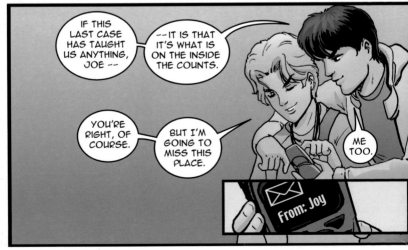

IF THIS LAST CASE HAS TAUGHT US ANYTHING, JOE --

-- IT IS THAT IT'S WHAT IS ON THE INSIDE THE COUNTS.

YOU'RE RIGHT, OF COURSE.

BUT I'M GOING TO MISS THIS PLACE.

ME TOO.

From: Joy

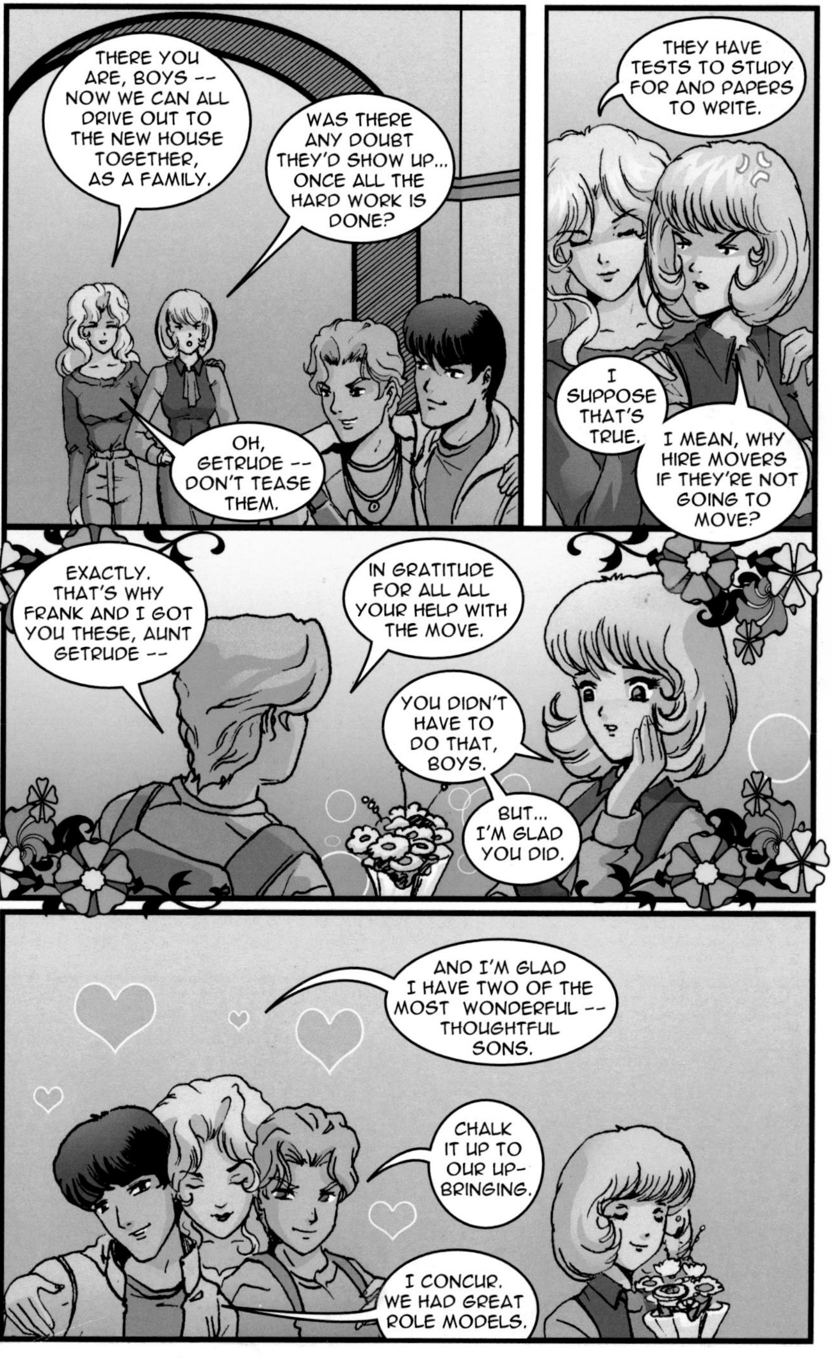
THERE YOU ARE, BOYS -- NOW WE CAN ALL DRIVE OUT TO THE NEW HOUSE TOGETHER, AS A FAMILY.
WAS THERE ANY DOUBT THEY'D SHOW UP... ONCE ALL THE HARD WORK IS DONE?
OH, GETRUDE -- DON'T TEASE THEM.
THEY HAVE TESTS TO STUDY FOR AND PAPERS TO WRITE.
I SUPPOSE THAT'S TRUE.
I MEAN, WHY HIRE MOVERS IF THEY'RE NOT GOING TO MOVE?
EXACTLY. THAT'S WHY FRANK AND I GOT YOU THESE, AUNT GETRUDE --
IN GRATITUDE FOR ALL ALL YOUR HELP WITH THE MOVE.
YOU DIDN'T HAVE TO DO THAT, BOYS.
BUT... I'M GLAD YOU DID.
AND I'M GLAD I HAVE TWO OF THE MOST WONDERFUL -- THOUGHTFUL SONS.
CHALK IT UP TO OUR UP-BRINGING.
I CONCUR. WE HAD GREAT ROLE MODELS.

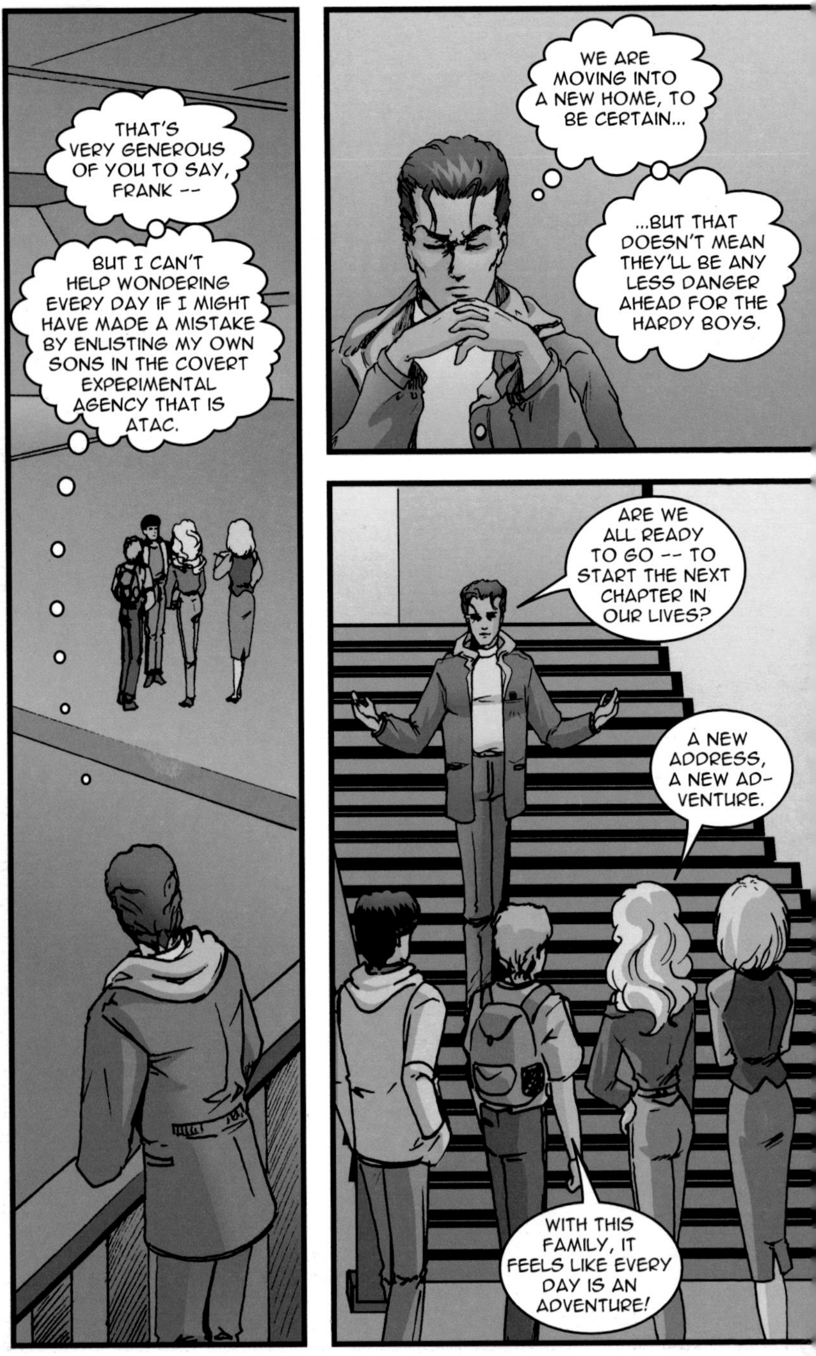

THAT'S VERY GENEROUS OF YOU TO SAY, FRANK --
BUT I CAN'T HELP WONDERING EVERY DAY IF I MIGHT HAVE MADE A MISTAKE BY ENLISTING MY OWN SONS IN THE COVERT EXPERIMENTAL AGENCY THAT IS ATAC.
WE ARE MOVING INTO A NEW HOME, TO BE CERTAIN...
...BUT THAT DOESN'T MEAN THEY'LL BE ANY LESS DANGER AHEAD FOR THE HARDY BOYS.
ARE WE ALL READY TO GO -- TO START THE NEXT CHAPTER IN OUR LIVES?
A NEW ADDRESS, A NEW AD-VENTURE.
WITH THIS FAMILY, IT FEELS LIKE EVERY DAY IS AN ADVENTURE!

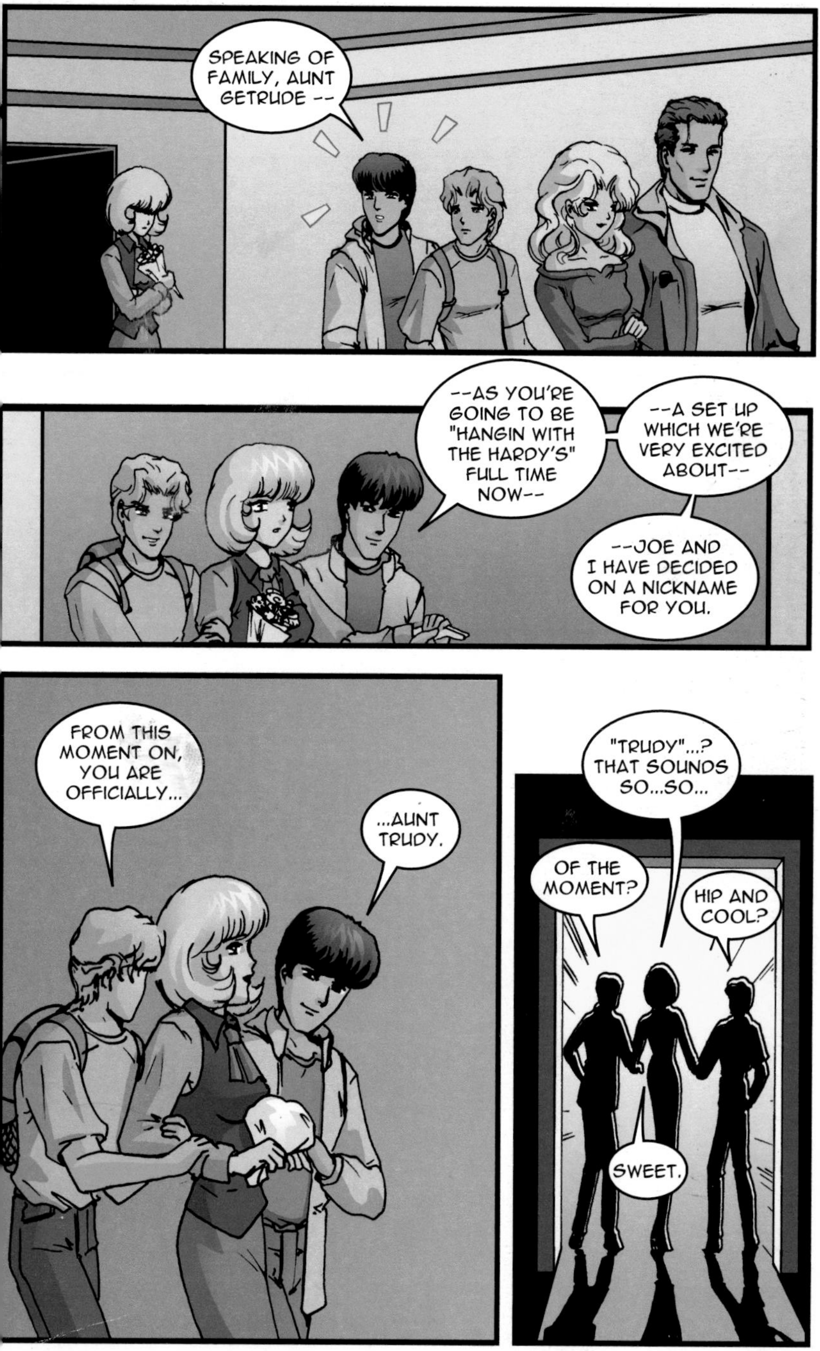
SPEAKING OF FAMILY, AUNT GETRUDE --
--AS YOU'RE GOING TO BE "HANGIN WITH THE HARDY'S" FULL TIME NOW--
--A SET UP WHICH WE'RE VERY EXCITED ABOUT--
--JOE AND I HAVE DECIDED ON A NICKNAME FOR YOU.
FROM THIS MOMENT ON, YOU ARE OFFICIALLY...
...AUNT TRUDY.
"TRUDY"...? THAT SOUNDS SO...SO...
OF THE MOMENT?
HIP AND COOL?
SWEET.

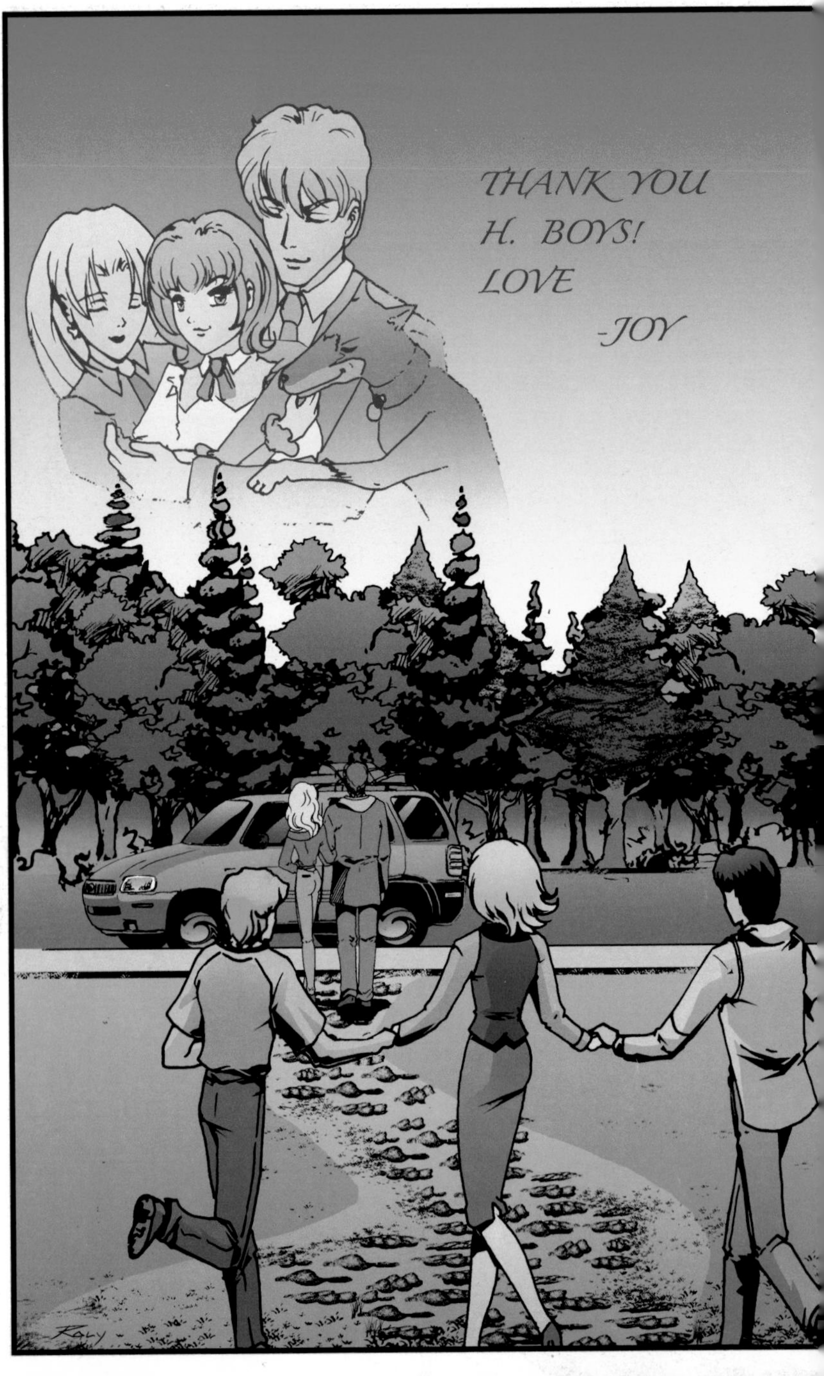
THANK YOU
H. BOYS!
LOVE
-JOY
Raly

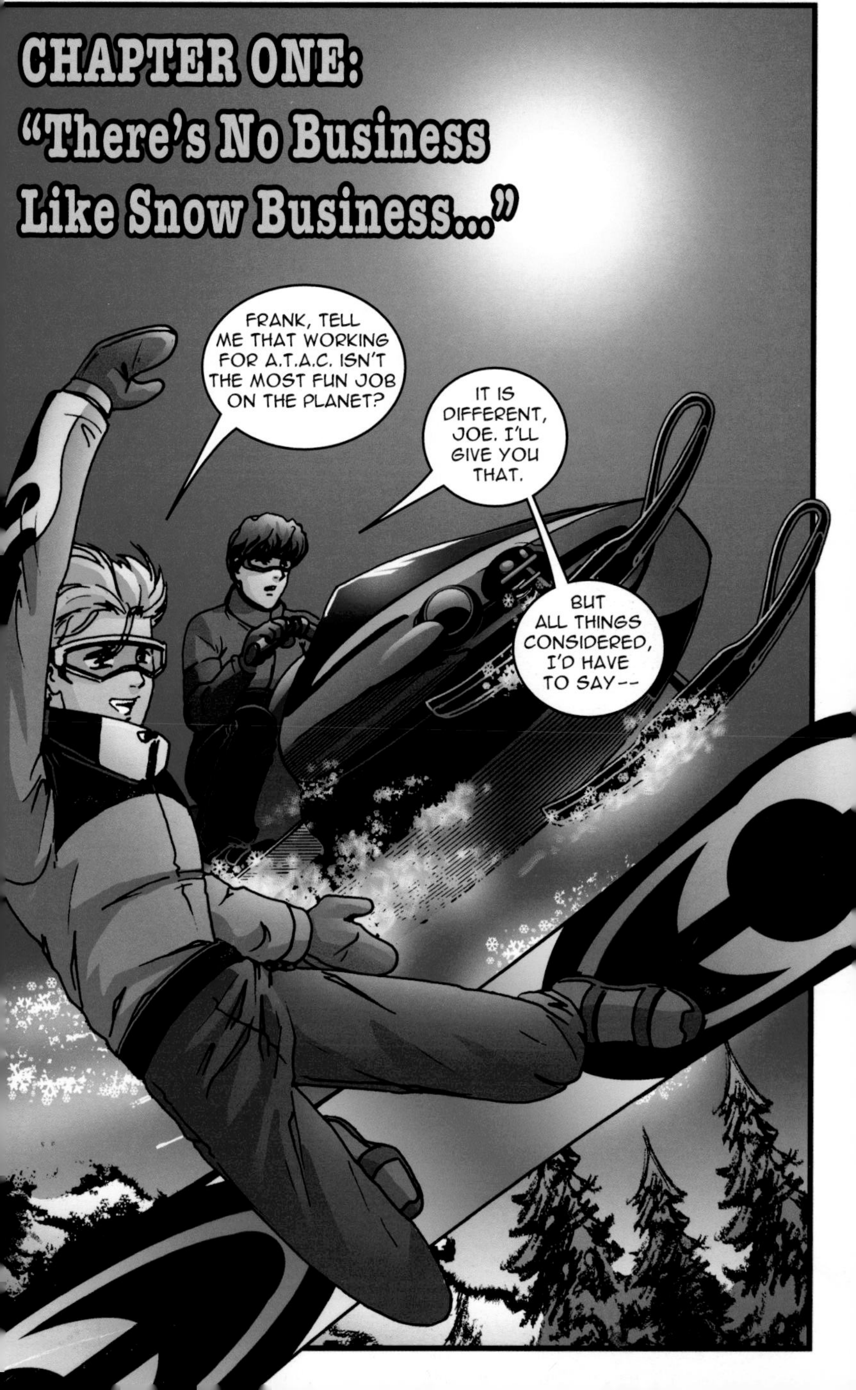
CHAPTER ONE:
"There's No Business Like Snow Business..."
FRANK, TELL ME THAT WORKING FOR A.T.A.C. ISN'T THE MOST FUN JOB ON THE PLANET?
IT IS DIFFERENT, JOE. I'LL GIVE YOU THAT.
BUT ALL THINGS CONSIDERED, I'D HAVE TO SAY--

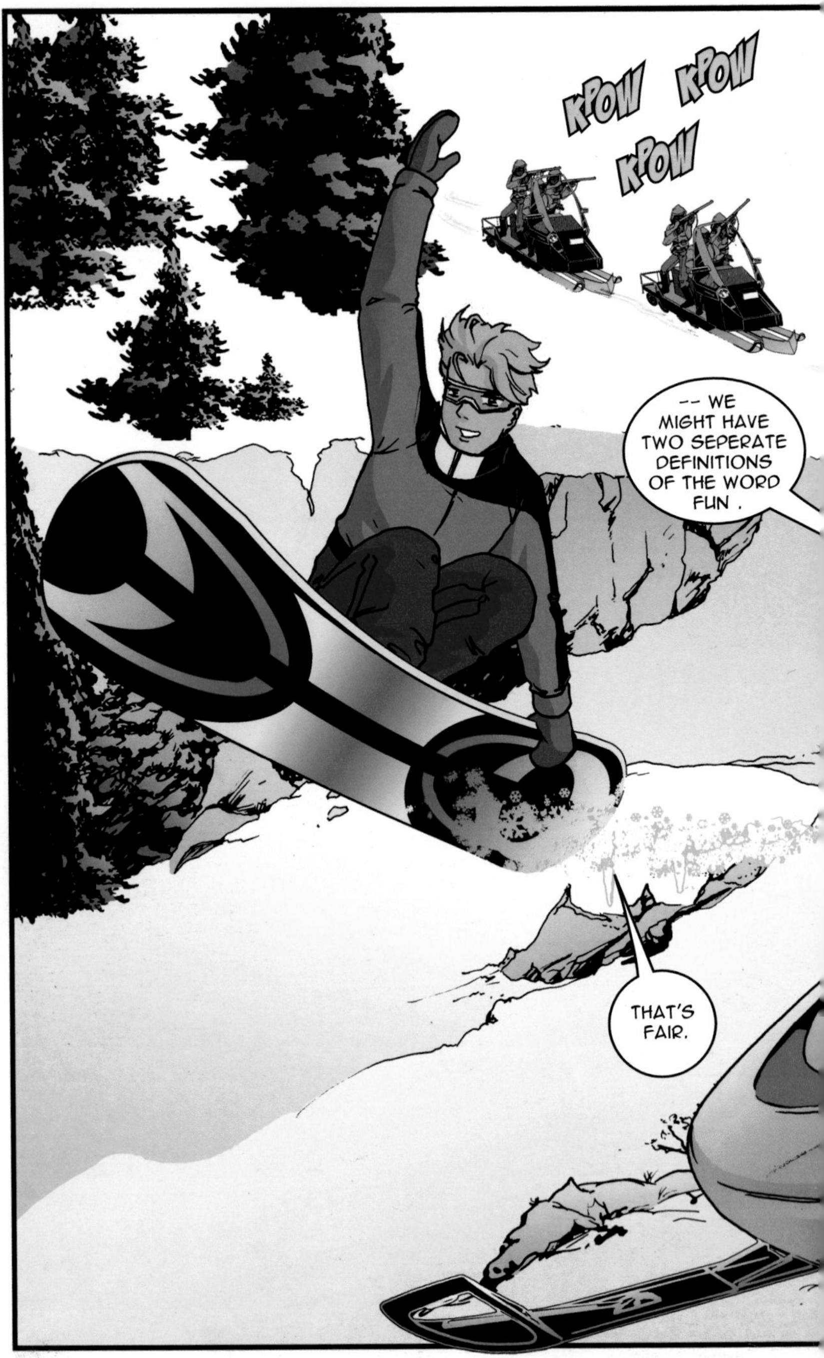

KPOW KPOW
KPOW
-- WE MIGHT HAVE TWO SEPERATE DEFINITIONS OF THE WORD FUN .
THAT'S FAIR.

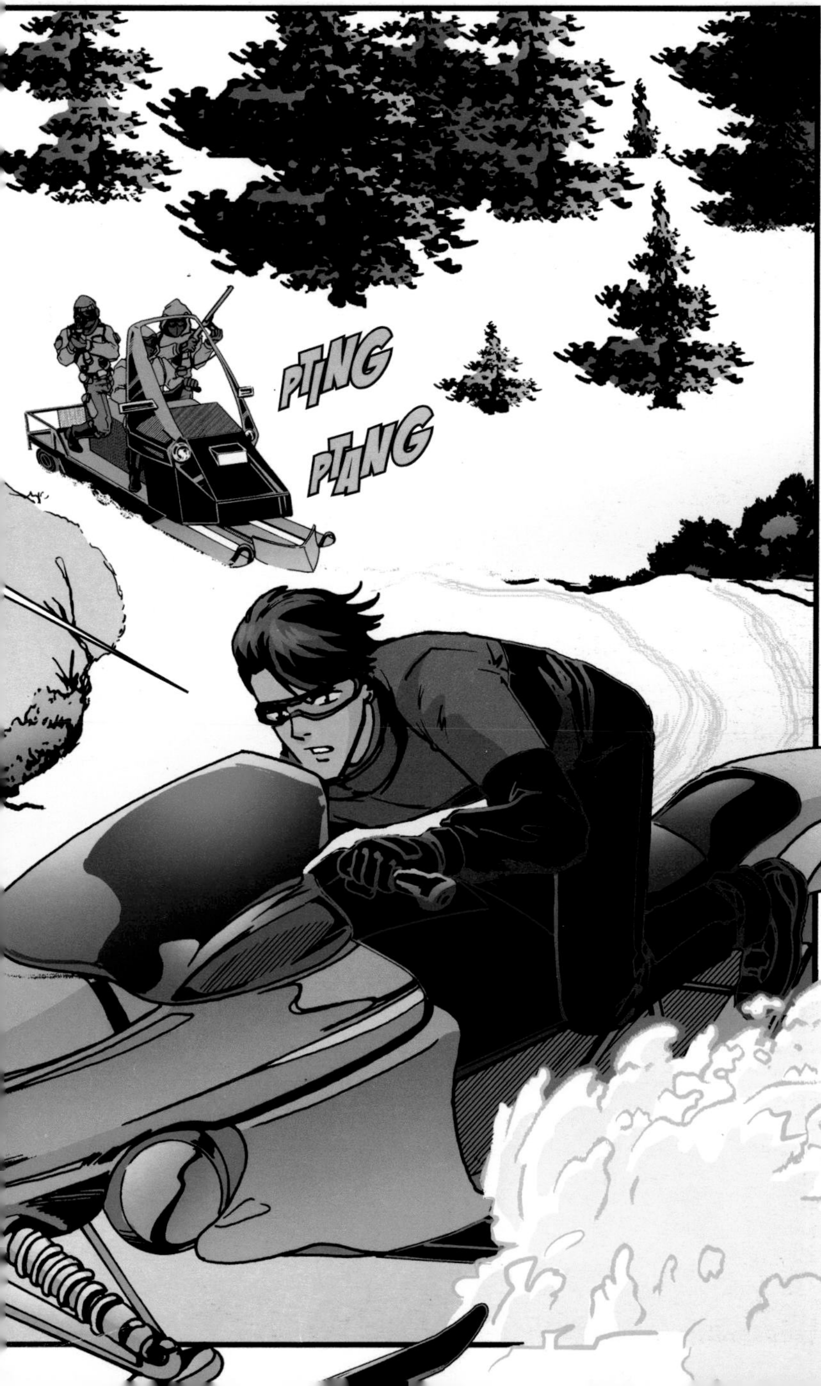
PTING
PTANG

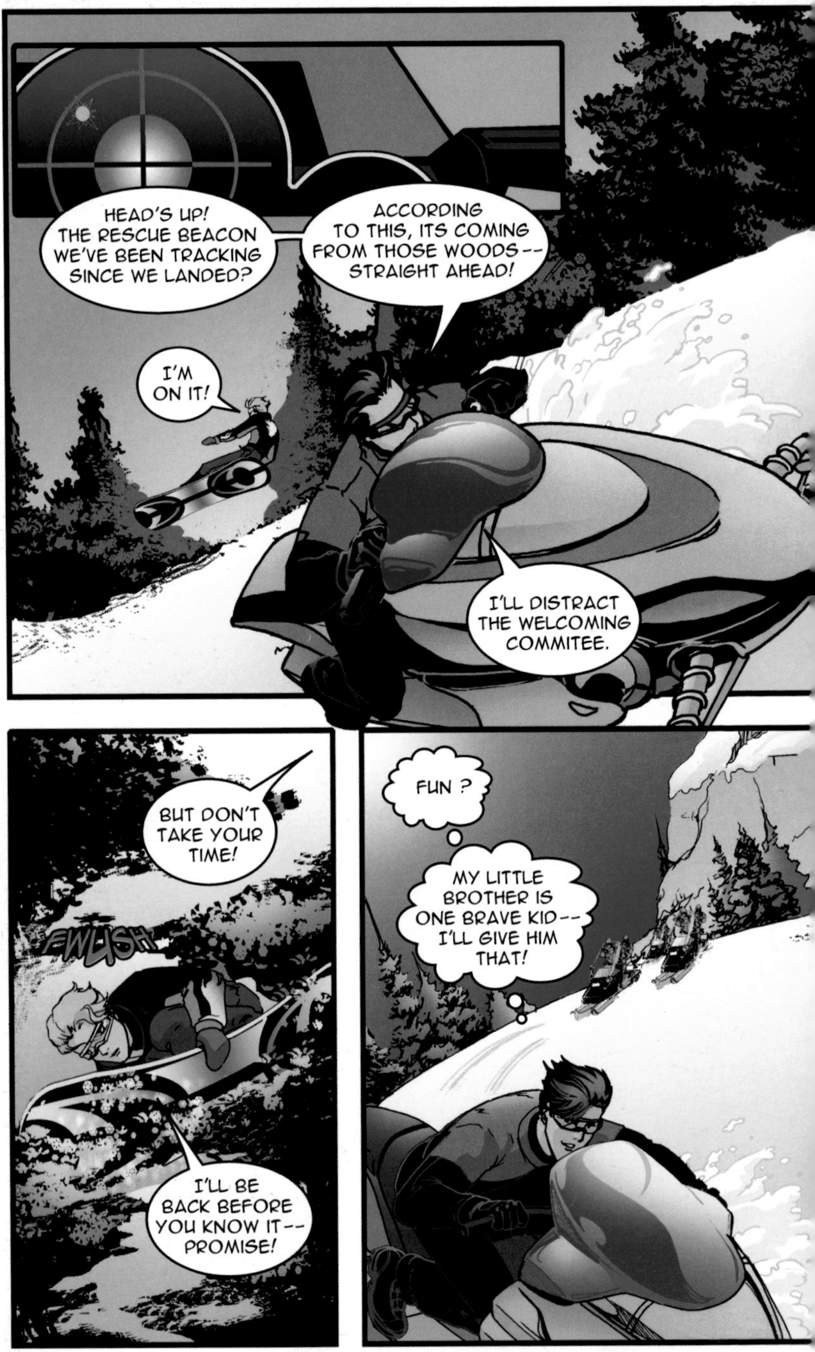
HEAD'S UP! THE RESCUE BEACON WE'VE BEEN TRACKING SINCE WE LANDED?
ACCORDING TO THIS, ITS COMING FROM THOSE WOODS-- STRAIGHT AHEAD!
I'M ON IT!
I'LL DISTRACT THE WELCOMING COMMITEE.
BUT DON'T TAKE YOUR TIME!
FWUSH
I'LL BE BACK BEFORE YOU KNOW IT-- PROMISE!
FUN ?
MY LITTLE BROTHER IS ONE BRAVE KID-- I'LL GIVE HIM THAT!

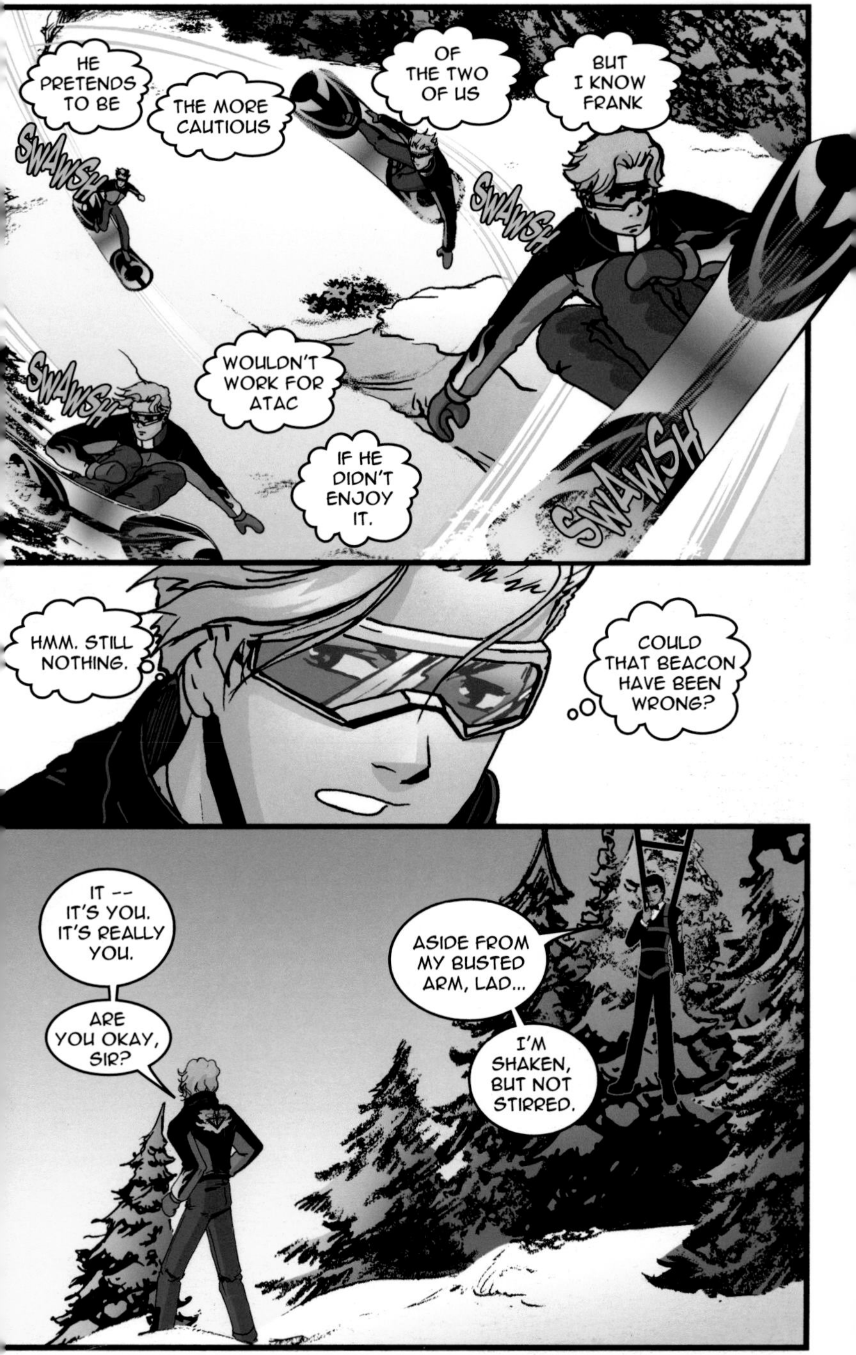
HE PRETENDS TO BE
THE MORE CAUTIOUS
OF THE TWO OF US
BUT I KNOW FRANK
SWAWSH
SWAWSH
SWAWSH
WOULDN'T WORK FOR ATAC
IF HE DIDN'T ENJOY IT.
SWAWSH
HMM. STILL NOTHING.
COULD THAT BEACON HAVE BEEN WRONG?
IT -- IT'S YOU. IT'S REALLY YOU.
ARE YOU OKAY, SIR?
ASIDE FROM MY BUSTED ARM, LAD...
I'M SHAKEN, BUT NOT STIRRED.

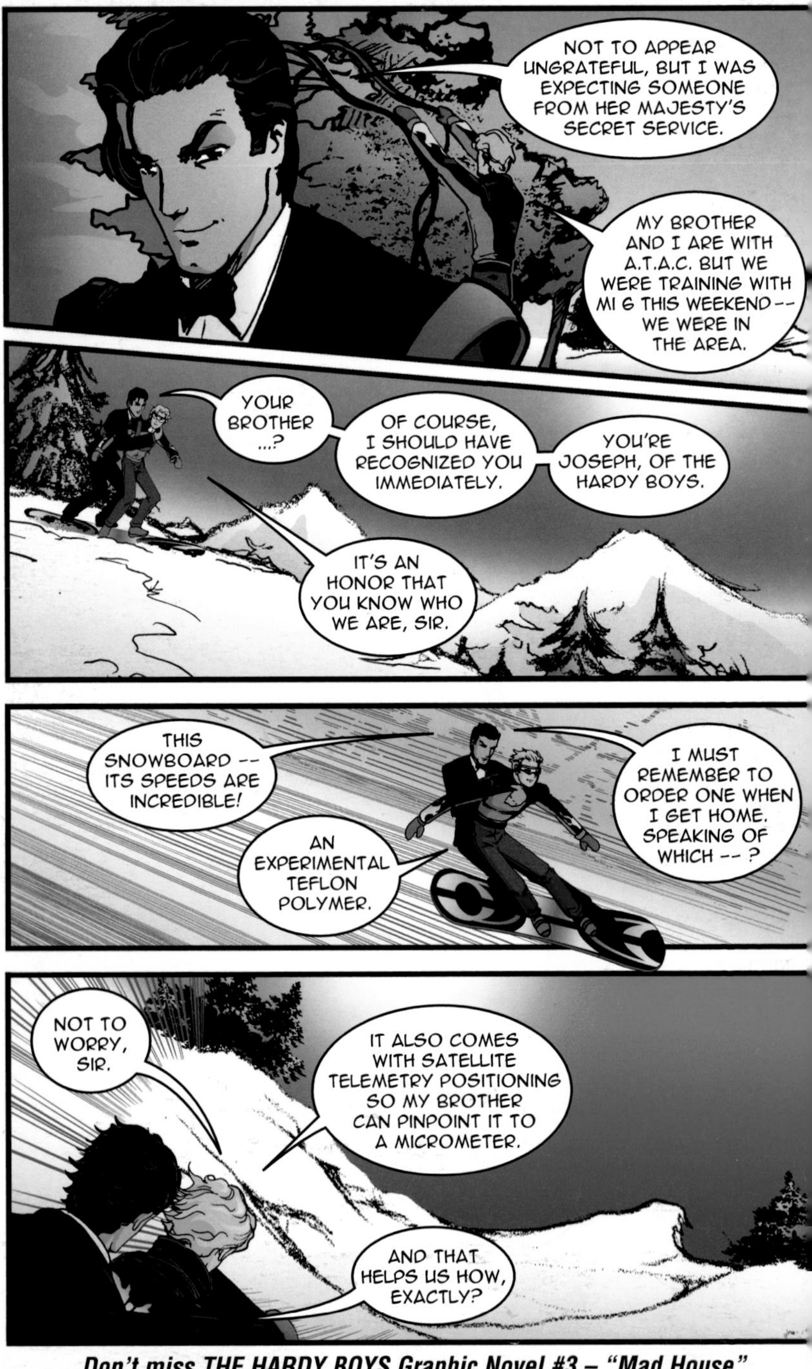
NOT TO APPEAR UNGRATEFUL, BUT I WAS EXPECTING SOMEONE FROM HER MAJESTY'S SECRET SERVICE.
MY BROTHER AND I ARE WITH A.T.A.C. BUT WE WERE TRAINING WITH MI 6 THIS WEEKEND -- WE WERE IN THE AREA.
YOUR BROTHER ...?
OF COURSE, I SHOULD HAVE RECOGNIZED YOU IMMEDIATELY.
YOU'RE JOSEPH, OF THE HARDY BOYS.
IT'S AN HONOR THAT YOU KNOW WHO WE ARE, SIR.
THIS SNOWBOARD -- ITS SPEEDS ARE INCREDIBLE!
I MUST REMEMBER TO ORDER ONE WHEN I GET HOME. SPEAKING OF WHICH -- ?
AN EXPERIMENTAL TEFLON POLYMER.
NOT TO WORRY, SIR.
IT ALSO COMES WITH SATELLITE TELEMETRY POSITIONING SO MY BROTHER CAN PINPOINT IT TO A MICROMETER.
AND THAT HELPS US HOW, EXACTLY?